PENGUIN BOOKS

COMFORT WOMAN

Nora Okja Keller, author of *Fox Girl,* was born in Seoul, Korea, and now lives in Hawaii. In 1995, Keller received the Pushcart Prize for "Mother Tongue," a piece that is a part of *Comfort Woman.*

Praise for *Comfort Woman*

"Lyrical and haunting. . . . A powerful book about mothers and daughters and the passions that bind one generation to another."
— Michiko Kakutani, *The New York Times*

"A beautiful first novel, lovingly written and lovingly told. *Comfort Woman* speaks eloquently for everyone who tries to imagine a parent's past, who tries to piece together a history that involves as much the dead as it does the living. Told with great grace, poetry and, yes, even humor, Nora Okja Keller has honored her ancestors and her readers with this book. *Comfort Woman* is not simply a story, but medicine for the spirit."
—Sandra Cisneros, author of *The House on
Mango Street* and *Loose Woman*

"*Comfort Woman* may have the elements of a classic mother-daughter tale, but it is so fresh and powerful that it reads like uncharted territory. And the storytelling is as rich as the story itself."
—*San Francisco Chronicle*

"Powerful and beautifully rendered."
—*The Women's Review of Books*

"Terrifyingly vivid . . . *Comfort Woman* is a novel that demands intense reaction. Disturbing and beautiful, it takes its place in the American canon as a unique and exquisite tale."
—*The Seattle Times*

"There is nothing comfortable about Nora Okja Keller's *Comfort Woman*. A beautifully orchestrated, elegiac novel about a mother-daughter relationship that survives holocaust, madness, and death. Nora Okja Keller can write her way into the heart of darkness without losing her way. Her sense of humor, her lucid and graceful writing, her spunky characters keep our hearts from breaking."
—Julia Alvarez, author of *¡Yo!* and *How the
Garcia Girls Lost Their Accents*

COMFORT

WOMAN

NORA

OKJA

KELLER

PENGUIN BOOKS

PENGUIN BOOKS
Published by the Penguin Group
Penguin Group (USA) Inc., 375 Hudson Street, New York, New York 10014, U.S.A.
Penguin Books Ltd, 80 Strand, London WC2R 0RL, England
Penguin Books Australia Ltd, 250 Camberwell Road, Camberwell, Victoria 3124, Australia
Penguin Books Canada Ltd, 10 Alcorn Avenue, Toronto, Ontario, Canada M4V 3B2
Penguin Books India (P) Ltd, 11 Community Centre, Panchsheel Park, New Delhi – 110 017, India
Penguin Group (NZ), cnr Airborne and Rosedale Roads, Albany, Auckland 1310, New Zealand
Penguin Books (South Africa) (Pty) Ltd, 24 Sturdee Avenue,
Rosebank, Johannesburg 2196, South Africa

Penguin Books Ltd, Registered Offices: 80 Strand, London WC2R 0RL, England

First published in the United States of America by Viking Penguin,
a division of Penguin Books USA Inc. 1997
Published in Penguin Books 1998

20 19 18 17 16 15 14 13

Grateful acknowledgment is made to the following publications in which portions of
this book, in slightly different form, first appeared: *Bamboo Ridge*; *Into the Fire: Asian
American Prose*, edited by Sylvia Watanabe and Carol Bruchac, Greenfield Review Lit-
erary Center, Incorporated; *On a Bed of Rice: An Asian American Erotic Feast*, edited by
Geraldine Kudaka, Anchor Books; *The Pushcart Prize XX*, edited by Bill Henderson
with the Pushcart Prize editors, Pushcart Press; and *Writing Away Here*.

PUBLISHER'S NOTE
This is a work of fiction. Names, characters, places, and incidents either are the
product of the author's imagination or are used fictitiously, and any resemblance
to actual persons, living or dead, events, or locales is entirely coincidental.

THE LIBRARY OF CONGRESS HAS CATALOGUED THE HARDCOVER AS FOLLOWS:
Keller, Nora Okja.
Comfort woman / Nora Okja Keller.
p.   cm.
ISBN 0-670-87269-5 (hc.)
ISBN 0 14 02.6335 7 (pbk.)
I. Title.
PS3561.E38574C66   1997
813'.54—dc20   96–35458

Printed in the United States of America
Set in Adobe Garamond
Designed by Sabrina Bowers

FOR TAE KATHLEEN

COMFORT

WOMAN

I

BECCAH ·~

On the fifth anniversary of my father's death, my mother confessed to his murder. We had been peeling the shrimp for his *chesa,* slicing through the crackling skins, popping the gray and slippery meat, ripe as fruit, into the kitchen sink. My mother, who was allergic to my father's favorite food, held her red and puffy hands under cold running water and scratched at her fingers. "Beccah-chan," she told me without looking up, "I killed your father."

My mother picked at her hands, rubbing at the blisters bubbling between her fingers. I turned the water off and wrapped her hands in a dish towel. "Shh, Mommy," I said. "Don't start."

"Never happen like this," she said, trying to snap her fingers under the cloth. "I had to work at it."

I led her to the kitchen table, clearing a place for her by pushing the stacks of offerings we planned to burn after I ate the remembrance feast my mother made to appease my father's spirit. My father died when I was five, and this yearly meal, with its persistent smell of the ocean, and the smoke and the ash that would penetrate our apartment for days after we burned the Monopoly money and paper-doll clothes, supplanted my dim memories of an actual man. Even when I unearthed the picture I had of him from my underwear drawer, stealing a look, I saw him less and less clearly, the image fading in almost imperceptible gradations each time I exposed it to light and scrutiny.

What stays with me, though, is the color of his eyes. While his face, his body, sit in shadows behind the black of the Bible he always carried with him, the blue of his eyes sharpen on me. At night before I fell asleep, I would try to imagine my father as an angel coming to comfort me. I gave him the face and voice of Mr. Rogers and waited for him to wrap me in that cardigan sweater, which would smell of mothballs and mint and Daddy. He would spirit me away, to a home on the Mainland complete with plush carpet and a cocker spaniel pup. My daddy, I knew, would save my mother and me, burning with his blue eyes the Korean ghosts and demons that fed off our lives.

But when he rolled me into the sweater, binding my arms behind me, my father opened his eyes not on the demons but on me. And the blue light from his eyes grew so bright it burned me, each night, into nothingness.

•⟶

I don't remember what I felt the day my mother told me she had killed my father. Maybe anger, or fear. Not because I believed she had killed him, but because I thought she was slipping into one of her trances. I remember telling her, "Okay," in a loud, slow voice, while I listed in my head the things that I needed to do: call Auntie Reno, buy enough oranges and incense sticks to last two weeks, secure the double locks on the doors when I left for school so my mother couldn't get out of the house.

Most of the time my mother seemed normal. Not normal like the moms on TV—the kind that baked cookies, joined the PTA, or came to weekly soccer games—but normal in that she seemed to know where she was and who I was. During those times, my mother would get up when she heard my alarm clock go off in the morning, and before I pressed the second snooze alarm, she'd have folded the blankets on her side of the bed, poured hot water for the tea, and made breakfast: fresh rice mixed with raw egg, shoyu, and Tabasco. After eating, we'd dress and then walk down the water-rotted hallway of our building, past the "three o'clock" drunk asleep on the bottom stairs, to the bus stop. Instead of continuing straight to school, I'd wait with her until the number 8 came to take her to Reno's Waikiki Bar-B-Q Hut, where she worked as fry cook and clean-up girl.

The days my mother was well enough to catch the bus, I would eat all of my school lunch at one time instead of wrapping half of it to eat before bed. Working at Auntie Reno's, my mother was able to bring home leftovers from the daily special; Auntie Reno, who isn't a blood relative, was good to us in that way: she always made sure we had enough to eat.

I have a habit I picked up from those small-kid days, one that I can't seem to shake even now. Before eating my meals, I set aside a small mound of rice—or whatever I'm eating—as a sacrifice for the spirits or for God, in case either exists. Even eating out with friends, I push the food around on my plate, severing a small portion, and think the prayer I have prayed ever since I can remember: "Please, God—please, spirits and Induk—please, Daddy and whoever is listening: Leave my mother alone."

•‑

I loved my mother during the normal times. She laughed and sang songs she made up. Instead of telling me to clear my papers and books off the table for dinner, she'd sing it to me. We'd play *hatto*, and while she dealt the cards, she'd sometimes tell me stories about my father or Korea—stories that began "Once on a time" but occasionally hinted at possible truths. And she'd sit and watch me do my homework, as if I were the TV, and mumble about how smart I was, so smart that could I really be her daughter? Though I used to grumble at her—"What? What you staring at? I got two heads or something?"—inside I was really loving it, seeing how she smiled, how she looked at me.

But always, no matter how many piles of rice I left for the gods, no matter how many times I prayed, there came the times when—as Auntie Reno used to say—the spirits claimed my mother.

When the spirits called to her, my mother would leave me and slip inside herself, to somewhere I could not and did not want to follow. It was as if the mother I knew turned off, checked out, and someone else came to rent the space. During these times, the body of my mother would float through our one-bedroom apartment, slamming into walls and bookshelves and bumping into the corners of the coffee table and the television. If I could catch her, I would try to clean her cuts with *Cambison* ointment, dab the bruises with vinegar to stop the swelling. But most times I just left her food and water and hid in the bedroom, where I listened to long stretches of thumping accentuated by occasional shouts to a spirit named Induk.

•➘

It was worse when I was younger. When my father died, leaving us as guests of his most recent employers, at the Miami Mission House for Boys, my mother cashed what was left of his estate—several pieces of family jewelry, pearls mostly, and shares in a retirement village—paid off his hospital bills, and tried to return to Korea. She got as far as Hawai'i when—not knowing anyone, broke, and with a young child to care for—my mother had to put me in school and find work. I remember my mother drifting in and out of under-the-table jobs—washing dishes in Vietnamese restaurants, slinging drinks in Korean bars on Ke'eaumoku—stringing together enough change to pay the weekly rent on a dirty second-floor apartment off Kapi'olani Boulevard. I remember the darkness of that apartment: the brown imitation-wood wall paneling blackened from exhaust from the street, the boarded-up windows, the nights without electricity when we could not pay the bill. And I remember nights that seemed to last for days, when my mother dropped into a darkness of her own, so deep that I did not think she would ever come back to me.

At Ala Wai Elementary, where I was enrolled, I was taught that if I was ever in trouble I should tell my teachers or the police; I learned about 911. But in real life, I knew none of these people would understand, that they might even hurt my mother. I was on my own. At least until Auntie Reno discovered my mother's potential.

• ~

The way Auntie Reno tells it, she was the only person who would hire my mother. Though my mother could speak English, Korean, and Japanese—which was a big plus in Waikiki—she had no real job skills or experience. "Out of dah goodness of my heart, I wen take your maddah as one cook," Auntie Reno told me. "Even though she nevah even know how for fry hamburgah steak."

The first few months on the job, my mother did well, despite the oil burns on her arms and face. Then the spirits—Saja the Death Messenger and Induk the Birth Grandmother—descended upon her, fighting over her loyalty and consciousness. During these times in which she shouted and punched at the air above her head, dancing as if to duck return jabs, I was afraid to let her out of the house, both because she might never come back and because—like a wandering *yongson* ghost finding its way back to its birthplace—she might. After roaming the streets, she could have led everyone back to me, the one who would have to explain my mother's insanity. Each morning during her spell, I locked the door on her rantings and ravings, and each afternoon I raced home, fearful of what I'd find when I slipped back into our apartment.

The day Reno found out about my mother, I had just come

home from school to find her dancing. At first I thought that she was back to normal, having fun listening to the radio or trying out a new American dance step, the bump-and-grind the teenagers were doing on *Bandstand* every week. But then I noticed the silence. Arms flailing, knees pumping into her chest, my mother danced without music. She must have been dancing a long time in that hot, airless apartment, because she was drenched in sweat: her hair slapped against, then stuck to her blotchy face, and water seeped from her pores, soaking the chest and underarms of her tunic blouse.

"Mom," I yelled at her. When she didn't look at me, I tried to grab one of her arms. She wrenched herself away and kept dancing.

"I got something for you to eat." I held up the part of my school lunch that I had wrapped in a napkin and brought home: half of my pig-in-the-blanket and a peanut butter cookie. I could not remember the last time she ate. I remember hoping that she had eaten while I was at school, but when I checked the refrigerator and the cabinets, whatever food we had seemed untouched.

She danced away from me, hearing music I could not hear, dancing and dancing until her rasping gasps for breath filled the air and permeated each bite of pig-in-the-blanket I took. The food tasted like sweat and hot air, but I ate because I was hungry and because I could not let it go to waste. I ate everything, not even saving any of the cookie to place on the shrine on top of our bookshelf, because I was mad at the spirits and at God for taking my mother away from me.

While I tried to do my homework and my mother continued to dance, Auntie Reno came pounding at our door. "Let me in," she bellowed. "I know you in dere, Akiko! You slackah! You lazy bum! You owe me for leaving me short so many days!"

I ran to the door and yelled through the crack: "Mrs. DeSilva-Chung, my mom is sick."

"Lie!" she yelled back. "How come when I wen call, I heard her laugh and laugh and den hang up?"

"Uh," I answered, trying to remember if I had forgotten to unplug the phone before I left for school.

Sweet Mary, the woman who lived next door, kicked the common wall between us so hard that the dishes in our sink rattled. "Shaddup!" she screeched through the walls. "I goin' call dah police! Whatchu think this is, Grand Central Station?"

Mrs. DeSilva-Chung, my Auntie Reno, yelled back, "Eh, *you* shaddup!" but she stopped banging the door and made her voice real sweet: "If you don't let me in, Rebeccah honey, I dah one goin' call dah police."

I unsnapped the locks and pulled the door open. "Won't you please come in?" I told her. Behind me, I could hear my mother panting and wheezing.

"Ho," Auntie Reno said as she pushed her way past me. The blue-and-silver scarf she had wrapped around her poodle-permed head snagged on the doorframe. "Goffunnit," she grumbled, yanking the scarf away from the frame. She folded the scarf over her hair, tucking the tight curls under the cloth. "Where's your maddah?" she growled, and when she looked up and saw my mother twirling in her see-through clothes, Auntie Reno breathed, "Ho-oly shit," and let the scarf float to the floor.

I closed the door and watched Auntie Reno watch my mother. A spider's line of spittle swung from my mother's gasping mouth as she swayed from the top of the coffee table. When she finally dropped to the ground, her chest heaving as she gulped air, Auntie Reno said, "Wow. I never seen that before."

"Shut up!" I marched over to where my mother lay and folded my arms across my chest. "She's not crazy!"

Auntie Reno looked at me, then blinked her eyes slowly, so that I could see the wings of her sparkly-blue eye shadow. "Honey girl, no one evah told you nevah jump to conclusions?" She walked forward. Stopping in front of me, she bent down and touched my mother's face.

My mother's eyes opened. "Why have you come here? Dirty person from a house full of mourning, tend to your own mother: Teeth are biting at her head, and rats are nesting at her feet."

Auntie Reno gasped. "What dah hell dat crazy woman saying?"

"Bad girl, bad daughter!" Rolling into a crouch, my mother yelled at Reno. "You pretended to take care of her, wiping her drool and her *gundinghi,* but you only wished for her to die! You only wish to save money for yourself. You wouldn't buy your mother a decent bed in life, and look, now, you won't buy her one in death—"

"No!" I rushed forward to put a hand over my mom's mouth. "She doesn't know what—"

Auntie Reno waddled quickly to the door. "I jus' go now. Uh, I call her wen she feeling better." She bent to pick up her scarf.

Before I could stop her, my mother rushed toward Reno and grabbed the scarf. She twined it around her own neck, closed her eyes, and started to rock back and forth on the cushions of her feet. "You, Baby Reno, you always wanted dis scarf. So did your sister, but I nevah wanted for you two for fight over um. 'Bury it wit me,' I told you. You made me one promise, you good-for-nuttin', and still you wen tell yoah sister I gave um to you."

Reno dropped to her knees. "Oh my God," she groaned. "Eh, Mama, wasn't li' dat, I swear on your memory."

"Mommy, stop," I said, jumping up to untangle the scarf from her neck. I pulled it from her, felt the sweat that had soaked into the material, and offered it to Reno. "I'm sorry," I said. "My mother is sick, and sometimes she just starts talking about nothing, rambling on about anykine stuff."

"Try wait, Mama—please no leave me again." Auntie Reno crawled to my mother's feet. "Mama? Akiko-san? Please," she whispered, "you can tell me anyting else?"

My mother hummed, then went to lie down on the couch.

Reno wiped at her eyes, smudging her makeup, and listened for a while to my mother's monotonous buzzing. "Your maddah might be one crazy lady," she said, holding up her hand when she thought I would protest, "but she got dah gift. She was right, you know." She glared at me, knotting the scarf in her fist and quickly adding, "Not about everyting: my maddah did say I could have dis as one—whatchucall—keepsake; my sistah only tink I was suppose to bury em wit dah body. But—and I stay shame for dis—I nevah put my maddah's remains where she asked, and now the city moving all dah graves where my maddah stay. Tractahs digging em up now."

When I frowned, inching away from her, Reno scowled back. "You dense or what? Don't you get it—dat's dah teet' stay biting at her head." She crossed her legs, leaned forward to prop her chin in the cup of her hands, and studied my mother. When my mother's eyes drifted shut and her breathing settled into a rumbling rhythm, Auntie Reno spoke: "All my life, I heard about people like dis. You know, my maddah said dis kinda thing supposed to run in our family, but I nevah seen anyone wit dah gift dis strong." She touched the tip of her finger to my mother's forehead. "Some people—not many, but some—get dah gift of talking to the dead, of walking true worlds and seeing things one regulah person like you or me don't even know about. Dah spirits love these people, tellin' em for 'do this, do that.' But they hate em, too, jealous of dah living."

·~

Auntie Reno likes to say she saved my mother and me from life in the streets, and I suppose she did. "Out of dah goodness of my heart, I'm telling you," the story goes, "I became your maddah's manager. I saw how she could help those in need, and I saw how those in need could help your maddah and you." Which is true, I guess, but Auntie Reno also saw a way that she could help herself.

Whenever the spirits called my mother to them, Auntie Reno insisted I dial her beeper, punching in 911 to let her know my mother had entered a trance. After the lunch crowd and before the dinner rush, Auntie Reno would phone the people who waited sometimes for months for my mother to deliver messages to and from the city of the dead. Then Reno closed the store and rushed over to our place.

While my mother wandered through the rooms talking to ghosts, Auntie Reno would place the large ceramic Wishing Bowl and a stack of red money envelopes on the coffee table, and I would stack oranges and light incense sticks in the corners of the apartment. Auntie Reno, who asserted that atmosphere was just as important as ability, hung bells and chimes and long banners of *kanji* on our walls. When I asked her what the characters meant, she shrugged. "Good luck, double happiness, someting like that."

Then we'd catch my mother, dress her in a long white or blue or yellow robe—whichever one we could throw over her body without protest from the spirits—and turn on the music that would start my mother dancing. She liked heavy drumbeats, and once she got going, my mother could tell all about a person and the wishes of the dead that circled around her.

It got to be that whenever my mother slipped into her spells, we'd have people camping in our kitchen and living room and out in the apartment hallway, all waiting for my mother to tell them about the death and unfulfilled desire in their lives. "Your father's mother's sister died in childbirth, crying out the name of the baby who died inside her," she'd tell one elderly customer with a growth in her uterus, "and she hangs around you, causing sickness and trouble, because she is jealous of all your children and grandchildren." Or she'd tell someone else that her husband was cheating on her because of her bad breath, caused by the vindictive first-wife ghost who died craving a final bite of *mu kimchee.*

For each of the seekers, my mother would pray and advise. And before they left, she would fold purified rock salt, ashes from the shrine, and the whispers of their deepest wish into a square of silk as a talisman against the evil or mischievous or unhappy spirits inhabiting their homes. In return, to ensure the fulfillment of their wishes, they folded money into a red envelope and dropped it into the Wishing Bowl.

And milling through all the mourners-in-waiting—the old ladies with their aching joints and deviant children, the fresh-off-the-boat immigrants with cheating husbands and tax problems, and, later on, the rich middle-aged haoles looking for a new direction in life—was Reno, who served tea or soda and collected the fee between her shifts at the restaurant.

Everyone seemed so respectful of my mother, so in awe of her, and Auntie Reno played it up, telling people my mother was a renowned fortune-teller and spirit medium in Japan and Korea. "Akiko Sonsaeng-nim," she'd say, attaching the Korean honorific to my mother's name—something she would never do when my mother was conscious—"stay famous in dah old country."

Auntie Reno's words impressed so many people that customers would wait for hours in the dank hallways and decrepit stairwells. Finally the apartment manager, fearful of the potential liabilities and lawsuits related to substandard housing and building codes, evicted us. And Auntie Reno saved us from the streets once again, informing us that my mother's share of the money enabled us to put a down payment on a small house in Waipahu, Kaimuki, Nu'uanu, or—if we weren't too choosy—Manoa Valley.

As long as my mother's trance lasted, Auntie Reno would show up at our door every morning before I went to school, leading a new gathering of people. After she organized the customers, packing them tight against the railing and down the stairs so that the line coiled from our second-story apartment into the alley below, she'd pull me aside and hand me a pastry and a small bag of money collected from the Wishing Bowl.

Always, when I went to hide the money in my room, I'd slip out a dollar bill, roll it tight as an incense stick, and lay it in an ashtray on the dresser. Careful to hide from Reno's eyes, I'd strike a match and burn the money for the spirits. Then, pulling out my father's picture, I would begin to pray to my only connection in the spirit world. "Please please please, Daddy. I'll give you everything if you give my mother back." I begged, reasoning that as a dead preacher, my father would be able to get God to intercede on my mother's behalf, or—as a spirit himself and in collusion with the other vengeful ghosts holding my mother captive—he might be persuaded by my own burnt offerings and bribes to free her.

dad was a preacher   •⁓

When my mother began talking about how she killed my father, I thought that the spirits were coming to claim her again. "Stop, Mommy," I said, rubbing the shrimp juice from her fingers. "You don't know what you're saying." At ten, despite all the people coming to hear her talk this way, I was still afraid that someone would hear my mother's craziness and lock her up. It wasn't until I reached high school that I actually started hoping that that would happen. "You're not yourself," I said loudly.

"Quiet!" My mother smacked my hand, just as she did when I couldn't memorize the times table. "Who else would I be? Pay attention!" She took the dishcloth, folded it into a rectangle, then a square, smoothing the wrinkles. "I wished him to death," she said. "Every day I think, every day I pray, 'Die, die,' sending him death-wish arrows, until one day my prayers were answered."

"Oh God," I groaned, my eyes rolling toward the back of my head. "So you didn't actually, physically kill him. Like with a knife or something."

She whacked my hand again. "I'm teaching you something very important about life. Listen: Sickness, bad luck, death, these things are not accidents. This kind stuff, people wish on you. Believe me, I know! And if you cannot block these wishes, all the death thoughts people send you collect, become arrows in your back. This is what causes wrinkles and make your shoulders fold inward."

She looked at me slouching into my chair, shoulders hunched into my body. I straightened up.

"Death thoughts turn your hair white, make you weak and break you, sucking out your life. I tell you these things," she said, touching my hair with her blistering hands, "to protect you."

She leaned toward me, and as she bent forward to kiss or hug me, I could see veins of white hair running through her black braid. Before she could touch me, I pushed away from the table, turning toward the sink to prepare the shrimp for the annual meal that made my mother's hands crack open and bleed.

• ~

I look at myself in the mirror now and see the same strands of white streaking across my dark head. I squint, and the lines in the corners of my eyes deepen, etching my face in the pattern that was my mother's. And I think: It has taken me nearly thirty years, almost all of my life, but finally the wishes I flung out in childhood have come true.

My mother is dead.

2

AKIKO ·~

The baby I could keep came when I was already dead.

I was twelve when I was murdered, fourteen when I looked into the Yalu River and, finding no face looking back at me, knew that I was dead. I wanted to let the Yalu's currents carry my body to where it might find my spirit again, but the Japanese soldiers hurried me across the bridge before I could jump.

I did not let them get too close. I knew they would see the name and number stenciled across my jacket and send me back to the camps, where they think nothing of using a dead girl's body. When the guards started to step toward me, I knew enough to walk on, to wave them back to their post, where they would watch for other Koreans with that "special look" in their eyes. Before the Japanese government posted the soldiers—"for the good of the Koreans"—the bridge over the Yalu had been a popular suicide spot.

My body moved on.

That is why, twenty years after it left my spirit behind at the recreation camp, my body was able to have this baby. Even the doctors here say it is almost a miracle. The camp doctor said I would never have a living child after he took my first one out, my insides too bruised and battered, impossible to properly heal.

So this little one is a surprise. This half-white and half-Korean child. She would be called tweggi in the village where I was born, but here she will be American.

· ~

When the missionaries found me, they thought I was Japanese because of the name, Akiko, sewn onto the sack that was my dress. The number, 41, they weren't sure about, and thought, Perhaps an orphanage? They asked me—in Korean, Japanese, Chinese—where I came from, who my family was, but by then I had no voice and could only stand dumbly in front of their moving mouths as they lifted my arms, poked at my teeth and into my ears, wiped the dirt from my face.

She is like the wild child raised by tigers, I heard them say to each other. Physically human but able to speak only in the language of animals. They were kind and praised me when I responded to the simple commands they issued in Japanese: sit, eat, sleep. Had they asked, I would also have responded to "close mouth" and "open legs." At the camps where the Japanese called us *Jungun Ianfu,* military comfort women, we were taught only whatever was necessary to service the soldiers. Other than that, we were not expected to understand and were forbidden to speak, any language at all.

But we were fast learners and creative. Listening as we gathered the soldiers' clothes for washing or cooked their meals, we were able to surmise when troops were coming in and how many we were expected to serve. We taught ourselves to communicate through eye movements, body posture, tilts of the head, or—when we could not see each other—through rhythmic rustlings between our stalls; in this way we could speak, in this way we kept our sanity.

The Japanese say Koreans have an inherent gift for languages, proving that we are a natural colony, meant to be dominated. They delighted in their own ignorance, feeling they had nothing to fear or learn. I suppose that was lucky for us, actually. They never knew what we were saying. Or maybe they just didn't care.

•⌐

I'm trying to remember exactly when I died. It must have been in stages, beginning with my birth as the fourth girl and last child in the Kim family, and ending in the recreation camps north of the Yalu. Perhaps if my parents had not died so early, I might have been able to live a full life. Perhaps not; we were a poor family. I might have been sold anyway.

My father was a cow trader. He traveled from village to village, herding the cows before him, from one farmer to the next, making a small profit as the middleman. When he was home, my older sisters' job was to collect the dung and, after we parceled out a small portion for our own garden, sell the rest to our neighbors. Sometimes we dried the dung for fuel, which burned longer and cleaner than wood. Most of the time, though, we used sticks that my sisters collected from the woods.

My job was to help my mother wash clothes. We each had a basket, according to our size, which we carried up the river we called Yalu Aniya, Older Sister to the Yalu. Going up was easy, the load light on our heads. Coming home was harder, since not only were the damp clothes heavier but we were tired from beating the clothes clean against the rocks. I remember that as we crouched over our wash, pounding out the dirt, I pretended that my mother and I sent secret signals to one another, the rocks singing out messages only we could understand. *washing clothes c̄ Mom*

•⌐

My mother died shortly after my father. I didn't see my father die; he was almost thirty miles away. As with his life, I know about his death primarily through what others have told me. The villagers who took him in say he had a lung disease, coughing up blood as he died. They also said he called for my mother.

She was always a good wife; she went to him quickly in death,

The language of Touch
for useless wds

just as she did in life. One night after we had carried home the wash, she kept saying how tired she was, how tired. Come, Mother, I told her, lie down. I kept asking her, what could I do? Do you want soup, do you want massage? Till finally she put her hand over my mouth and guided my fingers to her forehead. I stroked her softly, loosening her hair from the bun she tied it in, rubbing her temples where I could feel the heat and the throb of her beating heart. Even when the erratic tempo slowed, then finally stopped, I continued to pet her. I wanted her to know that I loved her.

I touch my child in the same way now; this is the language she understands: the cool caresses of my fingers across her tiny eyelids, her smooth tummy, her fat toes. This, not the senseless murmurings of useless words, is what quiets her, tells her she is precious. She is like my mother in this way.

Because of this likeness, this link to the dead, my daughter is the only living thing I love. My husband, the missionaries who took me in after the camp, my sisters, if they are still alive, all are incidental. What are living people to ghosts, except ghosts themselves?

My oldest sister understood this. When my second and third sisters ran away together to look for work as secretaries or factory workers in Pyongyang, the oldest sister tried to keep our father's business going by marrying our closest neighbor. The neighbors didn't have much money, but they had more than us and wouldn't take her without a dowry. How could they buy cattle without any capital, they reasoned.

I was her dowry, sold like one of the cows before and after me. You are just going to follow second and third sisters, she told me. The Japanese say there is enough work for anyone in the cities. Girls, even, can learn factory work or serve in restaurants. You will make lots of money.

Still, I cried. She hugged me, then pinched me. Grow up now, she said. No mother, no father. We all have to make our lives. She

sister
soldier

didn't look at my face when the soldiers came, didn't watch as they herded me onto their truck. I heard them asking her if she wanted to come along; your sister is still so young, not good for much, they said. But you. You are grown and pretty. You could do well.

I am not sure, but I think my sister laughed. I hope that she had at least a momentary fear that they would take her too.

I am already married, she said.

I imagine she shrugged then, as if to say, What can I do? Then she added, My sister will be even prettier. She didn't ask why that should matter in a factory line.

I knew I would not see the city. We had heard the rumors: girls bought or stolen from villages outside the city, sent to Japanese recreation centers. But still, we did not know what the centers were like. At worst, I thought, I would do what I've done all my life: clean, cook, wash clothes, work hard. How could I imagine anything else?

At first that is what I did do. Still young, I was kept to serve the women in the camps. Around women all my life, I felt almost like I was coming home when I first realized there were women at the camps, maybe a dozen. I didn't see them right away; they were kept in their stalls, behind mat curtains, most of the days and throughout the night. Only slowly were they revealed to me as I delivered and took away their meals, as I emptied their night pots. Hanako 38, her name given because her face was once pretty as a flower. Miyoko 52, frail and unlucky as the Miyokos before her. Kimi-ko 3, with hair the color of egg yellow, which made the officers laugh when they realized the pun of her name: Kimi the sovereign, Kimi the yolk. Akiko 40. Tamayo 29, who told the men she loved them and received gifts and money that she, stubborn in her hopes for a future, would bury in the corner of her stall.

Unless they had to visit the camp doctor, their freedom outside their stalls consisted of weekly baths at the river and scheduled trips to the outhouse. If they needed to relieve themselves when it was not their turn to go outside, they could use their special pots. It became my job to empty the pots. I also kept their clothes and bedding clean, combed and braided their hair, served them their meals. When I could, I brought them each a dab of grease, which they would smooth over their wounds, easing the pain of so many men.

I liked caring for the women. As their girl, I was able to move from one stall to the next, even from one section of the camp to another, if I was asked. And because of this luxury, the women used me to pass messages. I would sing to the women as I braided their hair or walked by their compartments to check their pots. When I hummed certain sections, the women knew to take those unsung words for their message. In this way, we could keep up with each other, find out who was sick, who was new, who had the most men the night before, who was going to crack.

•⁓

To this day, I do not think Induk—the woman who was the Akiko before me—cracked. Most of the other women thought she did because she would not shut up. One night she talked loud and nonstop. In Korean and in Japanese, she denounced the soldiers, yelling at them to stop their invasion of her country and her body. Even as they mounted her, she shouted: I am Korea, I am a woman, I am alive. I am seventeen, I had a family just like you do, I am a daughter, I am a sister.

Men left her stall quickly, some crying, most angrily joining the line for the woman next door. All through the night she talked, reclaiming her Korean name, reciting her family genealogy, even chanting the recipes her mother had passed on to her. Just before daybreak, they took her out of her stall and into the woods, where we couldn't hear her anymore. They brought her back skewered from her vagina to her mouth, like a pig ready for roasting. A lesson, they told the rest of us, warning us into silence.

That night, it was as if a thousand frogs encircled the camp. They opened their throats for us, swallowed our tears, and cried for us. All night, it seemed, they called, Induk, Induk, Induk, so we would never forget.

Although I might have imagined the frogs. That was my first night as the new Akiko. I was given her clothes, which were too big and made the soldiers laugh. The new P won't be wearing them much anyway, they jeered. Fresh poji.

Even though I had not yet had my first bleeding, I was auctioned off to the highest bidder. After that it was a free-for-all, and I thought I would never stop bleeding.

That is how I know Induk didn't go crazy. She was going sane. She was planning her escape. The corpse the soldiers brought back from the woods wasn't Induk.

It was Akiko 41; it was me.

·~

My husband speaks four languages: German, English, Korean, and Japanese. He is learning a fifth, Polish, from cassette tapes he borrows from the public library. He reads Chinese.

A scholar who spends his life with the Bible, he thinks he is safe, that the words he reads, the meaning he gathers, will remain the same. Concrete. He is wrong.

He shares all his languages with our daughter, though she is not even a year old. She will absorb the sounds, he tells me. But I worry that the different sounds for the same object will confuse her. To compensate, I try to balance her with language I know is true. I watch her with a mother's eye, trying to see what she needs—my breast, a new diaper, a kiss, her toy—before she cries, before she has to give voice to her pain.

And each night, I touch each part of her body, waiting until I see recognition in her eyes. I wait until I see that she knows that all of what I touch is her and hers to name in her own mind, before language dissects her into pieces that can be swallowed and digested by others not herself.

• ✐

At the camp, the doctor gave me a choice: rat poison or the stick. I chose the stick. I saw what happened to the girl given the rat bait to abort her baby. I did not have the courage then to die the death that she died.

As the doctor bound my legs and arms, gagged me, then reached for the stick he would use to hook and pull the baby, not quite a baby, into the world, he talked. He spoke of evolutionary differences between the races, biological quirks that made the women of one race so pure and the women of another so promiscuous. Base, really, almost like animals, he said.

Rats, too, will keep doing it until they die, refusing food or water as long as they have a supply of willing partners. The doctor chuckled and probed, digging and piercing, as he lectured. Luckily for the species, Nature ensures that there is one dominant male to keep the others at bay and the female under control. And the female will always respond to him. He squeezed my nipples, pinching until they tightened. See?

I followed the light made by the waves of my pain, tried to leave my body behind. But the doctor pinned me to the earth with his stick and his words. Finally he stood upright, cracked his back, and threw the stick into the trash. He rinsed his hands in a basin of water, then unbound my hands and mouth. He put the rags between my legs.

Fascinating, he said thoughtfully as he left the tent. Perhaps it is the differences in geography that make the women of our two countries so morally incompatible.

•~

He did not bother tying me down, securing me for the night. Maybe he thought I was too sick to run. Maybe he thought I wouldn't want to. Maybe he knew I had died and that ropes and guards couldn't keep me anyway.

That night, with the blood-soaked rags still wedged between my thighs, I slipped out of the tent, out of the camp. Following the sound of my mother beating clothes against the rocks, I floated along the trails made by deer and found a nameless stream that led in the end, like all the mountain streams, to the Yalu.

← caop dr.
about her baby
c̄ a stick

3

BECCAH:~ *writes obits*

I record the lives of the dead:

Severino Santos Agopada, 65, retired plumber and member of the Botanical Garden Society of Hawaii, died March 13, 1995.

Gladys Malia Leiatua-Smith, 81, died April 9, 1995. Formerly of Western Samoa, she is survived by sons Jacob, Nathaniel, Luke, Matthew, and Siu Junior; daughters Hope, Grace, Faith, and Nellie; 19 grandchildren and 5 great-grandchildren.

Lawrence Ching III of Honolulu, died April 15, 1995. Survived by wife, Rose, and son Lawrence IV. Services Saturday, Aloha attire.

When I first started writing the obits for the *Honolulu Star Bulletin*—as a graduating journalism major in awe of my first adult lover, U of H legend and the *Bulletin*'s managing editor, Sanford Dingman—I read the certificates of death, faxed fresh from the mortuaries, with imagination: creating adventures for those born far from their place of death, picturing the grief of parents having to bury a child, feeling satisfaction when someone died old, surrounded by the two or three generations that came from his body.

Now, however, after six years of death detail, treading water in both my relationship and my job, I no longer see people, families, lives lived and wasted. I no longer struggle over the script, thesaurus in one hand, hoping to utilize obscure synonyms for "die" so that my obits would illuminate my potential, attracting praise and admiration from the great Mr. Dingman. Now I deal only in words and statistics that need to be typed into the system. The first thing I do each day after I log on is to count how many inches I have to fill, computing how many names and death dates need to be processed.

I have recorded so many deaths that the formula is templated in my brain: Name, age, date of death, survivors, services. And yet, when it came time for me to write my own mother's obituary, as I held a copy of her death certificate in my hand, I found that I did not have the facts for even the most basic, skeletal obituary. And I found I did not know how to start imagining her life.

• ~

When I was a child, it did not occur to me that my mother had a life before me. Always, when I asked for stories about her past, they were about me, starting from my conception. "How did you and Daddy meet?" I would ask her. "When did you know you were in love? When did you decide to have me?"

In those days, I believed my mother's story that my parents met when she was a famous singer in Korea. "Once on a time, I sang on stage," my mother would boast, "and your father came to see me. He was in love."

I imagined hot spotlights blinding her eyes, a large stage empty except for my mother, dressed in stripes and glittering sequins. When I was in elementary school, and easily influenced by Auntie Reno's sense of fashion, that was my idea of glamour. The first outfit I chose for myself was a plaid and denim bell-bottom pantsuit, which I wore three times a week in the fourth grade. I wore it despite the hoots of the boys and the stink-eye and snub-nose from Janice "Toots" Tutivena and her Entourage, until the crisscrossing stripes faded at the knees and the bell-bottoms flapped above my ankles.

I believed my mother's story, even though when I heard her singing to the spirits, I thought not of music but of crying, her songs long wails of complaints and demands and wishes for the dead.

I believed it because I wanted to believe that my voice would rescue me, transport me to a new world. I lived with the secret hope that I had inherited my mother's talent and that I would soon be discovered—perhaps singing "Rudolph the Red-Nosed Reindeer" in our school's Xmas Xtravaganza. When my class took its place in the cafetorium and began singing our carol, I knew my voice would float out above the voices of the other students. Slowly, one by one, the rest of the singers would fall silent. One by one, the parents and teachers in the audience would rise to their feet, drawn closer to the stage by my voice, as pure as a bell. Then, when the song came to a close, the audience would erupt into cheers and applause, and one man—preferably Toots's father (who in real life sold vacuum cleaners at Sears but in my perfect daydream was a movie agent)—would point to me and shout, "What a voice! What poise! What a smile! The new Marie Osmond!"

Whenever I was alone, I'd sing—usually something by the Carpenters or Elvis—in preparation for my discovery. I would sing so hard I'd get tears in my eyes. My singing moved me.

One afternoon I crawled into the bathtub, pulled the curtain to make a private cave for myself, lay down, and sang "Let It Be," over and over again. Somewhere between my third and seventh renditions, my mother came in to use the toilet.

"What's wrong?" she shouted.

"Nothing," I growled. "I'm singing."

My mother yanked open the shower curtain so hard the bar fell onto the floor.

"Hey!" I squealed as I sat up. My mother loomed over me, the curtain clutched in her hands and pooling into the tub. The bar, suspended by the curtain's rings, knocked against her thighs. I almost asked, "Are you crazy?" but stopped myself before the words escaped and became concrete, heavy enough to break into the real world.

"Are the spirits after you too?" she panted. "Do you hear them singing, always singing?"

"No!" I shouted at her.

"Sometimes they cry so loud, just like a cat cry, so full of wanting, that I worry you will begin to hear them, too." My mother closed her eyes and started rocking. "Waaaooo, waaaaoooo," she wailed. "Just like that." She stopped rocking and glared at me. "You have to fight it."

I put my hands over my ears. "I can't hear you, I can't hear you," I sang over and over again. "I can't hear you, I can't hear you," I chanted each time she opened her mouth to add something else.

Finally she shut her mouth and didn't open it again. Then she shook her head, just looking at me lying in the tub with my hands plugging my ears, singing tonelessly, "I can't hear you I can't hear you I can't hear you." When she turned and walked away, kicking the curtain out in front of her, I was still chanting, "I can't hear you," though the words had lost their meaning.

•⁓

I was discovered not during Ala Wai E's Xmas Xtravaganza but during the tryouts for the May Day Pageant. And not by Toots's father but by Toots herself.

I was not naive enough to try out for May Day Queen or her court. I knew that I never had a chance, since I wasn't part Hawaiian and didn't have long hair. But I did want to be in the chorus that stood next to the stage and sang "Hawai'i Pono'i" as they ascended their thrones.

During the after-school tryouts, as I waited for my turn to sing next to the vice principal playing the piano, I watched the kids ahead of me turn shy and quiet, their squeaky voices breaking under the weight of the accompaniment. I vowed my voice would be strong enough to fill the entire cafetorium and rich enough to eat for dessert.

When my name was called, I marched down the aisle, a long gauntlet of chewed sunflower seeds spit at my feet by the Toots Entourage. My slippers kicked up the littered shells so that they flecked the backs of my calves. I kept my eyes on the stage, on the piano, and on Vice Principal "Piano Man" Pili, who alternately smiled encouragement to each struggling singer and glared into the audience in an attempt to stifle whistles and hoots and shouts of "Gong." But as I walked past their seats, I heard Toots and Tiffi Sugimoto hiss, "Look dah fancy-pants! 'I stay blinded by dah light!' "

I tossed my hair and glided onto the stage. Clearing my throat, I nodded to Vice P Pili, smiled and waved to the crowd—right at Toots—and tapped my foot: one and a two and a three!

To this day, I am not sure what happened, or how it happened. I had practiced—in the bathtub, walking to school—until I knew I was good, until I made myself cry. But that day, some devil-thing with the voice of a big, old-age frog took possession of my throat, and "Hawai'i Pono'i" lurched unreliably around the cafetorium: "Hawai'i Pono'iiiii, Nana i Kou mo'i . . . uh . . . la la la Lani e Kamehameha e . . . mmm hmm hmm . . . Hawai'iiiii Po-oh-no 'iiiii! Aaaah-meh-nehhhh!"

At least I was loud.

As I slunk off the stage, I heard Toots and her Entourage laughing and howling like dogs. "Guh-guh-guh-gong!" they barked.

They followed me out of the building and pinned me against the wall. "You suck," said Toots.

"Yeah," said Tiffi, a Toots wannabe. "You suck."

"You gotta be the worst singer in the school," Toots said. "We don't want you in our chorus."

"We don't even want you in our school, you weirdo," said another Toots follower.

"You're the weirdo," I snapped back. "Just so happens I got the talent of my mother, who was a famous singer in Korea." After I said this, I realized some things were better left unsaid.

"Yeah, right," said Toots.

"Yeah, that's right," I said, then added, compelled to defend myself, "They just have different singing over there."

"Hanyang anyang hasei-pasei-ooooh," Toots screeched. "Yobos must have bad ears!"

The girls laughed and stepped closer, the half-moon made by their bodies tightening around me. "You're nothing but stink Yobo-shit," said Toots. "Nothing but one big-fat-shit liar. 'Oh, my mommy's a famous singer.' 'Oh, my daddy was rich, with a house on the Mainland, and I had one puppy.' 'Oh, next year my daddy going come get us and move us back.' Yeah, right."

Toots pushed my shoulder. "This is what's true: You so poor that every day you gotta wear the same lame clothes and the same out-of-fashion, stink-smelling shoes until they get holes and still you wear em. You so poor you save your school lunch for one after-school snack—no lie, cause we seen you wrap em up in your napkin."

By this time Toots was so close I could smell a mixture of seeds and the kakimochi she always ate in class on her breath. I gave her stink-eye, but she kept pushing me.

"You talk like you better than everybody else, but you not. We all know you live in The Shacks, and you prob'ly sleep with dirty feet in the same bed as your crazy old lady."

"Not!" At the one thing I could call a lie—that I went to bed with dirty feet—I called Toots a liar and punched her in her soft, newly forming chest. When she fell back into her friends, I ran away and didn't look back, not even to see if they were chasing me.

• ⟩

I don't think I ran home and asked my mother to verify her singing story right away. I probably went to my secret place, a spot under the Ala Wai Bridge, where runoff from the rains and the city drained into the canal. Underneath, I had flattened out a nest among the tall grass that stretched along the bank. Sheltered by the underbelly of that small pedestrian bridge, I would practice my singing. I liked to hear my voice bounce off the concrete that surrounded me.

I probably went there right after Toots and her Entourage told me I sucked. I know I would have wanted to hear the truth for myself.

Eventually, though it might not have been that night, I must have asked my mother to repeat the story of how she met my father. Because I have the distinct memory of another story.

We were at the kitchen table, sorting coins from the Wishing Bowl and packing them into paper sleeves, when, trying to sound casual, I asked her for the story of my parents' first meeting. "Mom," I told her, "tell me again that story, you know, that one about you and Dad meeting."

Without looking up from counting out a pile of dimes, she sighed. "Once was a hard time," she said, "but a happy time. I was helping to take care of all the orphans during the war—you know, so many children lost their mommies, lost their daddies at that time. Your father was one of the missionaries that gave us food and clothing. When he saw how good I was with the children, he fell in love with me, because he knew I would make a good mother."

She slipped the dimes into a roll, then began on the quarters. "When the war moved into my village, he helped us all, everyone, even the old mamasans, escape. We walked and walked, trying to escape from the communists. We hid in cemeteries and walked over the mountains of Korea until we were free to build a new home. In America."

My mother finished one stack of quarters, then looked up at me. She touched my cheek. "You remember anything about your father?" When I shook my head, she said, "Everything was nice and happy."

I don't recall if I challenged this new story or her old one. Sometimes I think I must have said, "Wait! That's not what you told me before! What's the truth?" because even then I must have recognized her story as an adaptation of *The Sound of Music.* Every year we'd watch that movie, after preparing a big bowl of boiled peanuts and a plate of dried squid as snacks. My mother liked the songs and would always cry at the ending.

Other times I think I must have said nothing, swallowing her new story without accusation or confrontation, even if I didn't believe her. When she spoke to me, calling me by name, I never wanted to do anything to spoil the moment. I feared my own words might break the spell of normalcy.

•➴

I grew cautious of my mother's stories, never knowing what to count on or what to discount. They sounded good—most of the stories she told me included the phrase: "It was a hard time but a happy time." In fact, I repeated several of her stories, telling teachers and other students versions of them that I supplemented with my own favorite movies: *West Side Story,* where Maria, my mother, was left pregnant with her love child, who was, of course, myself; *The Little Princess* and *The Poor Little Rich Girl,* where I, the brave and suffering orphan, am reclaimed in the end by a rich and loving father, who was alive.

But I knew they were just stories told to people who didn't really matter, those who couldn't see into our Goodwill-furnished apartment in the row of dilapidated tri-story housing units nicknamed The Shacks. Those who couldn't see into the past when my father was alive and drunk and yelling about God. Those who couldn't see into my dreams of drowning and sinking and struggling for breath while unseen hands wrapped around my legs and pulled.

• ✦

Not long after I started working for the *Bulletin,* I saw Tiffi Sugimoto. She wandered into the news building, looking for the marketing department, and even after all the years that had passed, I recognized her right away. With her spindly arms and her head that seemed overly large for her thin neck and scrawny body, she looked more like a ten-year-old as an adult than she had when she was really ten. When we were both ten, she seemed so big, her power as Toots's "right-hand man" larger than life.

I meant to look away when she walked near me, but I was caught staring. She smiled at me and sailed over to my cubicle. "Rebeccah!" she said as she bent over to hug me. She smacked the air near my ear. "You look exactly the same!"

I must have appeared dubious, because she leaned back and said, "Don't you remember me? Tiffany Sugimoto. Remember, me and Janice were always following you around, trying to be your friend?"

"Uh, yes, Tiffi," I mumbled.

Tiffi giggled, high-pitched and girlish, and as the men in the newsroom—including Sanford, who back then always seemed to be nearby and ready with encouragement and advice—looked up, she batted her lashes. "What a wonderful place to work," she cooed. "How stimulating! How exciting to be the first to know the news!"

I grunted. "What I do is not glamorous," I said. Then, throwing a glance, a challenge, toward Sanford, I added, "At least not yet it's not."

"No, really, Rebeccah," Tiffi said, frowning her sincerity. "Wait till I tell Janice and the others what you are doing now. Now that Janice is back from California, learning how to be an EST instructor, I know she'd, like, love to see you! We always wondered what happened when you moved away—you went to the Mainland to live with your dad, right?"

She patted my head. "We really missed you. You always had such presence, an individualistic sense of style and color, and what a wit! Remember when Vice Principal Pili ordered you to sing "Hawai'i Pono'i" and you made up your own words? I thought he would, like, flip!"

Tiffi laughed and added how great it was to see me, that we should keep in touch, and maybe the "old Ala Wai gang" could get together for a mini-reunion. Hey—would I be willing to, like, put together a newsletter?

As I smiled and nodded whenever she took a breath, all I could think was: Is this the way she really remembers it? Her sincerity made me doubt my own version of events. Perhaps what I thought was true had been colored by the insecurities of a ten-year-old girl. At any rate, at that moment, looking at Tiffi chatting at me like we were the best of friends, I realized that not only could I not trust my mother's stories; I could not trust my own.

4
―――――

AKIKO ·‿

I was strapped down when my daughter was born too. My hands
cuffed to the bed, flat on my back with my knees up, I heard the low
keening of a wounded animal in the etherized darkness. Surrounded
by doctors, unable to move, I felt my mind slip back into the camps.
You're a doctor, I screamed, help me, help me get home. But he
only laughed and pushed himself on top of me, using my body as
the other soldiers had done. Afterward, as he wiped himself on my
shift, he opened the screen partition and let others watch him exam-
ine me. This one is still good, he called over his shoulder. He pried
the lips of my vagina open with his fingers. See? he said. Still firm
and moist.

·‿

I tried to protect my daughter from the doctors, from their dirty
hands and eyes. I scissored my legs closed, wanting to keep my child
cradled within me, safe. But they roped my legs, stretching them
open into the Japanese character for "man." One doctor pushed on
my stomach, another widened me with a double-pronged stick, and
this time my baby came into the world fully formed and alive.

We caught her, someone said—and when I heard that woman's
voice in the roomful of men, I knew Induk was there. Slipping into

the body of a doctor, she stood beside me, shadowed by mask, gown, and a halo of light. And though I could not see her face, though it had been some time since she last came to me, I knew it was her, just as I've always known. Even the first time.

• ⤳

She comes in singing, entering with full voice, filling me so that there is no me except for her, Induk.

• ⤳

That first time, she found me sprawled next to an unnamed stream above the Yalu, the place where I had discarded my empty body, and invited herself in.

I saw her with my eyes closed, though how I knew she was Induk I do not know, for she looked like my mother, standing there next to the river with her arms outstretched, long strips of hair coming undone from the married woman's bun at the back of her neck. It was as if without their earthly bodies, the boundaries between them melted, blending their features, merging their spirits. Now I cannot remember what either my mother or Induk looked like when she was alive and a separate person.

Here, baby, here, Induk said, her voice creaking like a hundred thousand frogs. She shuffled closer, hands cupping her breasts, which turned into an offering of freshly unearthed ginseng.

It is not myokkuk, Induk said as I gnawed on a raw root. She stroked my head, combing out the tangles with her fingers just as I did for her when she was alive, then she said: But the seaweed soup is mostly good for making milk anyway. You don't need that now.

My stomach cramped, and I threw up what I had eaten. I rinsed my mouth with water from the stream, and my stomach rebelled at even the taste of water. Yet I could not stop my mouth from sucking at the root.

•~

Secretly, I think that is why I could not have a baby for so long after the Japanese recreation camp. Though the camp doctors said my insides were ruined from so many men, so many times, I think that the real reason I could not conceive for almost twenty years is because I ate so much ginseng. I became unbalanced with male energy. Finally the effects wore off enough to give me a baby girl.

•~

I make seaweed soup for myself now, for milk for my living daughter. Induk says my body is weakest after birth, but also at its most flexible. Our bones are as soft and changeable as those of the fetus we carried for nine months. This is the time we are most female, she says. Myokkuk is for women, for life.

My breasts tingle at my daughter's cry. I pick her up before she fully wakes, so that even before she reaches consciousness, she knows that her mother is here for her.

Her father says, Leave her to cry for a while. You're spoiling her. She needs to learn independence.

He tells me, parroting the doctor, Give her the bottle, better than breast.

But I cannot. I have heard what the doctor says, but I also remember my own mother shaking her small, limp breasts at each of her daughters, laughing as we bathed together. Look, girls! See what you did to me? she teased. See what will happen to you, too, one day when you give all of yourself to your own children?

All I know is that I do not want my baby to experience even a moment of insecurity, of want. I cannot take the time to prepare and heat a bottle while she screams with hunger. And if she drinks from the bottle, how will she know her mother's heart?

Beccah-chan latches onto me, her lips and tongue pulling my nipple, one hand kneading my breast as if to make the milk flow faster. The milk comes in too fast; she chokes. My baby breaks away from me, squalling. Her arms stiffen, and little fists strike out at me. She is noisy like her father, not afraid to yell and keep yelling. This must be a lingering effect of the ginseng. I do not know if it is a good thing.

•➤

There was no need for me to get up. I lay by the river, already feeling the running water erode the layers of my skin, washing me away, but Induk filled my belly and forced me to my hands and knees. She led me to the double rainbow where virgins climb to heaven and told me to climb. Below me, a river of human-faced flowers stretched so wide and bright I could not keep my eyes open.

She spoke for me: No one performed the proper rites of the dead. For me. For you. Who was there to cry for us in kok, announcing our death? Or to fulfill the duties of yom: bathing and dressing our bodies, combing our hair, trimming our nails, laying us out? Who was there to write our names, to even know our names and to remember us?

And now, said Induk, there is only the dead to guide us. Here, she said, giving me the image of a woman. I saw a fox spirit who haunted the cemeteries of deserted villages, sucking at the mouths of the newly dead in order to taste their otherworld knowledge.

This is Manshin Ahjima, Induk said. Old lady of ten thousand spirits. Go to her, and she will prepare you.

I wanted to say I didn't know where she lived, but then I saw the exact spot where Manshin Ahjima lived and how to get there. I'd have to cross over the Yalu, scale seven mountain peaks in the deep country, then follow the road to the outskirts of Sinuiju. Through a scattering of gray adobe houses, all identical, I would go to the house fronted with mulberry trees. There I would find the old lady and her ten thousand spirits.

• ⤙

I do not know how long I left my body by the river, stirring periodically with cramps and the need to vomit. It lay in its own filth, moving only to fill its mouth with ginseng and water, the instinct for survival in the blood and bones.

When I finally opened my eyes, I saw not heaven but partially chewed and digested bits of ginseng root in the dirt next to my face. I felt clear and empty, as translucent as the river beside me. Noticing the bleeding between my legs had stopped, I peeled the rags, stiff as scabs, away from my body and, carefully folding them, placed them on some rocks away from the running water. After taking off the rest of my clothes, I waded into the stream and rubbed at the dried blood caked on my legs from groin to calves. The mud-colored flecks turned liquid red in my hands, then dissolved under the patient licking of the river's tongue.

Rubbing handfuls of small pebbles against my head and skin, I washed my hair and body until I felt raw. I let the cooling air dry me. By the length of the day, I knew that soon it would be the season to replant the stalks of rice in the paddies. When my parents were still alive and I was still a child, everyone in our family worked to grow the rice. Where we lived, there was time only for one planting, one harvest, so everything had to be done quickly and well. As the youngest, I was responsible for feeding the workers their meals of rice and soup, carried to them on trays balanced on my head. When I delivered the food without spilling, I was allowed to play— a function also rooted in practicality; as I jumped through the rows of fragile plants, waving sticks into the air, I kept scavenging birds away from our future meals.

But as I grew and second and third sister were hired on neighboring farms, I took over more of the work. Mother, oldest sister, and I would spend hours bent over the knee-deep silt, our fingers cradling the baby rice, laying them into the oozing earth.

During one season of planting, my mother gave birth to a dead baby. Smaller than one of my mother's outstretched hands, the infant slipped between her fingers in a gush of blood and sour-smelling fluid. My mother wrapped it in a bundle, packing it neat as a field lunch, before I could see it, but oldest sister saw. It was deformed, Soon Ja whispered. Tail like a tadpole. Or maybe, she added as an afterthought, it was a boy.

We walked with our mother to the river, taking the clothes that needed to be washed. My mother divided up the clothes between my sister and me, and humming under her breath, she walked downriver. We listened to her voice, rising in waves above the rushing of the water, sing the song of the river: Pururun mul, su manun saramdul-i, jugugat-na? Blue waters, how many lives have you carried away? Moot saram-ui seulpumdo hulro hulro sa ganora. You should carry the sorrow of people far, far away.

And as we beat our clothes clean, we watched out of the corners of our eyes as she tightened the knot on her baby's shroud and set it into the water where the current pulled it down. Into Saja's mouth, oldest sister told me later in an attempt to torment me. An offering for the gatekeeper of hell.

∙⁓

When I was dry from my bath, I took the rags that had held back my blood and all that was left of my first baby, and instead of throwing them into the water, I planted them in a clean patch of earth next to the stream.

∙⁓

I like to imagine the face of my first child, what she would have looked like had the features evolved from fetus to infant. I imagine her as perfectly formed as my living daughter: her head, her hands, her toes, everything perfect and human-looking, except in miniature. No bigger than my fist, her tiny body crosses in on itself, arms and legs folded over her chest and belly. Her eyes flutter against closed lids, and her mouth opens and closes as she dreams of suckling. I like to imagine my first baby in this way: nestled in the crook of the river's elbow, nursing at its breast.

5

BECCAH ·‿

Like the rats and cockroaches that ruled The Shacks, Saja the Death Messenger, Guardian of Hell, lived in the spaces between our walls. Each morning before dressing, I inspected the clothes hanging in the closet for the light dusting of gray fur or pawprints, and for the poppy-seed shit or fragile rice-paper skin of molting roaches. In the same way, I looked for indications of the Death Messenger: As I brushed and beat the dresses hanging in the closet, or shook and sifted through the underwear drawer, I unearthed the jade talismans my mother pinned to the insides of my clothes, the packets of salt or ashes she sewed into my panties.

I imagined the Death Messenger as an ugly old man with horns and ulcerous skin, burning yellow eyes and a gaping, toothless mouth that waited to feed ravenously on the souls that lined up in front of our apartment. Our open door was Saja's gaping mouth, my mother his tongue, sampling each person for the taste of death. The demon waiting to snatch me off to hell if I did not carry a red-packeted charm, Saja was the devil my father had preached about and, through my mother's chants and offerings, became more real to me than my father ever was.

Sometimes when I could not sleep at night, I would hear the murmurings of the people who shared the building with us, or the shrieks of the cars in the street, and I would think, I would know, that it was Saja feeding on the dead. At those times I would squeeze closer to my mother, who continued to sleep, and listen for the true sounds of the night.

When I heard Sweet Mary come home from her shift at the Lollipop Lounge, the clicking of the lock next door and the gurgling of the pipes as she drew a bath became Saja cracking his jaws and slurping rivers of blood. And the pacing of the old man who lived above us—about whom the only thing I remember now is the way he smelled, like piss and fingernail polish, and the way his pants wedged into his crack as he shuffled through the halls, calling out "Three o'clock!" no matter what time it was—became Saja emerging from the walls to hunt.

•⤳

I must have woken my mother on one of those sleepless nights, or maybe we had just turned off the alarm clock and lay in bed, drowsing in an early-morning dark still heavy with sleep. I have a memory of the two of us wrapped in the covers, my head tucked into her armpit, listening to the old man creak across his floor, waiting for him to shout "Three o'clock!"

When he did, my mother giggled, but I clutched at her arm. "It's Saja the Death Messenger," I blubbered. "I heard him come into our apartment. He looked through our kitchen and opened our refrigerator. He got a drink of water. And now he's coming for me."

"Are you dreaming?" my mother asked.

"It's Saja, Mommy," I whispered. "I can smell him."

"Wake up, Beccah!" My mother grabbed my shoulders and shook. "Wake up from your dream!"

"He stinks, Mommy, with his bubbling skin, black and green, fermenting with pus!" I wanted her to know that I saw him, as clearly as she ever did, and that I knew he was real.

My mother untangled herself from the sheets and ran into the kitchen. I heard the suction of the refrigerator door opening, and then she came rushing back into the room. Held aloft in her hands, swinging by its legs, was a raw chicken.

"Sit up," she said. "Quickly." My mother waved the chicken at me, and its liver and gizzard plopped onto the sheets.

"Aigu!" my mother swore as she stuffed the innards back into the bird. Without looking up, she told me, "Take off your nightgown."

"Why?" I asked, but when she started pulling the material over my head with her bloody fingers, I wriggled out of it myself. She grabbed my shift, rolled the chicken in it, swung the bundle around my head, and, singing, ran back out of the room.

"Mommy?" Wrapping my arms around my bony chest, I followed her into the living room–kitchen area, praying that I had not pushed her into one of her trances.

With the chicken tucked under her arm, my mother fumbled with the locks on the front door. After wrestling the door open, she charged to the railing and flung the chicken out into the street. The arms of my nightgown flapped loose, as if trying to fly away from the body that dragged it down. "Goodbye, Beccah's ghost," my mother called after it.

She turned back toward our apartment slowly, humming what I think was the river song, the only song my mother ever taught me. I waited, watching as she refastened the locks on the door, her greasy fingers slipping over the brass. She wiped her hands on her nightgown, said, "Well, that's that," and then I knew that she was still in this world, still with me.

"If that was Saja bothering you," she said, "though I don't think it was, he should have been fooled into thinking that was you I sacrificed to him." My mother walked into the kitchen, closed the refrigerator door, turned on the water faucet. As she washed her hands, she explained, "Saja may be handsome, but he's not too smart."

My picture of Saja was correct only in the fact that he was a glutton. And though he craved the human spirit above all other foods, he could be fooled or placated with offerings of chicken or pork, heapings of barley and rice, oranges and whiskey.

According to my mother, Saja was neither old nor ugly, but young and handsome, a dark soldier, alluring and virile. When she told me this, I then imagined Saja looked like my father, the handsomest man I could imagine.

Though his picture showed someone tall and thin, with brownish-gray hair receding sharply from the steep bank of his forehead, I thought my father, because he was haole, looked like Robert Redford. At times I would hold the picture up to the mirror, trying to find my father's parts in my face, in my high, straight nose, perhaps, or my mouth with its protruding teeth. Not in my tilting eyes or my hair, a sheet of relentless black like my mother's.

If I imagined Saja looked like my father, it helped me understand why my mother flirted with death. She, too, must have thought my father was handsome above all other men, at least when they were newly married. I could see them when they first met, looking into each other's eyes, stunned with love, humming "Some Enchanted Evening," as their features melt into those of Liat's and Lieutenant Joe Cable's in *South Pacific*. Later, when I believed myself in love for the first time, it was this image I tried to call upon, but the only character I could see clearly was Bloody Mary, Liat's mother. Her body, materializing in lucid majesty between them, dwarfed the minuscule lovers who clamored over and around her, pitiful in their attempts to speak or to kiss.

When my mother entered into her trances and began to dance, she would cajole the soldier of death, tease him, beg him to take her with him. She would dance, holding in her arms raw meat—chicken, or pig's feet, or a pig's head—calling, "Saja, Saja," in a singsong voice. When I'd hear her call his name, as if she were summoning a favorite pet or a lover, I would cry out, "Mommy, what about me?" and throw myself across her body in order to keep her from floating away. Mother would step over me and continue waltzing with the pig's head, daring Saja to cut in.

⋅〰

Tired of waiting, my mother twice tried to meet the Death Messenger on her own terms. The first time, she almost drowned in the bathtub. Apparently, after toasting Saja with a bottle of Crown Royal, she tried to take a shower and passed out. Sweet Mary, mad as hell when the relentless clanking of the water pipes woke her up before noon, called the police, as she had threatened to do so many times before. When they broke into our apartment, they found my mother dreaming under a thin layer of water, her nose pressed to the sluggish water drain.

suicide attempts ?

The second time, like the first, no one could say for certain she had been trying to commit suicide. The doctors gave her the benefit of the doubt and said that she had fallen into the Ala Wai Canal by accident; she shouldn't have walked so close to the edge when she couldn't swim.

Only I knew she went swimming to try to catch death.

My mother was like that cat who could never catch the tail of happiness because she never stopped chasing it; despite all her begging and threats and wishes, she was snubbed by death until she stopped wanting it.

⋅〰

After the doctors pumped the yellow waters of the Ala Wai from my mother's body, I spent even more time by the canal, watching the water trudge by my space underneath the bridge. I spent hours on the bank, sitting cross-legged on the foot of the bridge's concrete support, trying to see what my mother saw in the brackish, polluted water. If I hung my feet over the ledge of the support, I would have been able to touch the water. But afraid of the stinging jellyfish that shimmered, ghostlike, underneath the surface, I never even tried.

I did, however, ask my mother what she saw in the water, why she tried to drown herself in the canal. Actually, I think I asked her why she wanted to leave me when she said I was the only thing she loved.

"Beccah," she told me, touching my hair, "it's not a matter of leaving you, but of retrieving something that I lost."

My mother looked so sad then that I wanted to take back my words, words I said without thinking, just because I felt them. "Mommy," I said, "I could help you look for it, if you told me what you lost."

Back then, I thought I was good at finding lost objects. "Remember?" I told her. "Remember when you lost the jade frog Auntie Reno gave you for good luck? And I found it under the bed, under all those old boxes? Remember the Wishing Bowl money you thought we lost, that I found in Auntie Reno's trunk?"

I named the specific things I'd found for her over the years, from ever since I could remember, but I was really asking her to remember me, her daughter, and how much I could help her. I was her finder, and she needed me. I wanted to remind her that she was bound to me.

Instead of telling me what she was looking for, my mother told the story of Princess Pari. She pulled me down next to her on the couch, partially cradling me as if I were a much younger child. When I tried to ask my questions, her fingers fluttered over my mouth in a gesture so soft and fleeting that even then I was not sure if she'd actually touched me.

"Once on a time, many, many years ago . . . ," my mother began as soon as I had wriggled into a comfortable space. With my knees tucked close to my body, I sat with my back nestled into my mother's bosom. As she spoke, I could feel her words tickle the back of my head. ". . . A king and queen with no sons had yet another daughter, their seventh. Full of despair, not knowing what else to do to turn away their bad luck, the royal couple offered this girl to the Birth Grandmother spirit."

My mother spoke often of the Birth Grandmother, the spirit assigned to protect and nurture the children of the world. Every year on my birthday, my mother would place an offering of sweet rice cake on our shrine, thanking Birth Grandmother for the blessing of my birth. I was taught to pray to her, calling her by name— Induk—if ever I was in trouble or frightened.

"Did you offer me to the Birth Grandmother?" I interrupted my mother.

My mother tapped me on the head. "Listen," she said.

"When Princess Pari's parents died without any sons, Saja the Death Messenger carried them to hell. The daughter felt sorry for her parents and dived through the skies, into the earth, and across the deep, dark river that flowed past Kasi Mun, the Thornwood Gate, which is the entrance to hell. At the gate, the princess threw handfuls of barley and rice, she rolled oranges and poured whiskey through the bars, until Saja, greedy for the offerings, opened the gate.

"Saja was so distracted by the feast, the princess was able to slip into hell and, once there, searched for her parents. She swam through schools of human souls trapped in fish bodies until she heard a song she recognized as the song her mother had sung when she was still in the womb. 'Mama!' she cried, and caught her parents with strips of long cloth that she tied around her waist. Quickly, before Saja could belch and close the gate, she dragged them back through the gates of hell, through the earth, through the skies, and into the Lotus Paradise, where they were reborn as angels."

After the story, I crawled out of her lap and turned to face her. "What was the song?" I asked. "The one that Princess Pari recognized."

"You know it." My mother laughed, and sang: *"Pururun mul, Kang muldo mot miduriroda . . ."*

I sang the last part with her. "The river song. I'll never forget it, okay, Mom? You sing that song, and no matter what, I'll find you, okay? I'll be like Princess Pari, and I'll rescue you."

• ✐

The first Saturday after my mother died, I went to the canal. I parked at Ala Wai School, retracing the path from the playground through the park toward the canal. Still used, probably by several classes of elementary school kids since I was there, the red-dirt path—narrower than I remembered, made by smaller feet than mine now—wandered through the park's date trees and ended at my old hiding place beneath the bridge. Bending over, I crawled under one end of the bridge and fit myself onto the same ledge I sat on those many years ago. Looking down where the water of the canal licked the rocks, I saw a handful of date pits. I remembered how I would search the ground under the date palms and how if I found some of the small, hard fruit, I felt that I would have good luck, as if they were pennies, only better, because they were a gift from nature. When I gnawed the thin flesh from its seed, I would thank the Birth Grandmother for looking out for me.

As an adult, I discovered that Foodland sold pitted dates in large plastic tubs. I bought one and couldn't wait to experience the taste I remembered from childhood. I opened the tub in the car, ripping the seal with my teeth, but when I popped a date in my mouth I was disappointed. The fruit was too sweet, too thick in my mouth, and I missed being able to suck on the seed.

Next to the pile of seeds, half swallowed by the mud, was a once-white satin shoe, the kind girls wore to their wedding or to the prom. And next to the shoe, draped limply among twigs and mush, a condom. I'd seen all these things in the canal before, along with the arms and heads of Barbie dolls, beer bottles and soda cans, shit, newspaper boats and hats, and dog-paddling rats. Occasionally I would spy a jellyfish or a tilapia, the trash fish, and before it flipped away, my heart would beat faster as I waited to see if it would sing me the river song, thus revealing itself as a soul in disguise.

•~

The Saturday after my mother died, I watched the water of the canal lap at the trash under me and waited for something, some sign from my mother. I don't know what I was thinking, but I never caught a glimpse of a fish that might have carried her spirit.

When the time came, when she needed me, I had failed to rescue her. No Princess Pari, I could not swim to the far shores of death to pull my mother back to life; I could not even put my feet in the water.

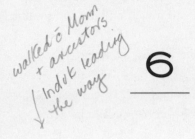
walked ō Mom + ancestors / Induk leading the way

6

AKIKO ·~

The day after Induk called me out of the river, I went looking for the spirit I knew I could never find. Go to Manshin Ahjima, Induk said as she dipped her hand into my chest and pulled out my maum, the force of my heartbeat, and led me forward by a silver thread.

I walked and slept, walked and slept, and throughout the journey kept my eyes fixed on Induk beckoning before me. At times, her form would blur until it doubled, then quadrupled, and she would become Induk and my mother, and in turn my mother's mother and an old woman dressed in the formal top'o of the olden days. I realized I was walking with my ancestors.

I tried running to my mother, but she shook her head and remained just outside my reach. It was then that I noticed that she held a small book, no bigger than the palm of my hand, which I recognized as the Ch'onja-chaek, the most basic school primer. When she began to turn the pages, I strained to read what it said, but to my surprise, I found I could not understand the words. Even concentrating on the rapidly moving pictures milked most of my energy.

As my mother flipped through the book, I saw myself and my sisters as children, hanging on to our mother as she moved through our barley field and tended to our garden. And I saw us holding on to her body as we cried the death cries for her spirit. I saw myself underneath the pumping bodies of Japanese soldiers and, in the later pages, saw my oldest sister beneath the same soldiers. I saw myself sitting in the river, and I saw myself walking and sleeping, walking and sleeping, until I died.

At this point my mother closed the book. When I asked her why I could not see the rest of the book, the oldest spirit, whom I knew to be my great-grandmother, said, If you read the final chapters, you would know the universe. You would be dead.

•⁓

When I looked up, I was alone and could smell the sea, so I knew I had followed the river west. Ahead of me I saw the cluster of small adobe homes Induk had told me about, nestled into the hillside. I knocked at the first house, wanting to ask if I could sleep in the courtyard. No one answered there, nor at the second home I came to. Finally, after failing to wake anyone at the third home, I entered the courtyard anyway and disrobed at the well. In the cold night, I laid my clothes on the brittle mud surrounding the well and bathed in the ice-cold water, wanting to purify myself and knowing I never could.

My skin felt waxy, as Induk's had the day after the soldiers killed her, the day after she reclaimed her name and I became the new Akiko. When the other camp women and I went to the river to bathe, we found her skewered body, abandoned alongside the path. We wanted to take her to the river with us to prepare her body for the separation of its spirit. Someone she loved should have cleansed her skin with her favorite scented oil. Someone who loved her should have laid her body out, with her head to the south, and prepared a feast to feed her soul for its next and longest journey.

The women from the camp wanted to do these things for her, but in the end we left her, just as the soldiers had, mounted on the pole, her nakedness only half concealed by the forest's undergrowth, her eyes dry and open and staring toward the river.

• ~

When my husband brings home toys for our newly born daughter, I pick out the dolls with the plastic skin and the unyielding, staring blue eyes and put them in the linen closet. Their skin feels like day-after-death skin, cold and hard though still faintly pliant. I feel sick thinking of my baby lying next to, gaining comfort from, the artificial dead. After I bury the dolls under the sheets and towels, I pick up my child, placing her against my chest. My body feels cold against her sleep-flushed warmth, yet she still snuggles, roots against me. As she nurses, her heat invades me and becomes mine, her heart beats against mine, becoming mine, becoming me, and gives me life. *Akiko + baby Beccah as one*

I try not to think of the dolls, stacked against each other in the closet, staring at us through the doors and walls with their unblinking, sightless eyes.

• ~

I woke at dawn with my fingers dangling like bait in the water at the edge of the river, and a rope looped around my neck. Old-lady breasts, flattened and elongated from years of childbearing, flapped against the side of my head. When I tried to sit up, the breasts squawked, Aigu! The dead is sitting up! and swung away.

Lifting my head against the noose, I could see that the breasts belonged to a gray-haired woman sitting cross-legged and naked on my clothes. Though her body was covered with wrinkles and age spots, her face was curiously unlined, youthful. I knew this was the Manshin Ahjima whom Induk had told me to find.

She tugged on the end of the rope.

Manshin Ahjima, I asked her, why am I tied?

E-yah! the woman cried. The dead knows me! the old lady jumped to her feet, and the rope between us stretched taut.

I lifted my hands to the rope, then pulled gently. The

rope slithered from her grasp and onto the ground. Please, I said, why?

The woman's hand jerked as if she still held the rope. You were lost, she said, between this world and the next, and I was trying to lead you back. She lifted her breasts and scratched her scarred belly. Besides, you were scaring me, growling like an animal one minute, crying like a baby the next.

The woman shuffled closer, then knelt to peer into my face. You aren't a tiger spirit, are you? She held her hands out, palms down. If so, I am ready to go. I've tended the mounds, burned the incense for the spirits whose families have been lost or run away. I've seen and I've remembered which son was taken by the Japanese, which son was killed by bandits, and which went to Shanghai as a freedom fighter. I've . . .

The old woman stopped talking, blinked, then touched my hair. I've seen the tiger spirit haunt the graves before, she said, but only at night. You are just a little girl.

When she called me a little girl, I remember I wanted to cry. I wanted to curl into a ball, cover my head, and call, Mother! Mother! as I did when I was very young and feeling alone, as I did from the rooftop of our home the night my mother died and I tried to catch her fleeing spirit. But I didn't, because I knew no one would ever again hold me in tenderness. Instead I stood up and looked around.

And I saw that we were not in a village but in a graveyard. When I realized that the homes that I knocked at the night before were houses of the dead, I started shaking, and perhaps then I did start to cry.

Here, Manshin Ahjima said, handing me my clothes. I don't suppose a tiger spirit would need these rags to keep warm. And I don't suppose a tiger spirit would have such messy hair. Tiger spirits are really rather prissy, you know.

Manshin Ahjima stretched her arms above her head, then began to braid her sparse hair. Hard to believe I was a beauty, huh?

she said. But it's true; my husband couldn't get enough of me, just like a dog. I had so many babies, I couldn't even count them anymore.

The old lady's lips flapped, then stopped. I knew she was waiting for me to say something, to respond with a smile or a nod, but I could only stare at her mouth, watching for when her lips parted in a certain way and I could see the black gap where she had lost some teeth.

Olppajin-saram, the mouth suddenly said. And again, louder, as if breaking a spell or casting one: Olppajin-saram. You've lost your soul. That is why you came to the graveyard. You were trying to steal someone else's spirit, a wandering spirit, maybe, one that was confused about where it belonged.

She lifted the rope from my head. This is useless, she said, throwing it to the ground. You need a pyong-kut, a healing ceremony.

I asked her if she could help me.

When she shook her head no, I became desperate. I begged her, telling her I would pay her for her services.

Manshin Ahjima wrapped her braid slowly around her head and seemed to consider the possibility. She looked down at me, then eyed the pitiful bundle of my clothes lying by the well. I was embarrassed, not by my nakedness or hers but because I knew and she knew I had nothing to pay her.

The old woman pulled her dress, white as death, around her freckled, flabby body and tied the sash tight across her chest. I cannot perform a kut for you, she said, because I no longer do the devil's work. But I will help you because that is the Christian way.

Manshin Ahjima bent to pick up a thin gold-plated chain, which she slipped around her neck. The old lady held the chain out so that I could see the tiny cross, smaller than my thumbnail, before she slipped it under the neckline of her dress. You see, she said, I've been saved.

She would help me, she said, because I reminded her of herself when she first got the sinbyong, the possession sickness. And of her daughter whom she sent away to live with her grandmother when the spirits first began to visit her, many years ago. The spirits are very jealous, Manshin Ahjima explained. They cannot stand it if you love someone more than them.

Manshin Ahjima touched my hair. Come, I will braid your hair for you, and then I will take you to the Pyongyang missionaries for food and clothes.

The missionaries had saved her from starvation and damnation, and in return Manshin Ahjima let them call her Mary.

Be prepared, she said. I think they call all of the girls Mary.

•‿

We followed the train tracks into Pyongyang, keeping mostly in the bordering woods, though sometimes slipping onto a side road to make it easier on the decrepit ox pulling her cart. We depended on that ox not only for transportation but also for sustenance. Some nights, after failing to forage anything to eat, Manshin Ahjima would nick the ox under its shoulder blade to siphon off some of its blood. I learned to savor the taste of blood.

To pass the days, Manshin Ahjima would tell me of the spirits who continued to talk with her. Sinjang-nim, the General, is the most powerful spirit, a giant-fighter, she said. And very sexy. He comes to me even now, waving his sword, demanding that I acknowledge him. It takes everything in my heart to call on Jesus Christ, Manshin Ahjima said, and even then, I can still hear the General whispering, whispering, planning his strategy.

One day, a day when we had not even talked about her spirits or about anything other than the food we dreamed of eating, Manshin Ahjima started screaming. She jumped off the oxcart and ran along the road, stopping to scoop up rocks, which she threw into the air. I yelled at her to stop, to tell me what was wrong, but she only screamed louder, covering my voice with hers until we were both hoarse.

After what seemed a long time but I know was not, she simply stopped. She dropped her rocks, stopped screaming, and climbed back into the cart. With scratched and bloody hands, she smoothed the wisps of hair that had escaped from her braid and smiled as if in apology.

Damn jealous, those men. The Satan General and the Jesus God fight over me, she said, thrusting her chest forward. I am the arena of their power contest. And in their battle to possess me, neither has any pity for me. I just can't take it sometimes.

That was the day she taught me to find lost things, something she taught all her daughters, because, she said, a woman must always find her own way.

Find the place of darkness within yourself, Manshin Ahjima explained, and imagine what you have lost. Then picture yourself in the last place you saw the object and spiral up and away, as if you were flying circles around that spot. Your spirit finds the object, so the better you can re-create the lost thing in your mind and in the spirit world, the more likely that you will find it in your hands again.

When Manshin Ahjima urged me to try to find something I had lost, all I could think of was my mother. I could not see her face clearly; even then, so soon after the time my sisters and I buried her alongside our winter's kimchee, the details of her face lacked focus in my memory. But she was all I could think of, and what I saw when my mind flew into its own darkness was a woman buried backward in a shallow forest grave, her face pressed against the earth, her mouth full of snakes. *vision of Mom buried face down*

Induk's voice erupted from Manshin Ahjima's mouth: It is an omen.

After I had described this vision to Manshin Ahjima, we no longer avoided people traveling away from Pyongyang. Instead

Manshin Ahjima greeted everyone who looked and dressed Korean. I've had a vision from the spirits, Manshin Ahjima would sing out, about Korean independence! If they gave her money she would tell them my dream and explain to them that the snakes in the body of Korea would be slithering north to bite at the head of the revolutionaries. Send the warning, she would say, tell them to beware.

One man, dressed in traditional yangban attire, seemed especially excited at the news. If your vision proves true, he said, I will be very rich. If your vision proves true, Sonsaeng-nim, Honored Teacher, I will repay you at the end of the year.

Manshin Ahjima gave me a sly look and wrote down the name of her cemetery. Months later, toward the end of war, I heard rumors that the Japanese had burned what they could in that cemetery, that they had dug up graves, desecrated bodies, and killed the caretaker, who might or might not have been Manshin Ahjima.

The yangban gave us a handful of coins, promising more as he scurried away, and for the rest of that day we did not talk, merely listened to the muffled jingling of the coins we had wrapped against our skin.

Manshin Ahjima told me that the people in Pyongyang were well fed, bigger and taller and bolder than the people from her village and mine. She told me that their skin was as pale as the milk they drank and smelled of, and that they never had to sweat in the fields. What I came to find out was that Manshin Ahjima was talking about the Americans, the missionaries, not about real people.

We entered Pyongyang through what people called tongk-kolchon, shit alley, because of the stench of rotten pumpkins, and unwashed bodies pressed against unwashed bodies, and, most of all, the piles of maggoty feces that dotted every bare patch of earth.

Animals, Manshin Ahjima said, hand over her mouth, as she stepped over a fresh mound of human dung.

We walked past old women, younger than I am now, who

missionaries not real people

picked through garbage and crowed when they found a scrap of food or material with which they could build a *hako-bang*, as the Japanese called the cardboard shacks a lucky few lived in.

And we walked past a woman lying at the side of the road, a begging bowl atop her still chest and two small children clinging to her bloated legs and hands. They cried against their mother's corpse, afraid to leave her side, afraid to stay, afraid to beg of the people stepping over and around them. I thought of my dream, and maybe I thought about my sisters and about what happened to me after my own mother died. I dropped the coins the yangban had given me into their bowl.

Manshin Ahjima swooped down and plucked back half of the coins. You crazy? Give them this much, and someone will kill them for it.

When I told her I only wanted to make sure they could buy something to eat, Manshin Ahjima told me that they would eat, that the missionaries would get them soon enough.

Just as they got me soon enough.

•➤

When we entered the Heaven and Earth Mentholatum and Matches Company building, where the missionaries hid from the Japanese, Manshin Ahjima began yelling.

She was half dead, Manshin Ahjima bellowed. Crazy out of her mind, dangerous. Thank the good Lord I was able to nurse her back to health and bring her here.

Manshin Ahjima pulled the cross out from under her blouse. Of course, she added, I spent all the money I had to feed her. I went hungry myself, you know.

You have such a good heart, Mary Ahjima, the missionary women cooed around Manshin Ahjima. You will surely be blessed.

Thank you, Manshin Ahjima said. I'm sure the good Lord will provide.

Yes, the missionary ladies agreed, as they pressed money into her hands. He always does.

Manshin Ahjima wrapped the coins in a strip of cloth, then slipped it under her skirt. After she had tied the cloth to her thigh, smoothed her skirts, Manshin Ahjima turned to go. Her eyes swept across me, but she did not look at me. I do what I can, she said. I do what I can, but my God is a jealous God, and I am in the midst of a war.

Wait, I cried, but I did not recognize my voice. Don't leave me, I yelled after her in words that did not sound like words.

The missionaries held on to my arms. *Cuckoo,* one of them said. Unsure of what she meant, I could not tell if she was referring to me or to Manshin Ahjima. I cried out again for Manshin Ahjima, and I cried for my mother.

In the end, I let the missionaries strip me down, burn my clothes, bathe my skin. I wanted to tell them that it would do no good; I would never become clean enough to keep.

•⤳

My daughter does not blink. She watches me with eyes that have not found their true color, changing from blue to gray, brown to green, with the light. I hold my finger in front of her nose; still she does not blink. My finger floats toward her open eyes, reaching until it touches the fringe of her lashes. Her eyes remain open with stubborn trust, and I think: How many betrayals will she endure before she loses that trust, before she wants to close her eyes and never open them again?

7

AKIKO ·‿

When Manshin Ahjima stumbled out of the missionary house, fondling her thigh where the money—the price of my trust—was tied, she took my hearing with her. By the time the echoes of her footsteps on the wooden stairs of the Heaven and Earth Mentholatum and Matches Company building had faded, I could not hear the sound of my own voice.

As the missionaries pulled at my hair, my clothes, my arms, I watched their chattering mouths but could not make out what they were saying. Eventually I turned my eyes away and gave my body to them. After bathing, dressing, and feeding me, the women pressed a Bible into my hands and led me to a small room, a closet in the women's sleeping quarters, that was not much bigger than the stall I had had in the camps.

In the darkness of that room, I cried for Induk. She, like me, must have been deaf, for she never came. But then again, maybe I had not even called for her, my voice lost with my hearing.

I considered finding her with the trick Manshin Ahjima had taught me, but I did not yet have the courage to envision the last place I saw Induk in this world.

·‿

In the days that followed, the missionaries assigned me to various tasks about the house. Sometimes they put a broom in my hands, and I would sweep until they took the broom away. If they put me in front of a tubful of dishes, I would wash them until the tub was empty and someone drained the water. Once, they positioned me at a table piled with matchboxes and labels. With big mouth movements and exaggerated gestures, one of the lady missionaries showed me how to glue the labels on the boxes. I sat and glued until all the boxes had labels, and then I glued labels on the table until I had run out of labels. I was considering what else to glue, when someone relieved me of my duty.

I would watch the broom scratch across the surface of the floors and on the stairs in front of the house. I could feel the water in the tub running down my hands as I rubbed my fingers across the smooth and resistant surfaces of plates and cups. And I smelled the pungent stickiness of the glue when I pasted the labels on the matchboxes, table, and chairs. But without the sounds of these actions, I had no way to connect them to myself. No way to judge time, distance, action, reaction.

As I swept, washed dishes, pasted labels, followed gestures and pointing fingers, instead of hearing the broom or the water or the fat sucking noise of glue on paper, my ears were filled with memories of the comfort camps.

•⁓

Invading my daily routine at the mission house, shattering the gaps between movement and silence, were the gruntings of soldier after soldier and the sounds of flesh slapping against flesh. Whenever I stopped for a beat, for a breath, I heard men laughing and betting on how many men one comfort woman could service before she split open. The men laughed and chanted *niku-ichi*—twenty-nine-to-one, one of the names they called us—but I heard the counting reach one hundred twenty-four before I could not bear to hear one more number.

Whenever I stopped cleaning or gluing to stretch cramping fingers or crack my stiff neck, I heard the sounds of a woman being kicked because she had used an old shirt as a sanitary pad. Or I heard a man sigh loudly as he urinated on the body where he had just pumped his seed.

And always, a low rumbling underlying every step I took at the mission house, I heard the grinding of trucks delivering more men and more military supplies: food rations, ammunition, boots, and new women to replace the ones that died, their bodies erupting in pus.

· ⌒

I remember thinking that I could not stop cleaning, washing, cooking, gluing, because if I did, the camp sounds would envelop me and I would be back there, trying to silence the noises I made eating, crying, relieving myself, breathing, living. As long as I was quiet, there was the hope that I would be overlooked and allowed to die in the darkness.

Each day, I woke in silence, not sure of where I was. Then, when I sat up, saw the Jesus-on-the-cross hanging on the back of the door, and realized I was in the Mentholatum building with the missionaries, I would begin to hear the thunder of delivery trucks and the grinding metal of gears shifting. The rumbling of the trucks would get louder and louder, and I knew that if I did not jump out of bed and hurry into action, I would be delivered into the camps once again.

I worked hard at the mission house, holding on to the labor to keep from spinning back into myself.

· ⌒

Because I could not risk looking away from my chores, it took me a long time to recognize the others staying in the home. Every day, I met the same people over and over again as if for the first time. No matter how many times I would glance at the faces floating by and away from me, I was never able to catch and hold on to the individual features of each person.

special tx by minister

The missionaries saved several girls by pretending to hire them as employees of the Heaven and Earth Mentholatum and Matches Company. Used as a shield from the Japanese, who, not trusting foreign influences, discouraged Christianity but encouraged businesses for the revenue that could be sent back to the Emperor, the Mentholatum and Matches building had been erected at the start of the Japanese occupation and now appeared generations old.

Roughly my age, the girls who were rescued were round-faced and pretty in their innocence, as I once had been. They braided their hair with bright-colored ribbons that flashed against their black hair and uniforms when they marched out of their common sleeping quarters and into the kitchen. Like children, they squirmed in their seats, stifling giggles and gossip when I swept past them.

Later, when I could once again hear what others heard, I caught their whispers flying against me: Why does the minister always save the sweetest pastry for the devil girl? And see how he always touches her head, gives her the prettiest ribbons for her braid?

Even the missionaries gossiped. I heard Sister Red Nose say, The wild child is possessed, a false light luring away the faithful. Sister Milk Breath, giving me the name that Manshin Ahjima predicted would be mine at the mission, muttered, *Mary Magdalene*, a curse, whenever I passed her way.

Once, when questioned to his face about his treatment of me, the minister smiled, a fleeting quirk of the lips, and said, What man of you, having a hundred sheep, doth not leave the ninety and nine to go after that one which is lost, until he finds it?

Putting his hand on my head, he looked at his sheep until they dropped their eyes. Rejoice, he said to them, for I have found a lamb that once was lost.

Later the young girls fluttered around me. Will the handsome minister save you? they giggled.

I wish he would save *me,* one said.

As long as he saves me some ribbon, another grumbled. Akiko must get more than her fair share, don't you, Akiko?

Oh, it's not fair, the girls cried. Akiko always gets more of everything because they say she's touched. I think you are just acting. You wait till the war is over, Akiko. Our families will find us and we'll marry rich men and have everything. What will you have, crazy Akiko, with no family and no mind?

Because they were still young, they had faith that the war would end and the Japanese would be defeated. That their lives would resume their prewar scripts, as if the war and their abandonment caused only a brief stutter in the opera they envisioned for themselves.

Because they were still babies, really, I did not tell them what I knew was true: The war would never end, because the Japanese, like all that was evil, would wait in the shadows, shape-shifting and patient, hoping for a chance to swallow you whole.

for Akiko, perhaps?

I could not seem to differentiate among the missionaries, with their pink skin, mud-and-straw-colored hair, and large noses that blocked the space between their pale, watery eyes. If not for the clothes, I would have had trouble distinguishing the men from the women, for even the women were tall, with big hands and knuckles.

Their actions, too, made it difficult to label them as men and women, for they did not behave as proper men and women. In the

Korean or separate *NOT uke that & the missionaries*

world before the camps, the unmarried women and men I knew lived separately. From the age of six, I was taken away from the babies of both sexes and taught the ways of women. Though we would play on the swing, standing tall as we were pushed high enough to see into the boys' courtyard, girls were not supposed to talk or look at boys. In our family's home, my sisters and I rarely saw my father. When he was home, we prepared his meals and served him first. After he finished eating and went into the back room to smoke or sleep, we would eat our meal. That was what was respectful.

Even in the camps, where the soldiers banged in and out of the comfort cubicles, in and out of our women's bodies, what was left of our minds we guarded, kept private and separate.

At the mission house, I was embarrassed by the disrespect between the men and the women. Lives overlapping, men and women ate and worked together. They looked into each other's faces as they spoke, laughing with mouths open. Even while worshiping, they sat side by side, unseparated by a curtain or sheet, on the same bench, thighs and shoulders almost touching.

• ➤

I began to recognize the minister because of the way the girls, forgetting or ignoring proper behavior, gathered around him. Like puppies, the girls would fall about his feet and legs, panting for a length of ribbon, a piece of candy, a box of chalk; for writing paper, toothpaste, a kind word. Thank you, Sonsaeng-nim, the girls would sing out, and as if they were pets, the minister would reach out, touching a nose, stroking the hair of those around him.

Stop, he would say. I am not an honored teacher. I am just a child, like you all, in God's eyes.

But the girls would cry out: No, no, not true! Look at your body, thin and long—an aristocrat's body! And your hands, so graceful—a scholar's hands! And your voice, they said, like God's!

The minister would laugh, saying, Stop! But his eyes would shine like blue glass. *girls would equate minister č God*

•~

Because I had begun to recognize him as an individual, I watched him carefully, intensely, as if memorizing his features, his gestures, were one of my chores. Often, as he gave away his gifts, he closed his eyes and lifted his chin. Pushing his chest forward, he would open and shut his mouth quickly, pursing his lips, blowing quick puffs of air. After a few days, I realized he was singing.

•~

Now, years later, I recognize those same body movements and hear the words to the songs he sings to our baby. When she is fretful, crying so loud that the only thing she hears is the pain within her, only he can quiet her. He holds her tight against his chest, pinning her arms within her blanket, and sings. Soon she stops struggling, and as her screams fade into hiccups, she lifts her head toward the sound of his voice singing about whales of Jo-jo-jonah. Noah's art-y art-y made out of go-phers barking barking. Jesus loving children.

They are silly songs that my husband sings to comfort our child, but I hate them and I hate him.

I hate that he can quiet her with his voice, the same voice that lulled and lured the girls from the Pyongyang mission. The same voice, sounding so honest and joyful that you want to believe, even when you know the truth. The same voice that fools everyone but me. I hate that voice because my daughter loves it.

I cannot sing to my daughter like that, in a voice full of laughter, for I never learned funny songs, songs that make you laugh and laugh. I remember only bits and pieces from those my mother sang when she was working. And they were songs that filled you with sadness, that made you want to cry until your throat swelled with salt.

⦁⌣

After one of the missionaries' communal dinners, the person who came to take the chopsticks from my hand was the minister the girls always followed. By then most of the people there had stopped speaking to or looking at me, unnerved by the silence by which I was surrounded. But when this man took the chotkarak away from me, he held my chin and looked into my eyes. He looked until I was forced to stop listening to the women crying in the comfort camps, until I looked back and saw him. And then he smiled, rubbed a napkin over my lips, and helped me stand. He took my hand and led me down the basement stairs, where the world turned on its side once again.

In the basement meeting room, he placed me on a bench between two other missionaries. I concentrated on watching him walk down the aisle to the pulpit, but my vision narrowed and buckled under the increasing intensity of camp sounds. During his speech, each time I saw him slap the pulpit for emphasis, I heard the sounds of women's naked buttocks being slapped as they were paraded in front of a new arrival of troops.

When the congregation stood, opening and riffling through their black books, I heard the shrieking of bullets ricocheting at the feet of women the soldiers were momentarily bored with.

And when the people around me all at once opened their mouths wide, I heard every sound from every day I spent in the camp all at once, so loud I felt I was drowning under a raging river, until, in a rush, my ears shattered.

After a moment of utter silence I heard singing, but singing like I've never heard before. The only songs I had heard before that day were sung by one person at a time, or by a group of people who all sang the same part in the same way.

What I heard after my ears cracked open was a single song,

ears open a crack

with notes so rich and varied that it sounded like many songs blended into one.

And in that song I heard things that I had almost forgotten: the enduring whisper of women who continued to pass messages under the ears of the soldiers; a defiant Induk bellowing the Korean national anthem even after the soldiers had knocked her teeth out; the symphony of ten thousand frogs; the lullabies my mother hummed as she put her daughters to sleep; the song the river sings when she finds her freedom in the ocean.

• ~

My daughter's cries filter into my dreams. Just before I wake, her crying turns into my mother's singing. My mother is crying and dancing and singing a song that I heard her sing repeatedly in my childhood, but in my dream I cannot quite make out the words. I try to embrace my mother, but she dances away from me again and again. Just as I finally reach her, her song erupts into the screams of an infant.

I look toward my husband's bed, see his unmoving form huddled beneath the blankets. Dazed with sleep, still seeing my dream, I go to my daughter. As I pick her up, her body stiffens with her screams, and out of my mouth comes my mother's voice, singing the song I forgot I knew:

> *Nodle Kang-byon pururun mul*
> *Kang muldo mot miduriroda*
> *Su manun saramdul-i jugugat-na*

It's a song full of tears, but one my mother sang for her country and for herself. A song she gave to me and one that I will give to my daughter. I want to shake my baby into listening, force her to hear, but I only sing louder and louder:

E he yo! Pururun mul, kang muldo
Na rul mit-go nado kang mul-ul miduriroda

Over my daughter's cries, I continue to sing and sing, until she begins to quiet. Her body falls into mine and the air in her room becomes sweet and heavy with the breath of her sleep, and still I sing. I sing until I reach the end of the song, until I can remember no more.

Moot saram-ui seulpumdo diwana bol-ga
Moot saram-ui seulpumdo hulro hulro sa ganora.

8

poison arrows at birth

BECCAH ↩

When I entered the world, bottom first, arrows impacted my body with such force that it took twelve years for them to work their way back to the surface of my skin. My mother said she tried to protect me from the barbs the doctors who delivered me let loose into the air with their male eyes and breath, but they tied her hands and put her to sleep. By the time my mother saw me, two days later, she said she knew the *sal* had embedded themselves deep into my body by the way my yellow eyes turned away from her breast. My mother spent two weeks in the hospital waiting, she said, to see how the arrows would harm me: so swift and deadly that she would never have time to fight their power, or slow detonating, festering for years, until I formed either an immunity or an addiction to its poison.

Years later, when the evil-energy arrows began to work their way from my body, I often wished the *sal* had killed me outright so that I would not have had to endure my mother's protection.

• ↩

At the start of each Korean New Year, my mother would throw grains of rice and handfuls of brass coins onto a meal tray to see my luck for the coming year. In the year of the fire snake, I turned twelve, and my mother missed the divination tray completely.

"Mistake! Mistake!" my mother yelled toward our ceiling as she scooted on her hands and knees to pluck coins and rice from the carpet. As soon as she collected enough to fill both fists, she held her hands above the tray, closed her eyes, and chanted, calling down the Birth Grandmother to reveal my yearly fortune. When my mother cast for the second time, she poured the riches from her hands rather than threw them, hoping to fill the tray with a better reading.

When she opened her eyes and saw that she had again missed the tray, she cried. She wrapped her arms around her body and rocked. "*Aigu, aigu,*" she moaned. My mother chanted and swayed until she fell into a trance. Then she got up and, eyes sealed, danced through the apartment: on the sofa bed, around the black-lacquered coffee table, over dining room chairs, around me. And as she danced, my mother touched our possessions, feeling—she later explained—for the red. My mother held her hands in front of her, and like divining rods, they swung toward the color of blood. She ripped red-bordered good luck talismans from our walls and furniture, where they fluttered like price tags. She knocked over our altars, sending the towers of fruit and sticky rice crashing to the floor, and rummaged for the apples and plums. Clawing through the bedroom closets and drawers, she collected everything red, from T-shirts and running shorts to a library copy of *The Catcher in the Rye* to the bag of Red Hots I bought with my own money and stashed in my sock drawer.

When she was through piling the red things into a mountain in our living room, my mother said, "We need to burn the red from your life. Everything."

At first, I didn't understand what she meant to do; sometimes she said such things to her clients, then just waved a lit incense stick or a moxa ball over their heads. But when my mother took an armload of clothes to the kitchen sink and lit a match, I scrambled to the floor and rooted through my possessions, trying to save something.

When the material in the sink caught fire, my mother came and took the one thing of mine I had managed to find: the tie-dye T-shirt I had made with rubber bands, melted crayon, and Rit dye in Arts and Crafts the year before. "Beccah," she told me, "*honyaek*, the cloud of Red Disaster, is all around you. I am trying to weaken it so it won't trigger your *sal* and make you sick."

Red Disaster, the way my mother explained it, was like the bacteria we had learned about in health class: invisible and everywhere in the air around us, *honyaek* was contagious and sometimes deadly. Burning the red from our apartment was my mother's version of washing my hands.

The fire in the sink kept sputtering out, held in check by flame-resistant clothing, until my mother added her talismans and money envelopes and a dash of lighter fluid. When she held a match to this kindling, the fire licked, hesitant at first, and then devoured what was offered. Flames shot up amidst coils of thick smoke that blackened our kitchen walls and ceiling. When this first batch had almost burned down, the smoke alarm sputtered to life with grunts and whines and a final full-strength shriek before my mother whacked it with a broom. After she cracked open a window, my mother continued to burn our possessions, even the Red Hots, which melted like drops of blood-red wax, filling the apartment with the stench of burning cinnamon.

• ‿

Since I was particularly susceptible to Red Disaster that year, my mother did not want me wandering about in unknown places, picking up foreign *honyaek* germs. I was not allowed to ride the bus without her or to swim at all. Consequently I was not supposed to attend school field trips. When my classmates went to Bishop

Museum and to Foster Botanical Gardens and to Dole pineapple cannery, where they sampled fresh juice and fruit slices, I stayed behind in the school library, reading and helping Mrs. Okimoto shelve books according to the Dewey decimal system.

But when my sixth-grade social science teacher arranged a snorkeling expedition at Hanauma Bay, I signed my own permission slip after practicing my mother's signature for so long that even now I cannot write her name without my letters cramping into her small, painfully precise script. I remember my hands shook when I turned in this first forgery on the day of the excursion, but Miss Ching just shuffled the form and the fare I had stolen from the Wishing Bowl into her carryall folder. Pushing me into line with the rest of the class, she counted our heads and led us like ducklings onto the bus.

Since my mother had burned my red-heart bathing suit, I wore an olive-green leotard—not the sparkling Danskin kind with spaghetti straps, which might have passed, but one that was cap-sleeved and frayed in the butt. I knew I would catch stares and snickers from the Toots Entourage (led now by Tiffi Sugimoto, since Toots spent all field trips in detention hall for smuggling packs of cigarettes to school in her tall, frizzy rat-nest hair), but I also knew that this trip would be worth it. And even though I had to pair up with Miss Ching in the walk down the winding trail from parking lot to beach, and even though I sucked in water each time I tried to breathe through the snorkel, and my mask fogged no matter how many times I washed it with spit, the trip was worth the teasing and the lies. Because when I trudged across the network of coral reef to dive into pockets of water as deep and clear as God's blue eyeball, I felt perfect, seamless, and as whole as the water that closed over me.

Only afterward, on the hike back to the parking lot, did I begin to feel the sting of Red Disaster. With each step, I felt a prick against my heel. By the time we reached the top, what had started out as an irritation had turned into bolts of fire shooting jagged through my leg.

In the middle of that night, my mother said she woke up on the couch in a suffocating heat, the sheets clinging to her body, a damp second skin. She fought to take each breath, her throat and lungs burning, and worked her way toward the bedroom, where the waves of heat originated.

"I thought there was a fire in there, that you were burning to death," my mother told me when I woke the next morning, my feet bandaged in strips of bedsheet.

"I swam through heat so heavy the room rippled before my eyes, and when I touched the bedroom door—*aigu!* Red hot!" My mother flung her hands into the air, showing off the raised welts on the palms. "I had to take my pajama, hold like this, then open."

The night of the terrible heat, sure that I was surrounded by a ring of fire, my mother wrapped the bottom of her nightgown around the doorknob and, waist bared, burst into the bedroom to rescue me. She was knocked immediately to the ground from the heat and enveloped in smoke that was not black but red. She pulled the collar of her nightgown over her nose and mouth to filter out the worst of the heat and the red smoke. "Just like a dust storm," she said. "Or like that plague curse in *The Ten Commandments* that killed off all the children—only red, not black.

"Red Death filled the room, thickening every breath I took, clouding my eyes so that I could barely see you—a motionless lump—on the bed. I called on the Birth Grandmother to help me beat a path through the *honyaek* to the windows. I tried to push some of the poison out, but the wind blew in even more *honyaek*."

My mother, who could not swim in water, would always pantomime the breast stroke when she told this part of the story. "I dove into red thick as blood pudding, fighting the tentacles of *honyaek* that tried to pull me under, and found you sweating and shivering under the blankets. I reached out to feel your forehead, but you burned so hot I could not touch you with my bare hands. I tucked the blankets underneath your body and carried you just like you were a baby again. But I could barely lift you; the Red Death sucked my energy, fed on my fear for you, so that I felt weak and unsure. I could barely force my legs forward as the fog of *honyaek* swirled around us, trying to trip my feet into missteps. I knew one wrong turn would lead us into the land of homeless hobo ghosts, *yongson*, where we could wander for ten thousand years without even one person knowing we were gone.

"I closed my eyes and told the Birth Grandmother to guide my feet, and when I opened them, she had led us to the bathroom. I placed you in the bathtub and turned on the water. At first the water evaporated as soon as it left the faucet, turning into red steam when it hit your body. I turned the cold on full blast, and finally enough trickled out to dampen the blankets and cool you off."

When I was out of immediate danger of "burning to ash," my mother said she needed to leave me in order to prepare her weapons. She opened the hallway closet, shook out our extra bedsheet, and, after studying it briefly, tore it into seven long strips. Then, with a felt marker, over and over again, she wrote my name, birth date, and genealogy—what she referred to as my "spiritual address." When I first looked at my feet in the morning, I thought they were bound in black-and-white striped material, so densely written were my mother's words.

"You needed to be tied into your body," she told me when I asked her about the linen around my feet. "And in case you slipped out, these words would have led you back." She pointed to one of the lines. "Look here—this character means you. This is me, this is the Birth Grandmother, this is each of her sisters. I linked us all together, a chain to fight the Red Death."

My mother said she forced the Birth Grandmother to call upon her sisters, the Seven Stars—each of them named Soon-something, which my mother said meant "pure"—to come protect me. "I didn't want to be rude," she said, "but really, if your spirit guardian can't protect you on her own, she should call for help, don't you think? I mean, I'm your mother, but I still ask her to help me watch you." My mother huffed as if disgusted and insulted by her spirit guardian's overbearing pride and lack of common sense. "Finally, I had to get rough with her.

" 'Induk,' I said, using her personal name to show how upset I was, 'this Red Death is too much for an old lady spirit like you!'

"When the Birth Grandmother did not answer, I knew I had been too blunt, but I could not waste time massaging the ego of a fickle spirit. 'Call on the Seven Stars, or I will find a new Birth Grandmother and you will be just another lost ghost,' I told her. 'My daughter is dying.' "

When I choked, my mother interrupted her story to scold me. "Pay attention." She scowled. "I told you this was serious."

The Birth Grandmother, responding to either her threats or her plea, must have listened to my mother, because a path of white light cracked the red cloud. My mother walked through—"Floated," she said. "I didn't even have to move my feet"—and found herself transported to my side in the bathtub.

She peeled the blankets from my body, stripping me naked. When I shivered, she placed each of the seven strips of bedsheet— one for each of the Star Sisters—on my body. Starting from my head, she smoothed the linen against my contours, asking for blessings from the protective spirits. She ran her hands down my face, throat, arms, torso, legs, and when she touched my feet, her hands vibrated.

"The Sisters were telling me where the *honyaek* entered your body. This," my mother said as she tapped at my feet, which I could barely feel under their wrap, "is your weak point. Didn't I always say you got them from your father?

"They were balloons—so swollen, red, and tender," she said, "they melted into pus when I touched them. I took a razor from the medicine cabinet and—zhaa! zhaa! just like gutting fish—opened your feet to let the sickness out." My mother brandished imaginary knives, slicing the air with sure, quick strokes, reliving her battle. "Red Death shot from your feet, fouling the air with its stench of rotting meat and rat feces. I cut deeper, catching and killing the poison with the bandages blessed by the spirits. At first, as soon as I placed the cloth by your feet, the whole thing turned red, becoming slick and saturated with Red Death. I was like a demon myself, possessed, pushing clean cloths against your feet with one hand, pulling away the ones drenched in Red Death with the other hand. And all the while, I could see the battle between the Sisters and the *honyaek* on the strips of cloth, as the good spirits fought to turn the bandages back to pure white.

"Finally, toward the morning, when all the Red Death had been sucked from the room through the balls of your feet, when all the bandages were white again—even the one against your feet, which by then wept only clear water—the arrowhead, the *sal* triggered by the *honyaek*, popped out. Wait, I'll show you." My mother scuttled off the bed and rushed into the kitchen. I could hear her rummaging through the glass cupboard, and when she returned, she held above her head like a small trophy a Smucker's jelly jar.

She shook the jar in my face, and what looked like bits of bone jumped and rattled around the bottom. *"Sal,"* she announced. "This is the shattered arrowhead working its way out, making all kinds of trouble. We've got to watch for more of these."

I took the jar from her, interested in something I could touch from the spirit world, something tangible from the place where my mother lived half her life. I looked into the jar, then shook the contents onto my palm.

"Don't make that face," my mother said as I stared at the *sal*. "Wrinkles will freeze in your forehead." When I didn't say anything, she knelt beside me and wailed, "It's not my fault! In Korea, everything is safe for the mother and baby—you're not even supposed to leave the bed for two weeks after you give birth! Here, anybody, any man, can come right into the delivery room and cut you, so how could I protect you when you first came into this world? At first I thought since you were half American you would be immune. But now I see that in your second life transition, the arrows are coming home."

I cupped my mother's chin in my hand, forcing her to look at me, worried that she was losing the present and drifting away from me. "Mom? What are you talking about? Where are you?"

She slapped my hand down. "Sometimes you ask stupid questions," she said. "I am explaining to you how the *sal* got in your body and what we can do about it. This is the critical year, the year you become a woman and vulnerable—just like when a snake first sheds his skin—so we got to purge the clouds of Red Disaster from the home—done—and then this building and then the school. Then we got to purify your mind. You got to—"

"Stop, Mommy, stop!" I held my palm toward her, displaying the white flecks. "This isn't *sal* or an arrow or whatever; it's coral."

"Coral?" My mother picked up a small piece and rolled it in her fingers.

"Yeah," I said, carefully dropping the rest of the rocks back into the jar so I wouldn't have to look at her. "You know, like stones from the sea."

"Yes," my mother said, her words measured, as if she were talking to someone mentally slow. "*Sal* is like stones from the sea."

"No, I mean coral is stones from the sea." I took a deep breath and exhaled in a rush. "I rode a bus and went swimming on a field trip. I lied to you before. I'm sorry. No need to watch me anymore."

My mother lifted the jar from my hands and swirled it until the coral skimmed across the bottom in an even hum. "I know you

"SAL"
poison

went swimming," she said. "The office called to tell me your bus would be getting back to school late."

"So you lied!" I yelled. "You know it's not *sal*."

My mother slammed the glass down on the night table. Bits of coral flew across the bed and onto the floor at her feet. "It is *sal*," she screamed back at me. "That's what made you lie in the first place. It's what made your feet swell up and stink. And I can see you still have more *sal* in your mouth, making it mean and stupid. Now—" Here my mother suddenly quieted and dropped down to kiss me on the forehead. "You are not well. Just rest. I'm going to keep you safe. I will watch for *sal* and pluck them out when you show the signs."

•~

My mother pounced on the signs of *sal* with quick efficiency, spotting the evidence of my decay in every shortcoming. Whenever I snapped at her, or overslept, or forgot something as simple as leaving an offering for the Seven Stars on the seventh day of the seventh month, she'd wave a lit incense stick about my head and yell, "*Sal!*"

Where earlier I had cherished the moments my mother paid attention to me, recognizing me as her flesh-and-blood daughter, I now began to cringe whenever she studied me, targeting a single part of my anatomy for any length of time. Because I knew that if I did not move out of her scope, she would hit me with another barb. Once, when I was about to kiss my mother goodbye before leaving for school, she grabbed my face, pressing my cheeks into my lips for a fish pucker. She held me that way for a blink or two, then announced, "Stink-breath. *Sal* from your father."

Sal seeped from the pores of my skin—proclaiming itself in feet that smelled like stale popcorn and armpits that smelled like fermenting potatoes—and pushed my body beyond its known topography. Knees and elbows erupted into sharp and dangerous angles. Zits bubbled onto my forehead and chin. Hair sprouted in damp, unexplored crevices. Knots of flesh fisted behind my nipples, punching up small hills.

And my mother's eyes and hands darted in to pinch and pull, poke and worry over each development.

I learned to study my body carefully in order to find and eliminate the signs of *sal* before my mother saw them. I sucked on breath mints, rubbed deodorant under my arms and on my feet. When my hands started to sweat, I swiped a layer of Secret across them too. And each night in the bath, I'd lie back and wait for strands of downy hair to float away from my body in exploratory tendrils, then pluck them out with eyebrow tweezers. The removal of each hair brought a flash of tears to my eyes, the sting of a tiny arrow.

I wore large, oversize T-shirts, which I pulled toward my knees to flatten my breasts. The kids called me a "mini-moke," because I slunk around the playground rolling my hands into the front of my shirts and slouched over my desk like one of the big, tough boys who smoked dope at the bus stop before school started. All of my shirts looked misshapen and distorted that year, even after Miss Ching announced during health education that "Some girls, who shall remain nameless, are ruining their clothes when they really, in the name of decency, should just go out and buy a bra." She looked right at me, and though I could feel my face burning red, I looked right back, sending a *sal* to strike her eyes. And her mouth.

•➤

My mother prayed for me. Alternately wailing over my out-of-control body and cursing my father, who passed on his *sal* to me, she berated the spirits and begged them for advice on how to save me. "Beccah," she told me after a long conference with Induk the Birth Grandmother. "No matter how much we cleanse the Red Disaster away from you, it comes back, because the *sal* keeps getting stronger." She sniffed at my skin, and under the mint and the "rain-fresh" scent of Secret, she detected another genetically embedded arrow, more evidence of impurity left by my haole father: the odor of cheese and milk and meat—animal waste. "You have to stop feeding the sickness in your body, and starve the *sal* out of you."

To cleanse the impurities from my system, I ate food blessed by the spirits. For breakfast and dinner, my mother set blocks of white rice cake, bowls of water, oranges, and mixed vegetable *namul* onto our altar, offering the Birth Grandmother and her sisters first helpings. After rubbing her hands in prayerful supplication, she'd bow stiffly from the waist. "Please share with us our food and your blessings," she'd say. "Please make this house peaceful. Please make the child turn out well." Then we would both kneel, waiting for the spirits to finish their meal. When the rice no longer sent spirals of steam into the air, we knew that the spirits were finished and that it was our turn to eat.

I tried cheating, eating the hot lunch at school. Pizza and Tater Tots, or loco-mocos—over-easy egg over gravy over beef patty over rice—cost twenty-five cents, so if I took only one money envelope from the Wishing Bowl, I could eat whatever I wanted for several weeks.

But my body always betrayed me. My mother listened to my stomach's noises, looked into my eyes, smelled my feet, and knew that I had eaten dirty food. "Rotten cow's milk, pig guts, and red-hot fat," she would comment, and that night I would have to drink endless bowls of blessed water while my mother chanted and sprinkled the ashes of burnt incense stick on my stinking parts. Sometimes this would go on through the night, so that when I woke in the early-morning hours to use the bathroom, I created landslides from ashes piled on the pillow near my mouth, on the sheets near my hands, on my stomach and crotch and feet.

When I stopped fighting and ate only what was acceptable to my guardian spirits, I wondered why I had fought in the first place.

Eating food that had been blessed, I began to feel the spirits fill my body, making me stronger, smarter, purer than my normal self. Each bite of the food tasted and tested by the Birth Grandmother and the Seven Stars seemed to ripen and bloom in my mouth, so that even one grain of rice, one section of orange, one strand of bean sprout, filled me to fullness.

I became so full that I consumed only what the spirits themselves ate, feasting on the steam evaporating from freshly made rice, on the scent of oranges and pears. I saw food take flight from its physical manifestation, turning into light that shot through my body. And I saw the light flow through me, swirling like blood under skin turned translucent as the shade of a lamp, until it eddied in the tips of my fingers.

My mother saw the light in my hands as well. "Your hands are so pale," she murmured once, "I can see the blue *hyolgwan* burning under its skin."

And when I massaged her back, my fingers migrated toward the *sal* hidden in her muscles, alongside her bones. "Saa, saa, saaa," my mother would groan with pain and pleasure. "Kill the *sal*." And I would press my fingers into the knotted muscles until I felt them loosen and dissolve under my heat. With the light, I could dip into her body to pull out the walnuts of pain lodged in her back, sucking like leeches against her spine or between her shoulder blades. Sometimes when I massaged my mother, I felt my arms disappear up to the elbows, my body reabsorbed by hers. In those moments, I knew I was truly my mother's daughter, that I nursed her with my light.

I aimed the light into myself, feeling for the poisoned arrowheads implanted in my body in order to kill my own pain. I fed the light with more spirit food, until it grew larger than myself. The bigger the light within me became, the smaller my body got, until I seemed to shrink into myself, becoming as elemental as the food offered to and consumed by the gods.

My body reabsorbed my hips, my breasts, the small belly that sloped between my pelvic bones. My hair fell out, leaving tufts of dry lifeless strands tangled in hairbrushes or in the shower drain. I knew that except for the down—like the woolly lanugo coating the fetus in the womb—developing on my arms and legs, I would soon become hairless as a newborn. I continued to devour the steam of rice, waiting until I would be tiny enough to slip completely into the world my mother lived in.

• ~

But no matter how clean, how small I became, the *sal*—too deep within me to uproot—remained, a seed burrowed low in my belly, to kill the light.

• ~

To ensure my safe passage through the critical year of the fire snake, my mother decided to meet me after school one day in order to purify the campus. Taking the same route as the morning bus, my mother walked and chanted her way from The Shacks to Ala Wai Elementary. Every few yards, she dipped into her shoulder bag and threw out handfuls of barley and rice—scrap offerings to lure the wandering dead and noxious influences away from the path I took to and from home every day. By the time she reached the campus, she had collected a gang of kids. "Eh, bag lady! Eh, crazy lady," they called out as they circled her. "Watchu doing? Feeding the birds?"

When my mother continued to chant and toss out grain, ignoring them, they must have grown bolder, pressing in on her with outstretched hands. "I like. I like," some teased. "Gimme some." And others, spurred by dares, came to slap at her bag or maybe her hands before scurrying back to the safety of the group.

Seeing that these devil children refused to be tempted by the meager handfuls of rice, my mother probably stepped up the exorcism. She had come prepared with talismans that attracted luck, incense sticks that purified the air and flushed out hidden pockets of Red Disaster, and lumps of moxa and red pepper to scare away troublesome imps. After first trying to bribe the children to go away by offering them her prized good luck packets, my mother took out a handful of moxa and red pepper balls. One by one, she lit the pellets with her Bic and threw them at the children.

"Shame on you! Your mothers must be so sad to have given birth to monsters," she scolded, flinging the smoldering lumps into the growing crowd.

"Hey, you crazy!" one or two of the kids yelled when a ball of moxa or pepper hit its mark, leaving a small ash-gray circle on a piece of clothing or a body part. The rest of the children edged in closer, howling with laughter at each word my mother spoke.

"Shame-u, shame-u!" they mimicked in singsong voices. "You maddahs mustu be so sad-u!"

When I first saw the frail, wild-haired lady in pajamas throwing handfuls of pebbles into the crowd, I did not realize she was my mother. Only when she raised her arms into the air and pivoted toward me for a moment, only when I caught the faint cry of "Induk," did I recognize her. I wanted to scream, to tell the kids to shut their mouths and go to hell. I wanted to pound the laughing heads into their necks. But I couldn't; looking at the only part of myself that I thought contained power, I saw my hands as the others around me must have seen them: feeble, scrawny, ineffectual. And I knew them then for what they were: the skeleton hands of death; and the light for what it was: Saja laughing just under my skin.

I wanted to help my mother, shield her from the children's sharp-toothed barbs, and take her home. And yet I didn't want to. Because for the first time, as I watched and listened to the children taunting my mother, using their tongues to mangle what she said into what they heard, I saw and heard what they did. And I was ashamed.

"Shame-u shame-u, sad-u sad-u!" my schoolmates chanted, unintimidated by the moxa balls or my mother promising vengeance from Induk, until they were interrupted by the vice principal and several burly teachers.

"What the hell is going on?" Vice Principal Pili demanded once the crowd had quieted. When no one spoke up, he looked around for familiar faces, children he recognized from detention hall. "You, Angelo Villanueva. You, Primo Beaton. You, Toots Tutivena. You causing trouble again?"

"No, Mr. Pili! Wasn't us. Was that crazy lady," said Angelo.

"Yeah, was her t'rowing fire at us," agreed Primo, who rubbed at a black mark on his forehead.

And Toots Tutivena, whom I dubbed my eternal archnemesis in that moment, said: "Was that crazy lady who I know for a fact is Beccah Bradley's maddah."

Vice Principal Pili scowled at them. "Okay, all of yous. Get out. I don't wanna see your faces hangin' around here after school no more unless it's in detention." After the three he singled out worked their way to the edge of the crowd, where they remained, reluctant to leave before the action died and the bag lady went home, he swung his face toward my mother. "Can I help you?" He frowned, his question almost mocking.

Recognizing authority, my mother straightened the strap of her shoulder bag and smoothed the front of her pajamas with fingers that left black streaks. "Yes, sir," she said. "I looking for daughteh. Name is Roh-beccah Blad-u-ley."

"Rebeccah Bradley?" Pili asked. "Is that right?"

When my mother nodded, he yelled out, "Rebeccah Bradley! Is Rebeccah Bradley here? Does anyone know Rebeccah Bradley?"

Before Toots Tutivena could finger me in the crowd I had joined, merely curious, when they started chanting, "Shame-u shame-u, sad-u sad-u," I slipped away. At the moment I was called upon to claim my mother, I couldn't. Instead I ran away, and the farther I ran from my mother, the smaller I seemed to shrink, until I was smaller and flimsier than the cheap moxa balls my mother burned to ward off the *sal* of malevolent beings.

9

AKIKO ·⤳

I undress my daughter slowly, taking care not to bend her arms at odd angles as I slip the shirt from her head, tucking my fingers between her skin and the pins as I undo her diaper. I dip a finger into her belly button, see her wiggle in surprise, and I remember how, just a few short weeks ago, she screamed with anger and fear when I peeled each piece of clothing from her body to reveal the red and wrinkly vulnerable skin surrounding the stub of her umbilicus.

Now she laughs as she stretches her legs and I tickle the rolls of fat on her thighs. I love nothing more than this: the velvet of her body underneath my fingertips, her powder-and-milk smell, her laughter and her perfect nakedness.

·⤳

The missionaries dressed the days in prayer. We gave thanks and praise-bes throughout the day and were taught to begin and end our day in communion with the Lord. After waking each day, we met in the basement, where we sat for a while in silent prayer before the sermon. And at the end of each day, we met in the basement again for singing and more communal prayer. We prayed for an end to hunger, for world peace, and for salvation. The minister taught that

in all things, whatsoever ye shall ask in prayer, believing, ye shall receive. That if we prayed hard enough, fervently enough, and to the
right God in the right heaven, our prayers would be answered.
Blessed were the meek, the persecuted, the reviled, for we would be
exalted in the Kingdom of Heaven.

Often the missionaries would describe heaven as a place of
spiritual freedom and God as Korea's own avenging angel. In chorus,
we sang out words like: Fight, O Lord, against those who fight me;
war against those who make war upon me. And what I remembered
most from each sermon were the verses that focused on justice:
When God arises, His enemies are scattered. As smoke is driven, so
are they driven; as wax melts before the fire, so the wicked perish before God.

I pictured heaven as a Korea liberated from domination,
where the angels trod over rivers littered with the charred bodies of
the Japanese.

Of God, I had no picture. But in the darkest part of the night,
when my prayers were peeled back and laid bare, the face I cried for,
called out to, was always Induk's.

• ✓

During the silences when we were supposed to commune privately
with God, I prayed for Induk to return to me. I spiraled my mind
away from my body, trying to find her, to catch a glimpse of her. I
listened for her in the empty spaces of my days and nights: in the
spaces between the beats of words and music, of my breath and my
heart. I waited, wondering if she had abandoned me; I called out,
Where are you, Where are you? until the words lost their meaning
and I was nothing but a bag of skin.

• ✓

During the silences, and in the privacy of the darkest part of night,
this is, as I came to know in the months and years that followed,

sin

what the missionary man prayed for: salvation from his sins. And the fulfillment of them. =

We all think we have our secrets, the minister said when I refused to tell him where I had come from, but we cannot hide from God. Only when we share our burden with Him, only when we give ourselves over to Him, are we uplifted and relieved.

He patted my head, brushing his fingers across my ear, and I jerked away.

Poor child, he murmured. You have suffered.

I am no longer a child, Sonsaeng-nim, I told him.

He forced his breath into laughs. Please, he said. I am not so much older than you.

I stared at the silver fanning across his temples.

Well, okay, he joked, his voice smooth as glass. I meant that in God's eyes we are all equal. Quick as a snake, he touched the end of my nose. So call me Richard, he said, or Rick. May I call you Akiko? Rick and Akiko, our names somehow match.

I felt as if he had slapped me with the name the soldiers had assigned to me. I wanted to shout, No! That is not my name! but I said nothing, knowing that after what had happened to me, I had no right to use the name I was born with. That girl was dead.

Akiko, the minister said, you are so different from the other girls. You look younger than many of them, yet you seem so mature. The way you carry yourself, the way you measure your words, as if you are always thinking, as if you know and have seen too much. How old are you?

I wanted to say that I was so old I was already rotting in my grave, but I shrugged and said nothing.

How old are you? he repeated, brushing a finger across my knuckles.

Eighteen, I lied. I did not want the missionaries placing me in an orphanage, where many of the older children were adopted by Japanese families looking for an extra worker.

The lids of the missionary man's eyes dropped until he looked at me through slits. If that's what you say, he said, nodding, though he seemed unsure. Sometimes war makes people older than they should be. I myself have been lucky, pampered and taken care of all my life. He said this with scorn, as if bitter, then added, As if God has never seen fit to test me.

But you! The missionary grabbed my shoulders. Just a child, and you have experienced tribulations equal to Job's so that you may feel the full measure of God's glory! Will you tell me what you have done so that I can help you? Confess and come to me and I will lead you into the Body of Christ!

I shrugged away from him, and he dropped his hands. Please, Akiko, do not forsake me or the one true God. Tell me! His voice fell to a whisper, and he leaned toward me. I have heard rumors, terrible rumors, about women being sent north of the Yalu—is that where you've come from? I mean, I noticed your uniform, and—if it is true, then know that God will love the greater debtor. He has said of the fallen woman, Her sins which are many are forgiven, for she loved much. Akiko, the minister cried, the sins of the body will be washed away by the blood of the lamb. His body will become your body; your flesh, His. Just give yourself to Him!

I watched him searching for words that would split open my silence. I looked at him, stripping away his mantle of piousness and humility, and kept looking until I could see the inside of his heart.

Forgive me, he stammered, if I press when I should not. I only want you to know that God does not judge, that I would not. I seek only to offer solace, knowing that God would not give you more than you could handle. Trust in Him. And me. Please, Akiko, welcome the Lord—and me—we who wait for you with open arms.

Even as words continued to spill from his mouth, the minister backed away, but not before I discovered his secret, the one he won't admit even now, even to himself, after twenty years of mar-

riage. It was a secret I learned about in the comfort camps, one I recognized in his hooded eyes, in his breathing, sharp and fast, and in
the way his hands fluttered about his sides as if they wanted to fly up
against my half-starved girl's body with its narrow hips and new
breasts.

This is his sin, the sin he fought against and still denies: that
he wanted me—a young girl—not for his God but for himself.

·~

I gave up eating, folding bites of food in my napkin so that I could
offer it to Induk later. I sipped water sparingly, leaving glass after
glass for Induk. When I lit the candles or the stove, I would
imagine that each flame ignited a stick of incense that burned for
Induk. And always, always I prayed her back to me. I needed her
protection.

One night, as I was on my knees for the last prayer of the day,
chanting her name in my head and my heart until her name ran together, seamless in its repetition, I fell to the ground. My body
turned to lead, so heavy that I could not lift a finger or a toe, much
less an arm or a leg. And then it was as if I liquefied; I lost the edges
of myself and began to soak into the floorboards. Waves surged
through my arms and legs, rushing toward the center of my body,
where I knew they would clash and explode out the top of my head.
I became afraid, knowing that I would feel naked and vulnerable
without my body.

The fear grew until it pressed against my chest, until I felt I
would drown under the weight of it, until it began to take shape
and I saw that it was Induk straddling me, holding me down to
the earth.

Afraid and angry because I could barely breathe, I still could
not ask her why she had abandoned me. I was too happy to see her
again. I tried to tell her this, but she began choking me.

Why did you leave me? Induk was the one to ask my question.

Induk

Why did you leave me to putrefy in the open air, as food for the wild animals just as if I were an animal myself?

Induk, I panted, I had to do what the soldiers told us to.

Liar, she sneered, why did you leave me?

Please, Induk, please, I cried: I was afraid of becoming you.

She rolled off me, then wailed so long and hard she blasted the air into my lungs. See me, she said as she stood up. See me as I am now.

I looked and saw: hair tangled through and around maggoty eye sockets and nostrils. Gnawed arms ripped from the body but still dangling from the hands to the skewering pole. Ribs broken and sucked clean of marrow. Flapping strips of skin stuck to sections of the backbone.

I forced myself to look, to linger over the details of her body. I found her beautiful, for she had come back to me.

I grabbed her hand, and my fingers slipped into bloated flesh. I kissed it and offered her my own hands, my eyes, my skin.

She offered me salvation.

• ✦

When my daughter still had her umbilical cord, my husband worried about infection. Thick and ugly, the color of dried blood and beef jerky, the cord was resolute and did not fall off when it was supposed to: after a month it was still there, dangling by a persistent thread of flesh. Though her navel turned pink around the edges, my daughter did not seem to be in pain, so we continued to dab it with alcohol, wiggling the umbilicus like a tooth loose in its socket.

Then one day I bent over my baby to change her diaper, and the birth cord was gone. Instead yellow fluid, sticky like glue, filled her navel. I swabbed at the glue, unveiling the indented star of her belly button, then undid the diaper to look for the umbilical cord. It wasn't there. I felt through her sleeper, checked the crib and the floor, but still couldn't find the cord.

I panicked, suddenly frantic to find this one piece of flesh that was both me and my daughter. I threw clothes out of drawers, dug through dirty hampers, and poked into the diaper pail, before I found it on the bathroom rug, already dusted with hair. I brushed it off and placed it in the center of my palm, where it looked tiny and fragile.

I cupped my hand over my daughter's birth cord and vowed to keep it safe, just as I would keep my daughter safe from harm and unhappiness. I would keep the cord so that as she grows into the person she will become, a person I do not know yet, we will both be reminded that we share one body, one flesh.

umbilical cord
A. Keeps it

IO

ＡＫＩＫＯ ·⌣

When my daughter cries in her sleep, caught in a dream of sorrow, I wonder what she has experienced in her short life to make her so unhappy, so afraid. I try to fold her into the comfort of my body, but she pushes away from me, startled into wakefulness. She watches me, her eyelids dropping solemnly until they shut her into sleep once again, taking her somewhere I cannot follow. Does she dream about her birth, about her expulsion from her first home? Or does she cry dreaming that she is there, trapped, once again?

·⌣

On August 15, 1945, as we pooled our rations to prepare bi bim kook soo for the afternoon meal, one of the missionaries turned on the radio for the news. Though most of the Japanese-controlled broadcasts still promised victory for Japan, explaining that they were retreating for covert military purposes, we heard what they did not say: that Japan was losing the war. When the Russian Allies and Korean freedom fighters had crossed the Yalu into Korea just a few days before, we knew that the end was near.

Yet when it came, I thought it was a trick, one more attempt to ferret out traitors to the Japanese state. The radio announcer called for everyone to stand by, and after a spurt of static, the

Emperor himself announced Japan's unconditional surrender to the Allied forces.

Unable to reconcile that thin, watery voice, the voice of a broken old man, with the Descendant of Heaven who had the power to sacrifice thousands like me, I did not trust the announcement. Still, I let myself be pulled along by the cheers. Mansei, Mansei, the missionaries and their charges yelled out the windows. Koreans ran into the streets, unfurling the blue-and-red Taeguk-ki into the wind that carried their shouts and cheers. Everyone became silent, though, when they saw that Japanese soldiers still lounged in the streets as if nothing had changed, as if they had not heard the news.

•~

The war was over, but the search for traitorous foreign sympathizers continued, with pressures and demands from the various People's Committees that struggled for political control. Day after day, as the Japanese were disarmed and replaced by Russian soldiers who stripped factories and farms, accusations and condemnations seeped through the walls of the Heaven and Earth Mentholatum and Matches building. Some of our neighbors—who had changed their names to Yamada or Ichida or Sakamaki during the war and were once again Kim or Pak or Yi and members of either the newly formed Nationalists' North Korean Five Province Administrative Bureau or the Independence League—threw rocks and shouts at our doors and windows. Outsiders go home, they yelled at us over and over, until the day the missionaries started to pack their belongings.

We are being called home, back to America, they explained to the girls in their care. We will find homes and sponsors for you, if you wish to come with us.

Most of the girls declined, saying they would try to find their families, saying they had somewhere they could return to, now that the war was over. They could pick up the threads of their lives, weaving them into a future as if the war had been a minor disruption in the fabric, but I knew I had to leave with the missionaries. I knew, had known the moment I crossed the Yalu and entered the recreation camps, that my home village of Sulsulham was as far away as heaven for me.

So when the minister told me I should marry him if I wanted to leave Pyongyang and come to America with them, I did, I made it easy for him to take me.

This girl, he explained to his fellow missionaries, has no place to go, no one to guide her. I can give her a new life. God is giving me a chance to save her, to guide her into the flock by yoking her to its shepherd.

Some of the women missionaries grumbled, Why not just adopt her?

No time. The minister smiled. Besides, she is eighteen, an adult.

One of the ladies blew—*Humph*—through pursed lips, and said something in English, too fast for me to follow.

The minister touched her arm, then answered in Korean. She says she is, and we will not be unevenly yoked; before the marriage ceremony, we will baptize Akiko.

He took hold of my hand and pulled me in front of the missionaries. His fingers slithered across my palm. No, he said, I am not sacrificing myself, for I am answering God's call.

God's call? said another missionary. Are you sure it is His voice you hear? Remember what He has said: Whosoever looketh on a woman with lust hath already committed sin in his heart. Cast her out, brother, for if the right eye offends, pluck it out so that the whole body can live.

The missionary's nails bit into my palm as he cleared his throat to hide his growl. I believe, he said, God also said: Why beholdest thou the mote that is in thy brother's eye but considerest not the beam that is in thine own? What is it, *brother,* that you see?

My hand clenched and sweating in his, I stood on display with my head bowed, unable to look into the faces of the missionaries and the Korean girls still remaining at the mission. But I felt their whispers and thoughts striking me in the chest.

.~

After a week of frenzied prayer and fervent packing, the Pyongyang mission was dismantled. We packed what we could as fast as we could and loaded up the carts. On the last day, we gathered on the front steps for a final prayer, and one of the missionaries pushed us shoulder-to-shoulder for a picture. *Cheese,* he said. I did not know what he meant, but all the missionaries smiled. The camera clicked twice, and then, as if on signal, the neighbors and their families swarmed into the building. They marched past us to look through the house, sorting through whatever was left behind. Jira-handa, those hama, those dungbo! I could hear them call to each other, loud enough for us to hear their insults. See how stingy those fat hippos are: hardly anything good left! Rags! Empty matchboxes! Dishes I wouldn't feed a dog off of!

.~

Years later, after the minister drove me through America, we received a copy of that picture in the mail. In it the minister and I are standing in the center of the stairs, surrounded by missionaries. One of his arms wraps loosely around my neck. He is smiling; I am not. Our heads have been circled in red, like ink halos. This is our wedding picture.   *wed. picture*

.~

Leaving Pyongyang, we hiked to the Taedong River, which was full and rushing because of the early fall rains. I wore a thin white gown that one of the missionary ladies had given me, because, she said, I was going to be reborn in the Spirit and because I was to be married. Two of the greatest events in a Christian woman's life.

I tried to push the dress away, but she said, Don't bother to thank me; it must be a dream come true.

She wrapped me in the dress, which kept slipping off my shoulders and dragged through the dust as we walked. Hold it up, the missionary lady kept whispering to me as she eyed the hem of what I think were her cast-off underclothes. You're getting it dirty.

I did not look up at her, even once. I kept my eyes on the trail and watched how the white cloth, the color of purity and death, soaked up the earth.

When we reached the river's edge, the congregation stopped, but I kept walking. I stepped onto the rocks at the shore and waded toward the center. Stop, I heard the minister yell. That's far enough.

The dress billowed around me, a bell on the water, and then, caught by the current, entangled me. I fell to my knees.

See how earnest she is, the minister shouted to the witnesses as he yanked on my elbow. What's the matter with you? he whispered. Get up!

Instead I threw myself facedown into the river. Stolen by the cold, my breath rushed out, bubbling in the river's froth. I held my body stiff, felt the waters turn me, testing my sturdiness against its rocks, and then I let go. I felt the pull of the river in my legs and my lungs, felt the need to dissolve into her body. I opened my eyes and my mouth to taste her—and then I was yanked by the hair and jerked upward.

I gagged on air. Nose streaming, eyes burning unprotected in the wind, I turned to look at the minister. Wet up to the chest, one hand clutching my hair, he delivered me unto the Lord. I baptize thee, he said, in the name of the Father, the Son, and the Holy Ghost.

He pulled me from the river by the hand and the hair, and as I stumbled away from the river and into the arms waiting along the bank, I felt empty, desolate, abandoned.

↑ baptism

Drenched and dripping, I heard someone ask me if I took the minister as husband. I nodded, unable to speak, and then I was led to the cart and given my own clothes.

You are born again, said the woman who had given me my wedding gown. As a Christian, as a wife, and as an American. Congratulations.

Before we left the river's edge, I reached down to touch the earth. I felt the mud under my hands, then quickly took a pinch into my mouth. I rubbed it across my tongue, the roof of my mouth, and I ground it between my teeth. I wanted to taste the earth, metallic as blood, take it into my body so that my country would always be a part of me.

•~

As thousands of exiled patriots from Manchuria returned to Korea to cheer the enemy's descent into their own lands, the Christian missionaries and those who followed them were in turn pushed south. We moved toward Seoul, hundreds of us, through a nation we thought free. And just as many people from the south moved north. In the months when all directions were open for travel, people roamed the country, searching for family members and homes, pieces of their lives and themselves that were severed and scattered during the war. Or they moved to escape memories, to search for new lives and new homes.

•~

Now, because I have my daughter to protect from restless spirits, I wonder about those dead. Did they follow their sons and daughters across the country? Or did they remain at home, abandoned and uncared for? I think of Induk, who somehow followed me not only across the country but across the world, to become my guardian. I think of my own mother and father, who stayed behind, or got lost, following another daughter or another family. I wonder if their spir-

its are fed and clothed, content, or if they have turned outlaw and
beggar, without kin, without home.

•⌐ *was the war when Korea split in two?*

Near Kaesong and Panmunjom, we passed roadblocks set up by the
military. I thought of the soldiers at the Yalu River and tried to run
away, but the minister husband pulled me alongside him. As we
moved toward them, I could feel their eyes studying me—my face,
breasts, hips, and poji—judging my worth as a *niku-ichi* P, and I
knew they would pull me aside, question me, ask me how I had escaped, and then send me south to hell, to Japan. But when we
moved past them, I saw that they were not even Japanese. Bored,
the guards did not look at me at all, or at any of the faces moving
past them, but stared instead at a point above the human river,
toward the mountains in the north.

And then the soldiers, rifles crossed against their chests, waved
us through the barricade, and we were on the other side. It still
seems strange to me to think of Korea in terms of north and south,
to realize that a line we couldn't see or feel, a line we crossed with
two steps, cut the body of my country in two. In dreams I will always see the thousands of people, the living and the dead, forming
long queues that spiral out from the head and feet of Korea, not
knowing that when they reach the navel they will have to turn back.
Not knowing that they will never be able to return home. Not
knowing they are forever lost.

•⌐

When we arrived in Seoul, we found a room in the Severance
Hospital Mission. Since we had left all the belongings from the
Pyongyang mission on the cart, we entered the room with nothing
but ourselves and the clothes we were wearing. The minister hus-
band pulled me toward the bed, saying, Tell me how to be with you.
As man and wife, we will be one flesh.

He held my face in his hands. You do not have to tell me of your past, for whatever you have done, you are now cleansed by the washing of water with the word.

His hands drifted down my neck and settled on my shoulders. He pressed his thumbs into my shoulder blades. I want to drink the water from your cistern and love your body as my own. But I do not know what you know of consummation, he whispered. Do you know what it feels like to take a man, how you will have to stretch and how it will pain you the first time? I will try to go slow.

He pressed me to his chest, tilted his hips toward mine. There will be blood the first time, he said. Do you know?

I knew what it felt like to stretch open for many men, and I knew about blood with the first and with the hundredth, and about pain sharp enough to cut your body from your mind. I could not form the words, but I must have cried out, for the minister husband pushed his lips against my head and said, Don't worry, sweetie, my little lamb. I will be gentle, he said, and then he bit my neck.

It is better to marry than to burn, he whispered, and I am burning for you. There is something about you—the way you look so innocent, yet act so experienced—that makes me on fire for you. You are not a virgin, are you? he asked.

He cooed to me and petted me, then grabbed and swore at me, as he stripped the clothes from our bodies. When he pushed me into the bed, positioned himself above me, fitting himself between my thighs, I let my mind fly away. For I knew then that my body was, and always would be, locked in a cubicle at the camps, trapped under the bodies of innumerable men.

* ~

Without the mission and the sermons that had structured his days, my husband became like a man without a head. We traveled from church to church, drifting toward the tip of the peninsula until we reached the port of Pusan. From there we crossed the ocean, pulled by the missionary's need to teach the word of his God, continuing his odyssey across the United States, from the Larchmont Presbyterian Church in New York to the Florida Chain of Missionary Assemblies, wherever we could obtain an invitation to teach or study or speak. I would stand by my husband's side in my Korean dress as he lectured on Spreading the Light: My Experiences in the Obscure Orient.

When we were not in a lecture, the minister husband dressed me in a white blouse pinched in at the waist and a dark-blue skirt that clung to my hips and barely covered my knees. I felt naked in the way the clothes touched my body, but this was the uniform I was to wear as the minister's wife. During the day, I pulled my hair back into a knot that reminded me that I was married. If I forgot and wore my hair in a long braid slung over my shoulder, the husband would scold me: You look like a little kid. And yet at night that is how he wanted me: hair down in braids to my waist; eyes wide and blank; lips dropped into a pout and ready to cry. At night, when he climbed on top of me, he'd take the ends of my hair, put them into his mouth, and suck. Afterward he'd pull the blankets over me, tucking them around my chin, and ask me to recite my prayers. Our Father who art in Heaven, hallowed be thy name, I would say, while thinking of Induk, her body bathed in a river of light.

For years, we traveled from the east coast to the west coast, from north to south, to every state of the Union. Rich enough to own a private car called a wagon, we drove through stretches of farmland so flat and yellow with grain that there was no way to judge time or distance. The land, smooth and bland as the dish called pudding, hypnotized me. Every once in a while, I would blink and rub my eyes, as if waking from a daze, and realize I was still caught in the dream: the same field, the same barns, the same cattle grazing along the same wire fence, endless. I felt that we were traveling in circles.

Trying to break the monotony, my husband pressed the car horn whenever we passed cows along the roadside. When we first entered the farm country, the beeps, sparse and irregular, jolted me. As we drove on, they became like the land, regular and lulling as a heartbeat.

I think it was the car horn that made me understand just how rich America was: in just a few hours, we beeped enough times for every family in Korea to have a cow, yet my husband said that only a handful of ranchers owned the cattle we saw. A country of excess and extravagance, America was so rich that one man could own a hundred cows.

America .

We packed and unpacked, living out of two bags and a box, sleeping sometimes in college guest rooms or motels, but mostly in the car at roadside rest stops. At these stops, I took a wad of Kleenex and ran behind the building to do my business, and I cleaned myself with napkins dampened at the drinking faucet. Though my husband complained, lecturing on how cleanliness was next to godliness, I could not bring myself to stand in line to use the toilets and showers. I felt cleaner skipping showers than remembering the way the Japanese referred to the recreation camps as public rest rooms.

Some of the rest stops and gas stations along the road had what were called vending machines, where anyone with a coin could pull a knob and receive candy—something that I thought only America must have. If the husband had money left over from filling the tank, he would give me the change so that I could practice using the vending machine. I memorized which coins to put in the money slot, learned to match the knob to the candy that I wanted, and watched as the belt rolled forward to push my selection off the shelf. At first I found it comforting that there was always another candy bar behind it, waiting to take its place. But the more of it I ate, the

vending machine

candy as comfort Q ?

more it began to bother me: it was so easy, so cheap, so easily replenished.

During the first few months of traveling, I ate only candy bars and salad with Tabasco sauce. Nothing else appealed to me; American food did not have any taste. I could not eat the food the husband ordered for me to put meat on my bones: potatoes fried or smashed and covered with gravy, bread so white and fluffy I couldn't remember swallowing it, meat I could not recognize. I did see meat that I could tell was meat, but it was something we never ordered. Once, at the counter of a diner that didn't turn us away because I looked Japanese, the woman sitting next to me ordered a plate of something that looked like kalbi. I watched out of the corner of my eye, and was surprised that she refused the best part: the chewy, tastiest meat—closest to the bone. When she pushed her plate away and touched the napkin to her lips, I picked up one of her bones and bit into it.

Excuse me, the woman said as she jumped up.

The husband grabbed the bone from my hand and put it back on her plate. No, Akiko! he said to me, and then to the woman: Excuse us. She is not from our country; her people tend to share plates.

She's a scrawny little thing; maybe you should feed her. The woman's eyes flicked at my stomach and breasts, and then lingered on my husband's face. She smiled. Where's she from? Where're you from?

Sorry I am, I said, my tongue stumbling in English in front of this woman who would not look at me. I not knowing you still wanting meat.

The lady did not look away from my husband. How quaint, she said, a poor little orphan Jap.

•~

To learn to be an American was to learn to waste. Food, paper, clothes—everything was thrown away when we got tired of it, because there was so much. The cities, especially, were places of waste; it seemed like everything everyone had ever thrown away collected in the cities. Looking up, you saw buildings so high they could catch the clouds, but then you stepped into side streets littered with rotting paper and old food and throwaway people wearing throwaway clothes. Rivers of cars snaked between buildings and blared at people as if they were cows. And the rivers of water were thick as sludge, slick enough with oil to catch fire. The cities all looked like shit alley to me.

In one of the cities, my husband took me to the highest building in the world. We rode to the top in a box that made me so dizzy I clutched at my husband's arm to keep from falling. See the numbers, he said. I looked up at the numbers lighting faster than I could count and dropped to my knees. At the top of the sky, everything glittered, the sun glinting off metal and concrete. From so far away, the city seemed beautiful, because you could forget about the waste and the dirt when you didn't have to step in it. Maybe that's what the earth looks like to people in heaven, to ghosts and to God.

That's what all of America was like to me. When you see it for the first time, it glitters, beautiful, like a dream. But then, the longer you walk through it, the more you realize that the dream is empty, false, sterile. You realize that you have no face and no place in this country.

My husband never talked about a home, about family, and I never asked. In fact, it did not occur to me that he might have a family, parents who loved him, until two letters from the place where he was born caught up with us at the First Friendship Bible Church in Illinois. The first letter we opened, from the manager of Cuyahoga Falls Sunnyside Retirement Community, told my husband that his mother had died. The second one told him she was ill.

We followed the letters back to their origin and found the last place where my husband's mother lived. After several false turns along roads that spiraled into dead ends, we entered the building's soot-stained parking structure. Someone had planted a handful of mugunghwa, the everlasting flowers, along the walkway that led into the three-story building. I took seeing them as a good sign, even though their stems seemed withered from the smell of burning tires and bent under the heavy eyes that looked down on them from the building's windows.

The lobby smelled of mildew and of old people without families to care for them, ancestors without descendants. It smelled like abandonment and loneliness and ghosts. It smelled like home.

As we waited for the elevator, old people flocked to us, eager to touch our young people's skin and smell our young people's breath as we received their questions.

You related to Mrs. Bradley? Never knew she had a son. Never knew he was married to a Chinee. All them people are so small, see? How adorable! You speakee English?

They crowded against us, eager to escort us to my husband's mother's door, eager to tell us of her death and her funeral, which was beautiful, just beautiful, even though none of her family saw fit to come.

·~

When we entered the mother's apartment, her ghost rushed out at us. She enveloped us with a heavy stickiness that sucked us into the room. A fat spirit, she demanded in death the space she had never had in her life as a thin, sickly woman. She pushed us up against each other, the furniture, the knickknacks and mementos that filled shelves and counters and floor spaces.

Jesus Above, Good Lord in Heaven, my husband said, trying to maneuver his way between a Dalmatian-dog lamp and thigh-high stacks of *National Geographic*s to get into the kitchen. What'll we do with all this junk?

A tower of magazines toppled onto the floor, knocking over several figurines and picture frames from one of the end tables placed in the middle of the living room. I stooped to pick up a wooden owl, a porcelain clown holding a bunch of balloons, a tea-cup, and the pictures. As I unfolded the backs of the silver frames to make them stand upright, I studied the people my husband's family once were: a gray-haired, thin-lipped man with heavy eyebrows, dressed in a military uniform; a bony woman with pointy glasses on a sharp nose, pressing a fat boy against her breast; the same fat boy, several years older and starting to stretch into the man who was my husband, with his hair curled about the high-necked collar of his private school uniform.

•~

For a long while after that first day, I could not live with the dead woman and her possessions. I could not touch her things, even the carpet that I walked on, without feeling her spirit trying to squeeze me out.

Help me tag and box everything, my husband would say, as he sifted through mountains of his mother's old magazines and letters, through her armies of tiny dolls and animals. And when I would not move, letting the dust fall and settle over everything like snow, he'd scold: Wife, be subject to your husband, as sayeth the Lord, for as Christ is head of the church, the husband is the head of the wife and savior of her body.

A good wife will turn a house into a home, he'd say. It's your duty as wife and helpmeet.

Then, after lecturing on cleanliness and godliness, he'd beg: Please, *please,* at least help me tidy up.

But I could not forge through the space filled by the mother. It was as if she sucked all the air from my body and pressed me down with the weight of her possessions. I spent most of my time hiding in the bed that had conformed to her body's indentations, under her mustard-and-green knitted blanket that smelled like lavender and must, dreaming of Induk and people who looked like me peeking in through the windows.

• ⤳

Finally, perhaps by way of my dreams, Induk slipped into the mother's apartment. After she rolled me out of bed, she slid her hands over the mother's desk, over the pictures, over the wooden animals and ceramic figurines, until her fingers were coated with dust. With the dust of all the mother's possessions cupped in her hands, Induk lured the ghost mother into her palms, where she pressed and pushed until the fat spirit became as small as a speck of dust. Then, bringing her fingers to my mouth, Induk told me to suck, to taste, to make this—the apartment, the city, the state, and America—home my own.   *make US home*

• ⤳

When I was pregnant with my daughter, I made tea with the black dirt from the garden outside our room at the Mission House for Boys. I drank the earth, nourishing her within the womb, so that she would never feel homeless, lost. After her birth, I rubbed that same earth across my nipples and touched it to my daughter's lips, so that, with her first suck, with her first taste of the dirt and the salt and the milk that is me, she would know that I am, and will always be, her home.   *dirt, earth, breast milk*
mom as home

II

AKIKO ·∽

I dreamed.

The sentries at the Yalu River checkpoint aimed their rifles at me instead of letting me hurry across.

Shall we make her eat a few beans? one of them asked, laughing.

I looked up at them just as the other mouthed, Pat-ta-ta-ta-tat. As his lips moved, I dreamed I could see the words leaping like the feet of a fire dragon from his gun.

When I turned to run, I felt the bullet words enter my back, burning through skin and blood, muscle and bone, so hot that I could feel myself evaporating. My legs still pumped but became heavier, denser, as the water in my body boiled into the air. Finally there was nothing left of me except for salt and the fire inside of me.

I heard more laughter. And felt pricks of brilliant heat from the dragon's teeth before a blessed coolness blew my body apart. When the grains settled, all that was left was the dragon, blue-white with its heat, chasing its tail around and around, faster and faster until it spun like the sun.

·∽

Because of that tae-mong, the first birth dream, I knew my baby was a boy. I was so sure of this, I told my husband. See, fire and dragon and sun, I said, all yang. And salt, really good luck because it's so valuable. I am having a boy.

He told me he had not heard such superstitious nonsense since leaving Korea. Didn't he teach me to leave all that behind, to give it up for the Lord? Ye cannot serve God and mammon.

But still, underneath the words of disapproval, I read the pleasure and the pride in his eyes.

Consequently we were both surprised when we saw the baby's genitals. I remember how hazy everything looked to me, how the faces of the doctor and the nurses blurred until they turned into those of Induk, my mother, my sisters. When they held my baby up to me, I remember first thinking: Oh no, something is wrong with his jajie—where is it? And then I realized I had a daughter and knew a fierce joy, more awesome because of its unexpectedness.

This baby was for me, mine, not my husband's son but my daughter.

I still feel that joy as if it were brand-new, so hot that it hurts, burning blue-white and brilliant, sharp as a dragon's teeth.

• ~

Like my mother, my daughter was born in the month of the dog. Fierce, loyal, bold, and fearless. If we were in Korea, and if I had married a Korean, I am sure my husband's father would have insisted on a name to counteract these traits, to inject meekness into the dominant natures of those animal signs.

I asked my husband to pick an American name that is very strong, one that will protect her throughout her life.

It does not matter that I cannot pronounce Roh-beccu.

I will call her Bek-hap, the lily, purest white. Blooming in the boundary between Korea and America, between life and death, this child, with the tendril of her body, keeps me from crossing over and roots me to this earth.

• ~

Watching my daughter sleep, arms and legs flung wide, her body like a star, I find myself fighting both overwhelming joy and over-whelming grief. I lightly touch each fold in her fat baby arms, stroke her wrists and fingers. I lift her hands to my face, inhaling her sweet, sweaty baby smell, and I know in that moment how much my own mother must have loved me—more than anything in this world or in heaven, including God.

• ~

I wonder if my own mother ever dreamed dreams so filled with yang that they could only mean sons, and I wonder whether she was happy or disappointed when yet another daughter emerged from between her legs. Did she feel betrayed by her night vi-sions, by the signs, by Samshin Halmoni, the grandmother spirit who takes care of babies and mothers? I know my mother and father would have made the appropriate offerings in hopes of a male infant.

Maybe by the fourth daughter, she could not feel the love that I now feel, all maternal instincts diluted with the disappointing birth of each successive child, all girls. Maybe by the time I was born, my parents had no need to pretend unhappiness to placate jealous spirits. There would have been no need to think of protec-tive, misleading nicknames like Dog's Dung or Straw Bag or Rock-head, because the truth, announced by the kumjul of pine branches and charcoal hung across our gate, would have been demeaning enough: one more girl for the mountain Kims.

• ~

I was born on the fourteenth day of the first month, the day before the first full moon of the year, and so it was doubly unfortunate that I was born a girl. Women in Korea take special care not to go visiting the day before the first full moon of the year, since bad luck will enter with them and stay for the year; because of me, a wrong-sexed baby arriving on an inauspicious day, bad luck moved in and became part of the family. *Akiko's bday inauspicious day*

Because of me, my oldest sister always reminded me, our family could not participate in what was to be the last full-moon celebration in our village; before the year was out, the Japanese soldiers arrived to enforce the Emperor's edict banning Korean holidays.

We all had to sit around and look at you, all crinkly red and ugly, she used to say, while outside we could hear nuts and firecrackers exploding in the bonfire, scaring away demons, wild animals, and mosquitoes into the next year.

Oldest sister was especially bitter, because that was the first year she had helped to weave the rope to be used in the male-female tug-of-war contest. She had even planned to position herself near the front—if not at the very front—of the rope so all the boys could see her; in this way she'd planned to lure a future husband and pull him to her side. She mentioned this every year until the year our parents died and she betrayed me, paying me back.

older sis betrayal.

Because I was the youngest and she was the oldest, my sister loved to torment me. The other two, second and third sisters, teased me too, but their taunts held no malice. They were just like little birds chirping out whatever words oldest sister fed them. They had each other and were happy, not having to worry about the responsibilities of oldest sister while at the same time having someone to order to refill the rice or water bowls.

Oldest sister, though, snapped at me out of anger. She was old enough to realize I should have been a boy. She was old enough to have traveled with my mother to Samshin Halmoni's shrine and old enough to pray. She was old enough to understand what my parents wished for and what the villagers would have celebrated.

If you were a boy, she used to tell me, we would have had a hundred-day party for you. We would have dressed you in a crown and a rainbow-sleeved hanbok as if it were New Year's or Harvest Day. We would have made a feast, with special red-and-black bean cake sprinkled with honey to show how much we loved you, if you were a boy. *I should have been a boy*

·-

I want my own child to know that I gave her a hundred-day celebration, that I love her and thank the spirits for her health, even though she is not a boy and not in Korea. Or perhaps I celebrate because she is a girl, an American girl.

·-

I sew her hanbok and crown out of the best satin on sale at Sears. I make special red bean cake topped with white sugar and place it at the four compass points in the house, to bar disaster and welcome happiness. And I prepare enough rice cake for one hundred people to ensure her a long life, even though I do not know one hundred people to invite to the party.

·-

My husband and the minister wives who come to the party do not care for the rice cake. My husband says, Tastes like Styrofoam. What blasphemous waste. The neighbor ladies say, No, no, it's not so bad, but they wrap their pieces in a napkin and leave it on the table. Then they take pictures of my Beccah-chan, a tiny face lost in voluminous clouds of color, and leave.

When my husband takes the newspaper into the bathroom, I

carry the baby and the platters of rice cake to the porch. I settle my daughter into her basket, then crumble each cake, precious in its own way as salt, until she is surrounded by miniature mountains of crumbs.

I place a bit of rice in my baby's mouth and throw a handful high over the railing. When birds fly in for the feast, my daughter flaps her arms and crows as the bravest swoop over her basket and into the piles of rice cake surrounding her. Faster and faster, I scatter crumbs by the fistful, calling more and still more birds to come and join us, until there must be well over one hundred pecking in a frenzy at the ground and at their tails, flapping along the porch railing, hopping next to the basket where my baby girl laughs and I sing over and over, into the ball of flurry and heat made by their beating wings: Thank you, thank you for coming, thank you for coming to my party.

12

↓ dream of swimming in wonderful blue BUT pulled under

BECCAH ·~

Since my mother died, I dream the dream from my childhood.

I am swimming in water so blue that even when you're dreaming you think nothing this pure exists in real life, a blue so translucent you can almost breathe it. I hunt black-and-white fish as they dart through red coral reef, when suddenly I am wrenched from behind. I try to kick away but cannot move my feet. Something pulls me under. I begin to feel dizzy with the effort of not breathing, and when I know I will drown, I wake up, gasping for air.

·~

I found my mother after she had been dead a night and a day and another night. I usually stopped by to check on her before and after work and during the day on the weekends, to see if she was lucid, eating, sleeping, combing her hair. Since moving into my own apartment last year, I missed only one day, and on that one day she chose to die. I think she did it on purpose, to punish me. Or, maybe, to release me.

I brought doughnuts that morning, my usual peace offering of maple bars, planning on having breakfast with her on the lanai. The lanai was the main reason my mother bought the house when we first saw it, almost two decades ago. When Auntie Reno badgered the realtor for a list of homes in our price range, this house was last on her list and so the first one we visited; Auntie Reno believed in saving the best for last.

The ten-year-old, white-with-blue-trim two-bedroom home in Manoa was relatively inexpensive but did not convey the image of spirituality Reno felt a prominent fortune-teller's home should. "You need a cottage in Kahala or, better yet, Nu'uanu—you know how many ghosts stay in Nu'uanu?" Auntie Reno sniffed. "Manoa not bad, but dis house, jeesh!" She snorted loud enough for the realtor to wince. "Jus' like one *Leave It to Beaver* house wit one open port garage, gimme a break."

"I like it, Auntie Reno." I hung on to my mother's arm and sniffed the air. I remember that the air was so fresh and alive it stung my nose, like I was smelling the rain through the sun. I think I thought that we could run away from Saja with his stench of Red Disaster, that the Death Messenger would never find us in this clean-smelling house that sang of green things. Now I think that it was just the first house I smelled that didn't stink of roaches. "It smells like my dream home," I said.

Auntie Reno ignored me, as she did—and still does—when what I say isn't useful to her. "Let me pick dah right house, okay? Image stay nine-tenths dah battle," she told my mother. "And dat's my job. You jus' predict dah future, and we goin' make it."

My mother drifted behind our realtor, a large, long-necked ostrich of a woman. As the realtor strutted through the kitchen and bedrooms of the house, swiveling her head toward the home's highlights—the "refurbished cabinetry" and "economic use of space" and "quaint powder rooms," all of which had Reno harumphing and rolling her eyes—my mother nodded her head and smiled politely. But when my mother peeked behind the pea-green curtains that hid the sliding glass doors of the master bedroom, she stopped smiling and nodding.

The saleslady fidgeted. "Well, sure, the back's not in the best shape now," she said. My mother unlatched the door and pushed until the doors screeched apart. As my mother stepped onto the faded wood deck, just avoiding a jutting nail, the saleslady hopped forward to lead her away from the termite-hollowed railing. "But, ah, notice the potential. It, uh, it leads right into the garden." We all looked into the backyard, where yellow-flowered vines of wedelia swelled in waves to drown out a border of fly-specked hibiscus bushes, where the heads of overgrown red ti shook on thin stalks above the roof. Banana trees dropped their rotting fruit, which lay one on top of the other, dying in layers. Pom-poms of white-and-blue 'uki 'uki lilies swayed on wiry necks above nut grass that grew as high as my knees. The realtor stammered, then, trying to distract us once more, pointed toward the sky. "Look up!" she almost shouted. "The mountains! Now isn't that a beautiful view of the Ko'olaus!"

Auntie Reno pressed her lips together. "Mmm-hmm," she said. "I tink we seen enough." She turned to go, but my mother continued to stand there, her eyes intense and far away, as if she were listening to something carried on the air.

"Can you hear it, Beccah?" my mother whispered as she moved down the steps and into the yard. She forded through the grass, the wedelia, and the banana patch, all the way up to the rusty chicken-wire fence that marked the boundary.

"Mommy?" I ran after her, brushing from my face and hair the mist of fruit flies that sucked on the rotting sweet bananas. "Do you hear Saja? Is he coming to get us?"

"Hush," my mother told me. She bowed her head, resting her forehead against the fence. Loops of wire pressed octagons into her face, just below the hairline, imprinting a headdress of chains.

Auntie Reno, trampling a banana sapling as she clambered up to the fence next to us, asked, her face sweaty and excited, "Is the girl right—you see spirits here?"

"Shh," my mother told Reno without looking up. "Listen."

Auntie Reno and I scowled at each other, but we quieted, trying to hear what my mother heard, trying to catch the wails of the
restless dead carried by the wind.

"There! Do you hear that?" my mother whispered. "The song
of the river?"

• ~

Although I was wrong in thinking that Saja the Soldier of Death
would not find us in that clean-smelling house, I am glad that my
mother did not die in our damp and dark apartment in The Shacks
before she could know what it was like to live in a house with shiny
wood floors and walls instead of mildewed carpet and peeling plastic
wall paneling. Before she could forget about washing clothes by
hand in a rust-stained bathtub and hanging laundry to dry out of
windows that sucked in the sound and soot of street traffic. In the
Manoa home, she marveled at the luxury of throwing laundry into
an automatic washing machine and hanging it on a clothesline in
the backyard to catch the smell of the sun among the banana trees
and heliconia, the 'uki 'uki and hibiscus.

My mother loved the expanse of her yard, her wild garden; except for weeding and pruning the wedelia and nut grass whenever
they threatened to choke the other plants, she let things grow how
and where they would. In the late mornings, when the traffic died
down, my mother would set up a lawn chair in that jungle and listen. She said that on quiet days she could hear the Manoa River and
would dream of riding it to the ocean.

• ~

When I walked into her room, shaking the bag of doughnuts, I
thought she was sleeping off a trance. After a two-week trance, my
mother would sleep for days; even after a brief spell, she would sleep
so deeply I'd have to pinch her nose to make her wake up.

"Hey, Mom," I said. "Got maple bars." She lay on her stomach, tangled in sheets, eyes closed and mouth open. I walked to her bed to fix her covers, planning to let her sleep, but when I saw her face, I knew she was dead. My mother was an expressive sleeper, quick to frown or smile in her dreams. When I found her body, its face was empty.

I am both terrified and comforted whenever I remember this emptiness. Because of it, I can hope that my mother did not die caught in a dream as binding as Saja's arms, gasping and afraid, unable to wake up.

People tell me it's a blessing she died in her sleep, at peace. But these are the things said by people who do not dream.

dies in sleep

My mother said she would watch me sleep at night when I was very young, afraid that I would suddenly stop breathing. The rhythm of my sleep was odd, she explained, unsteady as the steps of an old man. The long nights of my infancy were, for my mother, measured by my breaths. *mom watches bec sleep now vice versa*

Later, after my mother tried to drown herself the second time, I realized that our roles had reversed. Even at ten, I knew that I had become the guardian of her life and she the tenuous sleeper. I trained myself to wake at abrupt snorts, unusual breathing patterns. Part of me was aware of each time she turned over in bed, dreaming dreams like mini-trances where she traveled into worlds and times I could not follow to protect her. The most I could do was wait, holding the thin blue thread of her life while her spirit tunneled into the darkness of the earth to swim the dark red river toward hell. Each night, I went to bed praying that I would not let go in my own sleep. And in the morning, before I even opened my eyes, I'd jerk my still clenched, aching hand to my chest, yanking my mother back to me.

The part of me that watched my mother sleep, the part of me that still lives within my dreams, believes that if I had been home with my mother, holding on to her life with my bare hands, she would not have died. I would have been able to save her. Even now I wonder why I didn't know my mother was dying; after so many years of training myself to listen, why didn't I hear that she had stopped breathing?

And then I realize I was with Sanford that night.

• ~

The last time I sat with my mother in her garden, she told me she wanted to wait to die but wasn't sure she could. She said something about bathing in blessed water and rolling in ashes, preparing for the final transition. Something about how when she lay down to die, her body marked and open for Saja, she felt my hands pulling at her feet, holding her back. As she spoke, I squatted next to her and watched her prune the vines of the wedelia. I watched the sharp tugs of her hands ripping and tearing the reaching fingers of the plant, and, watching, I lost her voice. Now the only thing about her death talk that I can recall with clarity is the image of the sickle curve of her back bending toward the earth. And the way her bare hands tore at the wedelia, then massaged the black ground, as if she cared for it, as if she loved it.

Patting the earth, caressing the leaves of the plants she had worked on—saying "goodbye" and "thank you" for the day—my mother announced, "I been waiting a long time to see you settle down." She brushed a small wedelia flower against the side of her face, dabbing yellow pollen on the underside of her chin. "You need a good man to give you babies. Someone to take care of you."

I remember thinking how ironic and how convenient that my mother thought of taking care of me only when I was a grown woman. And even then, to delegate the responsibility of that care. But accustomed to nurturing my mother's bouts of coherency, I drowned the memories of myself as a child that rose to the surface:

huddling under the bridge at the Ala Wai, waiting for a fish to take me to an underwater kingdom where I would find my true mother, a mother who would make me dinner so I wouldn't have to buy Ho Hos and cheese nachos at the 7-Eleven; forging my mother's signature on school report cards filled with E's for excellence that she never saw because she was looking into another world; rocking my mother, cradling her head and upper body in my lap, her legs dangling over the bed, when she cried out for my father, for Saja the Death Soldier, for the spirits that teased her with their cacklings, for anyone who cared, to kill her.

I swallowed words soaked in anger. Instead of saying, "Why are you worried about me now, Mother?" or, "Where were you when I needed you?" I said, "This is the nineties, Mom." And: "Women need men like fish need bicycles."

My mother straightened, then arched her back, exposing her throat to the sun. I watched her hands come to the small of her back, kneading black dirt into a faded flower print. Her head dropped forward. "Fish?" she said, scowling. "You're talking crazy. Women need men for children. God listens to men, Beccah. It was your father, praying for forgiveness, wishing for a miracle, who finally pressured God into giving you to us. And when at last you came, your father fell to his knees, held your red body above his head, and thanked his Father in Heaven."

I pictured my father as an aging Charlton Heston in the role of Abraham, holding a black-haired Asian-eyed Isaac above the altar in heavenly sacrifice to a God who looked like my mother.

I laughed. Thinking of how I grew up—in a household of spirits, not one of them my father or the Christian God—I thought my mother was joking.

"What's so funny?" My mother reached into her bag of cuttings and flung a handful of nut grass, mud still clinging in clumps amidst the intricate tangle of roots, at me.

"Nothing," I said, brushing flecks of dirt off my shirt as I swallowed my laughter. "I just don't think I'll ever have children. I don't want the responsibility of having someone need me that much."

My mother dropped her weeds and turned to face me. "What? Don't you know that babies are the only way you know you're alive?" She gripped my hand, pressing dirt and flesh into my palm. I could see fine red welts from the wedelia across the back of her hand. "Beccah, how will you know how much I love you if you don't have your own children?" *only being a mom can u know mother*

When my mother moved us from The Shacks to Manoa, I changed school districts, leaving Ala Wai for Robert Louis Stevenson Intermediate. I was not upset about this but instead thought of it as a rebirth. I fantasized that by moving out of the orbit of Toots Tutivena and her Entourage, I would no longer be persecuted. In a way, I was right; I was now ignored. I drifted from class to class, sitting in the back row so quiet and hunched into myself that even the teachers forgot I was there. At Stevenson and then at Franklin D. Roosevelt High, except for the other misfits—the unpaired girls with concave breasts or thick granny glasses or hair that frizzed like the Bride of Frankenstein's—I was invisible. Safe. *at school*

At times we, the Unacceptables, would gather at the bottom of the library steps as if by accident, as if pulled by an innate instinct for self-preservation to see if we still existed. And there, perched on the lowest step, partially sheltered by the splotchy shade of a plumeria tree, we would practice at adolescence, filling our mouths with the names of boys we loved.

"Isn't Shaun Cassidy fantabulous?" one of the girls said. It was probably Cordelia, whom I remember as a giant of a girl with large red knuckles, who could never grasp the "in" lingo. After our high school's ten-year reunion, which neither Cordelia nor I attended, I heard a rumor that she worked as a scriptwriter for the children's show *Barney*.

"Totally cool," the rest of us agreed, pretending that we did not consider Cordelia—or ourselves—geeky.

"He's the utmost," Edith sighed. "Let's add your names together to see if they match." Edith, who was—at least in the uninspiring academic atmosphere of Stevenson Intermediate and Roosevelt High—considered a math genius, devised a system to establish the compatibility of prospective couples. Based on some numerical values assigned to consonants—vowels were worth zero—Edith would add and divide and multiply our names with those of the boys we loved, crossing out letters and mumbling to herself. The rest of us never quite understood the whys and hows of Edith's matchmaking rules but were content to wait until she produced the answer, because— no matter which name we gave her—it'd always come out right. An invariable perfect match.

If Edith was not at the stairs when we wanted to confirm that the boy we loved was our truest match, despite his not knowing of our existence, we would cast our fortunes with cards, the king of hearts representing the boy we loved. And we would read the sides of our fists to see how many children we would bear. My fist dimpled five times or zero times, depending on whether the reader was generous in defining the bumps. I chose to see five, one bump for each of the children who I knew would look like their father, the one I always named as the king of hearts, the only one I matched my name with: Maximilian Lee.

All through junior high and the first two years of high school, I watched him. Through eight semesters of advanced English classes, I watched the way he slumped in the chair nearest the door, as if to make an escape at the earliest possible moment. I watched how the shag of his black hair, the part that wasn't shaved to his skull, fell into his face like a dog's tail, wagging as he tapped a staccato beat on the desktop with the long, lean drumsticks of his fingers. While the teachers cast frowns at him during their lectures on Milton and Chaucer, Max played his music—ratatatat ratatatat—and smiled. When he smiled I would watch the three moles that framed his mouth dance around his lips, a connect-the-dots invitation.

Sometimes he would even close his eyes as if he were sleeping, and the teacher, if she was new, would finally slam the chalk down and yell, "Maybe Mr. Maximilian Lee can tell us about palindromes," or whatever topic she had chosen. And without opening his eyes, he would say something like: "Palindromes are like, you know, when you're in the tube, yeah? And you're jammin' down to the left, and whoom! it shuts down on you. So you maneuver to the right, yeah, but whoom! that shuts down too. Both sides are comin' in on you, like you're the candy twisted inside those cellophane wrappers—you know the kind I mean, yeah? Those butterscotch or peppermint-stripe ones. And it's totally cool being wrapped in the tube like that, even though you know you're gonna eat it, backward or forward. Like, that's my metaphor for palindrome, man: you're gonna wind up in the same place, eating sand, no matter which way you read that wave."

Max knew poetry.

And I knew Max.

I knew that he saw music on the inside of his eyelids and that he carried a notepad in his plaid flannel shirts so that, when he opened his eyes, he could capture the lyrics and notes with his black-ink Pentel fine writer pen. I knew that the music he wrote for his band, the Too Toned, all sounded like variations of "Stairway to Heaven." I knew his class schedule, and knew which water fountain to hang out at when his PE class let out. I knew that he brought sprout and eggplant sandwiches from home for lunch, then bought manapua and Fat Boy ice cream sandwiches from the lunch wagon. I knew he called his Ford Mustang "The Frog," not because of its color—which was a dull gray—but because of the way it hopped, its timing off. And I knew when he started watching me back.

It was toward the end of our sophomore year, when the Am Lit teacher's wife filed for divorce. Rumor had it that Van Dyke—whom his students called Van Dick because his zipper often slipped to half-mast—molested his daughter. From the time we heard that his wife had left him, taking the kids to the Mainland, until the end of the year, Van Dyke told us to write poetry in the "Man vs." series. On the board each week, Van Dyke scribbled either "Man vs. Man," "Man vs. God," "Man vs. Machine," "Man vs. Himself," or "Man vs. Nature," and underneath: "Write about it." Our final assignment—in the "Man vs. Man" category—was to create a tribute to fathers. The poems would be shared in class and the best selected for the special Father's Day issue of the school newspaper, printed just before summer vacation. I think Van Dyke planned to send a copy to his own children.

This, or something close to it, was the poem I read aloud:

Father
who art dead in heaven
because Mother wished it so
hollow be thy name
Father
the black hole
eating my life
from the inside out
feasting on whatever I feed it—
a platter of grasping fingers
a snack of salty eyes
the delicacy of a tongue, still warm from calling your name
Father

school poem B wrote f/ dad's day

When I looked up from my notebook, it was to find everyone staring at me, including Mr. Van Dyke. Including Max. After almost

four years of loving the way his eyes looked when closed, after innumerable fantasies in which I touched his flickering lids and heard
the music they shielded, he opened his eyes and looked at me. And I
didn't like it.

I sat down when Mr. Van Dyke pushed a tight thank-you out
of pursed lips and instructed Cordelia to read. Without bothering to
stand or even look up, Cordelia wilted over her notebook, mumbling into its pages:

> *Fathers are the best*
> *Even though they put you to the test*
> *Never let you rest*
> *It's because they want the best*
> *for you.*
> *Thank you.*

While Mr. Van Dyke warbled over Cordelia's poem, her sophisti-
cated structure and clever use of rhyme, and while the rest of the
class rolled their eyes at Van Dick's pet, Max continued to stare at
me. Every day for the next week, he looked at me. And every day the
week after, he'd comment on what he saw. "You have a sensitive-
looking nose," he told me once. Another time, he noticed how my
fingers matched my voice: quick and soft, breathless as a bird's
wings. Each time he pointed to something about me, it was as if it
fell away from me, foreign and unrecognizable. For days after he
mentioned my nose, I could feel it ballooning from and shrinking
into my face, quivering as if sentient. And even now, when I remember what he said about my hands and voice, my throat closes
and my hands fall heavy to my sides, as if afraid they will fly away
without me if I speak. By the end of the third week of Max's attention, I was in pieces, waiting for him to make me whole again.

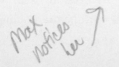

· ∾

The last time I sat with my mother in her garden, I wished to tell her that there was only one time in my life I wanted children. I was a child myself then, sixteen, and held together by the glue of Max Lee's love. I remember the way Max's fingers tapped his music on my body, until I sang the song he taught me. The nights my mother flew into her trances, Max would pick me up on the corner and we would chase the sound of Manoa Stream through winding streets until we dead-ended at Aku Ponds.

Recently, just before I moved away from Manoa, I drove in search of Aku Ponds. After several wrong turns, I let my mind wander and found myself on the dead-end street, in front of the chained bridge that led to the pond. I let my motor idle as I debated testing the picket that held the chain. When I went there with Max, we would wriggle the first picket of the bridge's railing like a loose tooth until it slipped, releasing the chain.

Now, as an adult, I am too conscious of the eyes of the neighbors, of the law, of the Kapu sign warning off trespassers. I am too aware that that is what I am now, a trespasser out of place and time.

In high school, I felt Aku Ponds belonged to Max and me, consecrated through our bodies. As we pressed ourselves against each other, we also pressed into the damp earth of the water's banks. When we joined, thick blades of sweet Manoa grass and liliko'i vines would tangle in our hair and limbs, urging and binding us tighter. And when we opened our mouths, deep enough to taste the heart of the other, we also tasted the water of the pond. Aku Ponds was the place where we learned about our bodies. Where I learned the sudden, blind animal taste of a man and the tart taste of myself from his lips.

After making love, we would sometimes slip naked into the water, lunging through the hip-high water toward the "surf spot," a place where the pond seemed to double back upon itself. Water from the stream pooled briefly on a shallow shelf before spilling into

Aku Ponds. Max would pull me under that cascade, into a gap between rock and rushing water. Pressed against my body, he would say, "This is what it's like in the tube, like looking through an ice-blue diamond with the sounds so pure you don't care you're about to get smashed." We'd hold on to each other, looking through water-spun glass and hearing nothing but our own breathing and the hollow sound of breaking water, until our lips turned blue.

I remember the time he told me that the tube was magical, that the water which poured in front of us would carry our wishes in its song, forever and ever until they came true. Shoulder-to-shoulder, we held hands and sang out our dreams. "I love you," I yelled into the sheet of water. "I'll care for you forever!"

And Max echoed, "I'll love you forever. We're gonna get married and have five children!"

When Max took me home that night, I let myself into the house, my hair still dripping the water of the stream. My body smelled clean, electric like a rainstorm on the Ko'olaus. But when I walked through the door, my mother yelled, "Stink *poji*-cunt!" and charged forward with a knife. I backed into the door and cringed, flinging a hand across my face as she sliced the air above my head.

"Mom!" I yelled. "It's me! Beccah, Beccah-chan!"

My mother waved the knife and shaved strips of air away from my body. "It's me, it's me," she mimicked, and I knew then she could not really hear me. "You cannot use my daughter as your puppet, Saja! Evil spirit, the stink of pus and men's waste!" She jabbed at my head and then lowered her hand until the point of the knife touched my crotch.

"I call you out!" my mother yelled, and threw the knife across the room. The blade stuck in the carpet, caught vertically for just a moment, and then fell, pointing toward me. *"E-yah!"* My mother screamed, and rushed to retrieve the knife. "Stubborn ghost," she muttered. She scratched the knife along the zipper of my jeans and

Mom smells sex, evil spirit after Beccah

threw the blade again. This time it landed pointing away from me. She left the knife as it lay and went into her bedroom.

That night I dreamed I drowned in blood, unable to fight the arms that pulled me under, while the fins of sharks sliced the water like knives.

My mother slept through the next day, and when Max came to pick me up that night, she still slept. We drove to Aku Ponds, and for the first time, I noticed the sign nailed to the bridge as we drove up to it: "Kapu! Violators will be prosecuted!" When I slipped out of the car to undo the chain, the picket stuck. "Someone must have fixed the bridge," I hissed to Max. I pounded on the railing until the chain swung like a jump rope.

Max opened his door, the light from inside the car creating an aura around his body until he stepped into the dark toward me. He lifted my hands from the bridge. "You all right?" he asked. When he tapped the top of the picket, it creaked sideways and the chain popped loose. He turned back to the car, leaving me to replace the chain after he drove over it, and I answered, "Are you?"

Though my voice seemed especially loud to me, Max didn't answer, only continued driving as if he didn't hear.

That night as we made love, I kept asking, "Are you all right?" sometimes not even waiting for an answer before asking again. At least I think I asked; I might have just been thinking it, beginning for the first time to doubt that he was "all right" for me. I remember thinking that this was supposed to be spiritual, but what I was most aware of was that his knees kept getting in the way, knocking against mine, and that the insides of his elbows seemed very white, very feminine in the dark. And that a mosquito kept buzzing in my ear, louder even than Max's fevered "I love you"s.

I held Max tighter, telling him I loved him even more than he loved me, and all the while I thought: What's wrong? and wondered if I had imagined the previous times, when I seemed to leave my body and float through a universe of colored sound. Now, after my subsequent experiences with sex, I am almost positive I am mistaken about the intensity I thought I felt when he slipped inside me, the way all sound and sight spiraled into blackness so that the only thing I knew was the rhythm of our bodies, elemental as the river's song.

⌁

Bbroke off w/ Max

After my mother sliced the air around me, cutting me loose from the demons she thought were holding me, I began to watch Max again. I discovered little things—the way he licked his top teeth before he smiled, the way his head lolled as if unanchored by his spine when he played the drums, the way his jaw slackened, then gaped when he slept—that started to bother me. And I began watching the two of us making love, the way we groped and lunged, as if from another's eyes. As if from my mother's eyes.

When I finally told him it was over, I could not bear to look at him; his face, hovering so close to mine, seemed grotesque. "Why, Beccah, why?" he cried, not caring that his nose had begun to run. "What did I do?"

Sickened, I hugged him so I would not have to see his blotchy, swollen face. "Nothing," I mumbled. "It's just time to move on." I held him, letting him cry, and it was like holding a stranger. I felt pity, uncomfortable about the pain I had no connection to, but also I was irritated, as if he were wasting my time.

⌁

I heard from someone who knew us as a couple that Max now sells electric guitars and drum sets at Harry's Music in Kaimuki, that he has a small place in Palolo, a wife, and three children under the age of five. In fact, the person who told me said he had heard a rumor that I was that wife. I laughed, joking, "Me with three kids? God forbid! I can barely take care of myself!" but I clenched my hand, thinking of the dimples on my fist that I once tried to count.

Years ago, I was the one who told Max that it was time to move on, yet it seems he is the one who has done so. He composed his life in steady measures, fulfilling with someone else the plans we made at Aku Ponds. And I am the one who is stuck, envious of the normalcy of his unexceptional life.

Auntie Reno, who has long since given up on pairing me with eligible bachelors, has come to the conclusion that I am "that way." She has now started hinting that Sweet Mary's daughter Precious—whom I sometimes baby-sat when we lived at The Shacks—is also "that way." I laugh, letting her think what she wants, then tell her I'll find someone on my own when I'm ready.

"Not supposed to live alone," she scolds me, trying to sound biblical, ominous. "Or die alone."

• ⤙

My latest lover, Sanford, will not die alone. I am sure that when Saja calls for him, he will be surrounded by his family: his boy and two girls and the tennis-playing wife with the lipo'ed thighs and Sun-In hair. But he will be looking out the window, waiting for me.

He says he has never loved his wife the way he loves me, but I know he will not leave her. Just as I know that, despite his avowals, his marriage isn't platonic; I can tell by the way he touches me, looks at me, even the way he E-mails me—quick and businesslike—when he has had sex with his wife. I wonder if I should be hurt, but realize I don't care. Already he is starting to irritate me. I cannot stand the way he combs his hair forward to disguise his receding hairline, then asks—uncertain and vulnerable—if he looks too old for me.

I resent this vulnerability, his attempts at youth.

When he first interviewed me for the job, Sanford seemed at once self-assured and shy, solidly suited and tied to middle age and family life. I loved to knock timidly at his office door, then enter boldly and stare at him over the desk, across the stacks of clippings and reports, the homemade lunch and framed family photos, until he blinked and blushed. I played with him, testing my sexuality, my attractiveness, yet was surprised—and flattered—when he responded.

Dignified and serious, at least at first, Sanford introduced me to cocktail parties, journalism conferences, black-tie fund-raisers. Though I could not, of course, attend in place of his wife, Sanford always made sure I received an invitation and an escort. And afterward, perhaps the next afternoon, during a "business meeting," we would discuss the event, then make slow, reverent love. He treated me with what I thought of as respect, as a grown-up.

He, in turn, received youth. Not just mine, but his own. I replaced his ties and long-sleeved pin-striped shirts with Polo and OP. I taught him to appreciate the same music—Boyz II Men and Big Mountain—as his children. And I'm the one who nicknamed him Sandy, after the most dangerous and unpredictable beach on the island. But only because I liked the irony; in his previous incarnation, I could not have imagined him near the water.

Now, when he visits my apartment, he struts in the Jams or OPs that I've bought for him, flexes in front of the bathroom mirror, and talks about taking up surfing or body building. "How else can I compete with the young stud you'll eventually leave me for?" he says, only half joking. If he were completely joking, attractive in his arrogance, I could forgive him. But it is that hint of seriousness, that insecurity in his looks, in the difference in our ages, in himself and me, that makes me know that I will leave him.

• ↝

I wanted to avoid him when I went in to work the day after I found my mother's body.

"Why are you here?" the police beat reporter said, drawing attention, when I sat down in my cubicle. Coworkers' eyes peeked into my compartment, then darted away. I thought I recognized Sanford's oily forehead bob in hesitation on the other side of the partition.

"Pretend I'm not," I snapped, and the reporter and the forehead backed away.

"Maybe she needs to work to get her mind off her pain," yelled Mirabelle Chun, food editor. She never did know how to whisper, when to keep quiet. "Lord knows I would not have the strength to go on like nothing happened if someone I loved died."

I ignored them and the condolences I received over the terminal—"We are saddened by your loss," "My sympathies in your time of grief," "Go home, have a good cry"—until I read Sandy's: "Need a shoulder—or anything else—to cry on?"

I typed, "No," and pressed Return. I can't stand when he tries to make flippant sexual innuendos, though I am the one who teased Sanford into a hipper, lighter version of his previous self. Into the Sandy who irritates me in direct porportion to how much I miss the old Sanford, the paternal Mr. Dingman.

"I want to see you," Sandy typed back, and before I could think of something to shut him down: "Let me take you home."

And suddenly I wanted to be home. Not at my apartment, which after a year had boxes yet to be unpacked stacked in closets and corners. And not back at the Manoa house or The Shacks. I wanted to be with my mother in her garden, when she knew she was my mother. I wanted to be held and comforted in a mother's arms, tended to the way she tended to her plants. "Sing the river song," I wanted to tell her, ready to be rocked and sung to sleep amidst the green growing things.

grief- wants to be rocked by Mom

"Okay," I told Sanford.

• ~

I let myself lean against him as he opened my door for me. When we entered, out of habit I played the answering machine, half expecting to hear my mother either ranting about spirits and bad luck arrows or asking what time I'll be by for supper. Instead Auntie Reno's voice blundered into the room.

"Hallo, hallo? Dis on or what? I dunno if I heard dah beep or what." After a long pause, Auntie Reno began talking again. "Beccah, we got to make dah arrangements. Dah guest list, dah body—you wanna bury it or what? Borthwick Mortuary got some fancy casket we can use for dah ceremony, den aftahwards, one cheap one we can use for dah ground. No matter, right? Call me."

I imagined Mother laid out in a fancy dress, her face made up in pinks and purples she would never use—Auntie Reno would probably pick out her outfit and insist on overseeing the makeup—on display for people who never knew her. And I laughed, realizing that despite her reputation and the hundreds of people who paid in time and money to see her, no one knew her. Not even Auntie Reno, who gave her her first job and decided she was a fortune-teller. Not even I, her daughter—the only person who loved her, at least part of the time—really knew her.

I doubled over with laughter, my sides hurting as I pushed the giggles out. "We are having a funeral for a *yongson!*" I gasped.

Unsure of how to touch me, Sanford awkwardly patted my shoulder. "Yes, your mother was a wonderful woman."

His attempt at comfort only made me howl louder. "No!" I managed to sputter before I rolled to the floor, unable to explain that a *yongson* is the ghost of a person who traveled far from home and died a stranger.

"There, there," Sandy crooned, acting as if I were hysterical. He carried me to the bed, and we ended up sleeping together, our bodies sticky in the heat of the afternoon. Afterward I peeled my body away from his, trying to find a cool spot on the bed. I'd forgotten to put sheets on the water bed, so that our sweat glistened and glued us against the plastic mattress. As usual, Sandy sprawled across the middle. I had to brace myself against the side to keep from getting sucked into the overheated pit he created with his body.

I listened to him breathe in his sleep, and my fist curled to my heart out of habit. I forced myself to open my fingers, to relax my vigilance, to fall asleep.

•✐

When I dive in now, I swim for only a few short seconds before I am trapped, kicking at the shark that pulls me under. I twist and turn, trying to land blows on its snout with my fists as well as my feet, when I see not the jaws of a shark but the nebulous folds of a giant jellyfish wrapping itself about my lower body, trying to suck me into itself. I can feel myself dissolving where the jellyfish stings me. I reach out to try to tear it off me, and my hand disappears in waves of black hair dancing in the water.

I realize that it is my mother wrapped around my legs, holding on to me as though I can save her. Instead I feel myself sinking. I cannot hold my breath any longer, and just when I open my mouth to drown, I wake and find my body sinking toward Sanford's once again.

13

AKIKO ·⁓

I lie straining against my skin, feeling its heaviness covering me like a blanket thick as sleep. I wait, paralyzed, for the popping of my blood that signals Induk is near, also waiting, wanting me.

When she was alive, she did not seem so impatient. But then I knew her only at the comfort stations, when she had to hide between layers of silence and secret movements. I want to say that I knew she would be the one who would join me after death. That there was something special about her even then, perhaps in the way she carried herself—walking more erect, with impudence, even—or in the way she gave the other women courage through the looks and smiles she offered us.

But I am trying not to lie.

There was nothing special about her life at the recreation camps; only her death was special. In front of the men, we all tried to walk the same, tie our hair the same, keep the same blank looks on our faces. To be special there meant only that we would be used more, that we would die faster.

Though we were not afraid of death, were afraid only of dying under them, like dogs.

One of the women there—I do not know her real name and will not use the one assigned to her—I think she came from yangban, high class. She spoke of a dagger her mother wore about the waist. Smaller than the length of her palm, the hilt encrusted with gems, it was to have been hers when she married. The knife would have shown her pride in her virtue; if she had failed in guarding it, she would have used the weapon on herself.

The rest of us were envious, not of the rich things she indicated having, not of her aristocracy, but of her right to kill herself. We all had the obligation, of course, given what had happened to us, but it didn't have the status of privilege and choice.

That is what, in the end, made Induk so special: she chose her own death. Using the Japanese as her dagger, she taunted them with the language and truths they perceived as insults. She sharpened their anger to the point where it equaled and fused with their black hungers. She used them to end her life, to find release.

7' Induk's death is fucked. Kill self

I cannot believe she chooses to come to me, a coward. But I am grateful.

•~

My body grows heavy, but inside I am crackling like hot oil. She is going to peel back my skin, then cover me, like steam; gentle, insistent, invasive.

I do not see her, but I know Induk is with me. She licks at my toes and fingertips, sucking at them until my blood rushes to greet her touch. I feel her fingers wind through my hair, rubbing my scalp, soothing me, while her mouth caresses my chin and neck. My body prickles.

With infinite care, Induk slides her arms around my back, cradling me into her heat. Her lips press the base of my throat, the hollow underneath my jaw, then travel lower to brush against my nipples. I feel them pulling, drawing my milk, feel the excess liquid trickle against my sides and down my belly. Induk laps it up, her tongue following the meandering trails.

She kneads my buttocks, shaping them to her hands, spreading them apart. Her fingers dip into and flirt with the cleft, from anus to the tip of my vagina, where my blood gathers and pulses until it aches. She combs my pubic hair with her long nails, pulling at the crinkling hairs as if to straighten them. I stifle a groan, try to keep my hips still. I cannot.

I open myself to her and move in rhythm to the tug of her lips and fingers and the heat of her between my thighs. The steady buzzing that began at my fingertips shoots through my body, concentrates at the pulse point between my legs, then without warning explodes through the top of my head. I see only the blackness of my pleasure.

My body sings in silence until emptied, and there is only her left, Induk.

• ➤

Once, I was not quiet when Induk came to me. I must have cried out, for I attracted the attention of my husband. He knelt by my bed, watching me until I became aware of the sound of his harsh breathing. When I looked at him, he moved the covers off me and crowded into my bed.

He pushed his forehead against mine and, firmly, unknowingly, replaced Induk's hands on my body. His fingers, rough and harsh, lifted my nightgown and pressed into the skin of my breasts and hips. When he felt the fabric of my underwear, he pulled it aside and fit himself between my legs.

I felt his arousal probing the entrance to my vagina and tensed. He found it slick, made ready by Induk's endless caresses, and thrust into me.

Jesus, he said. He pulled out slowly, then entered me again, stretching me. As he thrust and thrust again in long, slow strokes, he lifted my hips against his, forcing me into a counterpoint rhythm. Take me, he panted, for through a child will you be sanctified.

And, suddenly, it was as if Induk was still there, between us, inside him and inside me. The buzzing that I felt with her unfurled within me, gaining strength until I could not contain it. As it burst over me, I cried out against my husband's shoulder and was answered by his own shout of pleasure.

Afterward, when my husband had returned to his bed, I dreamed of Induk and of him and of his shouts that sounded too much like the shouts the men at the camps gave as they collapsed over the women in release and triumph.

The next morning, my husband told me in his sermon-preaching voice, Ah . . . self-fornication is a sin.

I blinked.

Sungyok un chae ok-ida, he repeated in Korean, an indication of how disorientated he was, to speak my language in his country.

Finally, realizing he was referring to what he had witnessed between Induk and myself, I laughed. How could he compare what went on between men's and women's bodies with what happened spiritually?

I was not alone, I said. Did you not see her touching me where your hands touched me? Suckling me where your mouth suckled?

When he asked, Who? I laughed harder.

He licked his lips and looked at my laughing mouth. Succubus, he whispered. And God gave them over to shameful lusts so that even the women exchanged natural relations for unnatural ones. Succubus.

I howled, and still in his eyes I saw the lust, dark and heavy and animal, that I'd seen in the eyes of men at the camps. But now I also saw the fear.

⸱⤳

Japanese

They came to us in fear as well as lust, lining up against our stalls to spend their scrip and themselves on our bodies. Some would spread our legs, pinch our vaginas, checking for discoloration, open sores, pus, disease—which meant, for them, not death but demotion in rank. Though each shipment of women included boxes of condoms, and though the doctors tried to control outbreaks of syphilis through injections of 606, venereal disease spread through the camp, manifesting itself in the labia and vaginas of the women. When the fist-sized eruptions swelled the women shut and spread to other body parts, climbing toward lips and eyes, the officers took the women out of the camp. Transferred, they called it, but I believe the officers abandoned them in the woods, disposable commodities.

Near the end of the war, they became less politic. Before I left the camp, I saw one more delivery of goods. After the trucks unloaded a half-dozen girls—looking dazed and frightened and younger than myself as they were packed into the service quarters— the commanding officer strode, his light automatic rifle swinging like a walking stick, toward the sick house.

Iriwa, iriwa, he shouted, luring those who could still walk outside with his Korean. Come!

One of the women, named Haruko, her wide, hopeful face distorted by blisters, and another woman—not infected but grossly pregnant—staggered against the doorframe. Before they could voice a question, he shot them, then he opened fire, showering the hut with a spray of random bullets. *not usable? die!*

Splinters of wood and blood exploded in rapid, concise bursts, the numbing reverberations of gunfire intermingling with the brief, shrill screams of the dying. When the screaming subsided into low, tentative moans, the commander gave orders to torch the remains of the hospital. And while it burned, smoke and ash soaking the camps with the smell of roasting meat, he whistled the *"Kimigayo,"* his national anthem. *hospital on camp*
shot then burnt the dying

o fear death
have sex all rite
pluck pubic hair
as talisman against
death + fear

But despite their fears of disease, the men still visited us, propelled by the greater fear of death. The day and night before a battalion was scheduled to leave, the women of the camp did not sleep. Again and again, the same men took their turns with us, until they could no longer create an erection. Touch! they would yell at us, Suck! and when nothing happened, some would beat us about our heads and pojis. Others, though, would merely want to spend their half-hour allotments burrowed into our breasts, being cradled like a child. And when their time was up, these were the ones to pluck curling wires of my pubic hair, which they would carry to the front with them, talismans against danger and against fear.

If they had asked, I would have pulled them myself, woven them into an amulet. Not to keep them safe from but to attract harm, each one of my hairs a wish for death and a call for justice.

•~

After the night Induk came to me, opening my body to her song, I saw the soldiers' fear of death and disease in my husband's eyes. His fear that instead of saving me, he had damned himself. That he could not pass the test his God devised for him. And I knew then that he would not use me again like that.

I knew then that he could not.

14

AKIKO ⌐

My baby's head is round—round as a rare and perfect river rock polished by the force of water.

I love her roundheaded perfection, my daughter's head shape so like mine, and like my mother's when she was a child.

⌐

While I was growing up, my mother would study her daughters for signs of herself, then make pronouncements binding us to her and to our fates. To oldest sister, Soon Ja, she would say: Our hair is like seaweed, so black and slick it can never hold a comb; watch that you don't fly away. To Soon Hi, she'd say: You've got my dimples. Life has to pinch your cheeks hard to make you happy.

My mother would tell third sister to hold out her hands, fingers pressed tightly together. See, she would sigh, see how the light shines through the cracks? Like me, you'll have trouble holding on to what you most want.

When she would look at me as if she was seeing both me and a memory, I knew what would come out of her mouth: Rockhead. Just like me, she'd say, shaking her head. You'll have a hard life, always banging against the current. Worse than a boy, more stubborn than a stone.

mom-daughter relationship

But she would say these things with pride, so I would know that she loved me.

And every time she called me Rockhead, I'd ask her, Why? How come? How do you know? What does it mean? pestering her for a story, hoping to learn more about my mother and, in turn, about the secrets of myself.

At night, when my mother unwound her hair, combing through the heavy silk with her fingers, I'd press against her, close as she would let me, and wait. If I was lucky, she would notice me. Baby Girl, she might say, pick out my white hairs. Or: Youngest Daughter, massage my temples.

I'd sit cross-legged on the floor and wait for my mother to lie down and slip her head into my lap. I'd stroke her forehead, the sides of her face, the top of her head where the spirit escapes at night. When she'd begin to tell her story, I'd part her hair into sections, using my nails to find and pluck the white strands. As she talked, I'd stick the oily roots onto a sheet of one of the underground newspapers—*Daedong Kongbo* or *Haecho Shinmun*—that found their way even into our village. And after the story, after my mother fell asleep, I'd crumple the paper into a ball and burn it in the underground flues that warmed our floorboards. As I drifted off to sleep, breathing in the scent of hair and smoke, I'd imagine that words wrapped in my mother's hair drifted into our dreams and spiraled up to heaven.

My mother was told that the most famous fortune-teller in Seoul, paid to read her head at birth, said that she was the most roundheaded baby she had ever seen. In a roundheaded family that valued head shape along with money and auspicious birth charts, this was the highest praise.

The fortune-teller predicted that because of her roundness, because of the class she was born into, and because of the sign she was born under, my mother would be very spoiled and very happy. Everything would roll her way.

This was true for perhaps the first seven years of her life.

Mother of akiko — wealthy? upperclass?

My favorite tales when I was growing up were my mother's own baby-time stories. When we played make-pretend, my sisters and I pretended to be our mother, whose early days were filled with parties in Seoul and candy and fancy Western dresses. I pictured most of the things she told us about by finding something in my own life to compare it to and thinking: Same thing, only one thousand times better. When she told us about a doll from France with blue eyes painted in a porcelain face, I took my own pine-and-rag doll, put a cup over her head, and imagined a toy a thousand times better.

The one thing my mother talked about that neither my sisters nor I could imagine or comprehend was ice cream. We just had no reference for it in our own lives, and when we'd push our mother for a definition, her descriptions left us even more dubious and mystified.

It's like sucking on an ice-cold, perfectly ripe peach, my mother once tried to explain.

Then why not just eat a peach? we asked.

Because it's not the same, my mother said. That's just what it feels like in your mouth. It feels like a ripe peach and like the snow, and like how a cloud full of rain must feel if you could bite into it.

I remember biting into my own honey-and-nut candy that my mother made for us during the harvest and watching her talk. She would shut her eyes, but I could see them move back and forth, back and forth, under their lids. She seemed very magical, like a princess from heaven, when she talked about ice cream.

●-

When I came to America, I was surprised to see how common and how cheap ice cream was. Once I found out what it was, I bought one carton of each flavor I could find—cherry vanilla, strawberry, mint, pistachio, Neapolitan, chocolate chip, butter brickle. We'd have ice cream every night after dinner. At first my husband encouraged me, glad that I was becoming American. But then he found out that I was also eating ice cream for lunch and for breakfast. And that I cried after eating a bowl of a particularly good flavor, because it reminded me that when my mother was a roundheaded child princess, she took a bite out of heaven.

After he found out about these things, my husband put me on a diet. He taught me about "Mulligan Stew," the four basic food groups, telling me, Your body is a temple.

• ✐

I try to maintain my baby's round head. I make sure her hats and headbands aren't too tight. When I shampoo her hair, I am careful that I don't use too much pressure and leave unintentional dents. I make sure she sleeps on her stomach, so her skull won't flatten out in the back, and I maintain a constant vigilance, checking on her throughout the night so that I can catch her when she flips over. This is hard work, and I do it in secret because I do not want to hear my husband talk about God and genetics. I know better, because of my mother, than to think that head shape is fixed for life.

• ✐

In the years before her head changed, my mother's father was a middle school official. He was the one who gave my mother her doll from France, her fancy dresses, her taste for ice cream. He was also the one who taught her her lessons, drilling her in math and history. Because of him, my mother wanted to be the best girl student in the primary school.

I studied, studied, studied, my mother would say, so I could be the best. But every time we took the tests, I always placed second. Number one was always my best friend, whom I hated at that time of year.

Every year, she said, I wished to be number one. One year,

though, I figured out that my wishing it wasn't enough to make it happen, because my best friend was also wishing to be number one. Her wish was blocking my wish. So that year, when it came time to write our wishes on the paper we would burn and send to heaven, I told my best friend she should wish to be the prettiest girl, since she was already the smartest. When she said okay and I saw her write this down, I snuck away and wrote on my own paper: I wish to be number one in the school.

• ✦

My mother would always become sad at this point in the story, and when my sisters and I asked if she got her wish, she'd always say, Yes, and I'm sorry.

The year my mother's wish came true was the year Japan invaded Korea. The year her father and his colleagues were taken away. The year that her best friend had to drop out of school because her family could not afford to pay the fee demanded by the Japanese Provisional Government, could not spare the money for a girl.

My mother's generation was the first in Korea to learn a new alphabet, and new words for everyday things. She had to learn to answer to a new name, to think of herself and her world in a new way. To hide her true self. I think these lessons, these deviations from the life she was supposed to lead, from the person she should have been, are what changed the shape of her head.

A's mother — JAPAN invade Korea, take away who she was — all things Japanese

Those are the same lessons my mother taught me, the morals of her stories, and because I learned them early, I was able to survive what eventually killed my mother. Hiding my true self, the original nature of my head, enabled me to survive in the recreation camp and in a new country.

• ✦

At the camps, both the women and the doctors always talked about the monsters born from the Japanese soldiers' mixing their blood with ours. When I became pregnant, I could not help worrying about what my baby would look like, wondering if she would be a monster or a human. Korean or Other. Me or not me.

• ✑

Now, as I look at my Bek-hap, my White Lily, I do not know how I could have doubted her perfection. Her hair, reddish brown at birth, is now growing in black. Her eyes, though brown, are neither my husband's shape nor mine, are instead what the face readers would classify as dragon eye, the best in size and curve. And her head is round. I cup her tiny head in my palms and whisper, I am so proud of you. You are a rockhead like your mother and your mother's mother. Only a thousand times better.

15

BECCAH ·~

I waited under the angels. In fat splendor, they lounged along the eaves of Reno's house in Kahala, peered over copper gutters turning green from rain and humidity, peeked out from behind marble columns imported from Italy. Toward the center of the courtyard, one of the heavenly imps—who Reno claims was modeled after her youngest grandson—frolicked in a fountain, spitting water at the koi that trembled at his feet.

I never pictured angels as carefree children, naked in their happiness. While my mother and I still lived in The Shacks, I had always imagined the angels in heaven as stern-faced men draped in beards and clothed in the voice of my father. In the dimness preceding sleep, they often visited me, looming over my bed to threaten me with the end of the world.

"Read this," an angel would say, shoving a stone tablet into my face.

I would try to open my eyes wide, try to focus on the tablet that melted even as I tried to read it. "Aaagh," I croaked, wanting to say something, anything, to delay heavenly retribution. But I was always too late, the tablet turning to water and the words hopping off the page like little black frogs before I could decipher even the first letter.

"Daddy, Daddy," I would call out as my bed was ferried down the river toward hell. "Save me." But the angel would only laugh, opening his mouth as wide as Saja's before a meal.

By my mother's stories, too, I knew angels sometimes came into the world as changelings: testing the worthiness of men's souls, they visited the world dressed in the skins of frogs, toads, and bums.

"Angels," my mother explained, when I asked her whether angels were good or bad, "come to collect the dead, carrying them off to either heaven or hell. This is what your father told me: if they're good depends on whether you are good." She stopped talking for a moment, considering, then added, "I have seen them, Beccah-chan. They are everywhere and could be anything, watching you, often disguised as the ugliest creatures on earth. If they ever catch the opportunity, angels will jump into the skin of humans, so remember to keep watch, keep track, take care. Never clip your nails at night. Burn the hair that falls from your head—don't leave any part of yourself laying around for an angel to absorb."

"Yeah, yeah, yeah," I said, sorry I had asked my mother anything. "You already told me."

My mother cocked her eyebrows at me. "Beccah," she said, "remember the Heavenly Toad." *threat spurs B into action!*

I was always reminded about the Heavenly Toad whenever I questioned my mother's wisdom, resisted her orders. "Tell your teachers to open all the north-facing windows," my mother would say at the start of every school year, and when I would balk, she'd add: "Remember the Heavenly Toad." Or when I was sent to demand payment for the yearly blessing my mother performed for neighbors who never asked to be blessed: "Remember the Heavenly Toad." Each time I heard the reminder I jumped, ready if not willing to do the dreaded task. The threat of the Heavenly Toad suctioning his arms around my body and propelling me away from my mother was enough to spur me into action.

The Heavenly Toad meant deception and separation. Although the dead often remained with the living, sharing the same home as their loving descendants, the Heavenly Toad sometimes tricked and kidnapped the unwary, spiriting them toward heaven or hell and away from the family.

"I am telling you this," my mother said, "so that you will know what to do when I am dead."

"Mommy," I said, running to her, as I did when I was younger and she talked of her death, "don't leave me, don't die." My arms circled her hips, my body a weight anchoring her to life.

My mother placed her hand on my head. "When I die, I will become your *momju,* guarding and guiding you. I will not leave you. Unless."

I clung harder. "Unless what?" I breathed, almost afraid to ask.

"Unless you forget about the Heavenly Toad," she said. "When I die, you must prepare my body and protect my spirit before the Heavenly Toad angel grabs me and jumps to heaven."

When I groaned, she said, "Remember what happened to the parents in the story? Remember what happened to the daughter?"

I had heard the story many times, but I still circled it carefully, as I would a real road. Though the story remained consistent, I could not decide what it meant.

In the story, a poor fisherman pulled a giant toad from a dying river, and instead of killing it, the man brought the toad home, where he and his wife raised it as the son they never had. The toad grew and grew, and when it was as large as a man, he decided to marry one of the daughters of the richest man in the village. "Make a deal with her father," the toad son urged his parents.

But they hemmed and hawed. "How can poor people like us propose marriage to such a great family?" they said and, though they felt guilty for mentioning it, added, "And you know, you are not even a human being."

The toad persisted until his father shuffled off to the rich man's house to ask for a marriage arrangement. The rich man and his family refused, of course, and beat the father.

When the father returned home broken and bloody, saying, "See? What did I tell you?" the toad son apologized and said that he would take care of everything.

That day he caught a hawk, and that night he carried the bird to the rich man's house. Sneaking into the courtyard, the toad climbed the tallest persimmon tree in the garden. Once settled in the branches, hidden by leaves and shadows, he tied a lighted lantern to the hawk's foot and released it into the air.

As the bird hovered just above the house, tethered to its master's arm, the toad called out, "The head of this household shall listen to this message from the Heavenly King. Today you rejected a proposal of marriage, and now you shall be punished for your arrogance. I shall give you one day to reconsider your decision. As the Heavenly Messenger, I advise you to accept the toad's proposal, for if you do not, you, your brothers, and all your sons will be killed. Your family name will be destroyed and you and your ancestors condemned to an afterlife as *yongson.*"

The people in the house, startled by the booming voice coming from the sky, opened their windows and saw a dim light hovering overhead, like the tip of an accusatory finger. Right at this moment, the toad released the string, letting the hawk soar skyward, with the lantern still tied to its foot.

After seeing with his own eyes the Heavenly Messenger fly back to heaven, the rich man ran into the courtyard and pressed his forehead into the dirt, promising eternal obedience. He asked each of his older girls to sacrifice herself for the family. The girls cried, fought among themselves, pleaded and begged, until, finally, the youngest daughter—who was still considered too young for marriage—offered to give herself to the toad.

The next morning, after the wedding ceremony, the toad told

his bride to plunge a knife into his back. At first she hesitated, but when the toad urged her once again, the girl stabbed him. When the skin of the toad split open, a young man as handsome as an angel and truly one of heaven's messengers jumped out. Before they could react with joy, the toad angel embraced his bride and his parents and leaped up to heaven, with the three bound tightly to his chest.

• ⁀

When I think of this story now, as an adult, I realize that the Heavenly Toad is meant to be a benevolent character, rewarding his adoptive parents for their kindness and his bride for either her sacrifice in marrying him or her obedience in stabbing him. But when I was a child, the toad—in his ability to transform himself, to hide in the skin of others—seemed more frightening to me even than Saja, who at least appeared as himself.

Whenever I walked along the Ala Wai, I searched for frogs and toads hiding in the damp mulch, in stagnant pools along the water. Spotting them squatting in bright-green slime, with only their heads showing, I'd grow dizzy, overwhelmed at the possibility that I was looking at an angel. But I'd always turn and hurry away, repulsed and panicked: what if they turned and saw that in my heart of hearts I found them disgusting? Or worse, what if one of them turned and saw something it liked in me? I kept my face averted and still, neither grimacing nor smiling—not wanting to give insult or false encouragement to any possible toad angel that might want to marry me, kill me, or take me to heaven.

• ⁀

It was Auntie Reno who gave my mother her first frog. "Heah," Reno said when she came to our apartment to give us our share of money from the first month of fortune-telling. She dug through her handbag, a Gucci knockoff from the swap meet, and pulled out the small jade piece hanging from a thin gold chain. "Took dis to

Vegas—dah city, not my daughtah—but dah money no jump back to me like one frog. Shit, what those Japs"—here Reno flicked her wrist above her head—"eh, scuze me, Great-Auntie Asami, may you rest in peace—talkin' about?" She jiggled the chain, and the frog jumped in front of my mother's face.

The spirits accepted the frog and allowed my mother to wear it during her trips into their world. The customers who visited my mother while she was in a trance, waiting for her to read their lives, saw the frog swinging from her neck. The next time they came, they brought a frog of their own to her, thinking she collected them. Ceramic frogs, pewter frogs, stone frogs, wood frogs—enough frogs to give bodies to however many angels wanted to spy on us—soon infested our home.

"Whatchu goin' do wit all them frogs?" Reno had asked when I told her I planned to sell my mother's house.

"I dunno," I told her. "Goodwill, I guess."

"Girlie," Reno said, "let me have em. I sell em, fifty-fifty. All the old customers goin' want a souvenir from your maddah, the famous frog psychic. I find all the frogs good homes." Reno laughed like she'd said something funny, then said the same thing she told me when it came time to make funeral arrangements: "Your maddah woulda wanted it dis way."

• ⌣

I visited Reno at her old apartment off Punahou only once. It was before we thought of installing the double locks on our apartment, and my mother had wandered away while in one of her trances. I buzzed Reno from the lobby and waited by the intercom for her to come down and help me. Then Reno moved to Hawaii Kai, and the few times I drove over to drop off money for her to deposit, I waited on the porch, watching the long-haired cats she had tried breeding watch me through the large picture windows.

In my first visit to the house that loops off Kahala Avenue, I circled the courtyard of the angels, waiting for her to come and help me dress my mother's body. In all the years I have known Reno, I have never been past the entrances of any of her homes, though I suppose she would have invited me in had I asked.

"Sorry, sorry, girlie!" Reno called out as she wrestled empty boxes and several glittering dresses cellophaned in Hakuyosha Dry Cleaning wrap out the front doors of her home. "Eh, come help!"

I ran past the fountain and picked up the empty boxes she kicked out in front of her. "What?" I teased, jerking my head toward the clothes draped across her arms. "You can't decide what to wear to the service? Gotta outdress the bride at every wedding and the corpse at every funeral?"

Reno folded her lips downward and looked to heaven. "Dis for your dearly departed maddah, may she rest in peace."

I almost dropped the boxes. "Don't tell me you actually bought these!"

Reno clucked her tongue and held the dresses up like an offering. Her underarms wobbled under the burden. "Puh-lease, honey," she said. "You tink dey make glamour like dis now-days?" She sniffed, her eyes skittering disdainfully over my T-shirt and cut-off jeans. "Dis from my Hong Kong glory days. Had um made special when I was deah years ago wit dah Royal Hawaiian Dance Company. I was keeping um for when I lose some weight, but . . . you know how dat goes. And Vegas, she no want um, telling me, 'Ma, out of style,' as if she one fashion arbitrator. I telling you, you young kids dunno the meaning of classic."

I looked side-eyed at Reno's jowls, her wildly gesturing arms, her ample apple-shaped torso, and when she caught me, I raised my eyebrows.

"Shaddup, you," Reno growled. "I know whatchu tinking: your maddah and I slightly different size. But a tuck heah, deah, fold dah extra under dah body, and nobody goin' notice. Not like she goin' dance around in deah, right?"

Reno laughed, but I didn't say anything. I opened the hatch on my Tercel, threw the boxes in, and took the dresses from Reno.

"Eh, watch yoah fat fingahs!" Reno screeched. "Watchu tinking? Dat beadwork fragile, all hand-sewn—no treat em like one football."

I laid the gowns in the back seat, careful to keep the plastic around each of the glittering skirts, the sequined and beaded bodices.

I cannot imagine my mother wearing Reno's old bar girl clothes, cannot imagine her in the sequins and flash I once dreamed of wearing myself. Though it is true my mother was accustomed to wearing clothes assigned to her by others. When my mother lent her body to the spirits, they each demanded a different color. The Seven Stars preferred the yellow robe, a tent of sunrise that swallowed my mother's body from neck to toes. The Birth Grandmother craved the clarity of blue. And Saja, the pig of death, grabbed at anything red, forcing my mother's body into whatever material—my T-shirts or shorts, a torn pillowcase, a fabric remnant from Kress my mother had planned to sew into a border for our drapes—fed his desire for red.

When I found my mother's body, she wore an orange-and-green mu'umu'u bought from Hilo Hattie's Christmas sale. The bright flowers, the mix and clash of colors, was a sign that she was in her body before she died. Yet I cannot believe that in the end she died alone, without the spirits she lived with surrounding her, without the daughter she had trained to pray over her journey holding her hand.

Everything that my mother had taught me about protecting the dead, preparing the body and spirit for the final transition, I forgot when I saw her body. "Remember the Heavenly Toad," she had said, and I did, but it only made me afraid without telling me how to save her. I knelt beside her bed and draped an arm around her waist. "I'm sorry," I said, half apologetic, half accusing. "You said you would remind me what to do when the time came, Mommy. But you didn't, and I don't know what to do."

Someone once told me that you have to weigh down the eyelids of the dead so that they will sleep forever in peace. After a while that was the only thing I could think of. I dug through my pockets for some change and, though her eyes were already closed, placed a penny on one and a dime on the other. And then I noticed her dress was twisted around her body, tangled about her thighs. She would have been embarrassed to be so exposed. I tugged at the hem and had to wrestle her hips to get it down around her ankles. The coins slid off her eyes and nested in her hair. I plucked them up, deciding they made her look undignified, like a cartoon character. I arranged the hair around her face, folded her arms across her chest in the correct posture of the dead, and called the paramedics.

Not once did I think about changing her clothes. The mu'u-mu'u was the dress she had chosen for herself; I would not assume the same power that the spirits did, as Reno did, by dressing her as if she were a doll to be played with, then posed and displayed behind a case of glass. *compares ma to doll, play*

• →

I left the engine running in front of Borthwick Mortuary, partially blocking the traffic pulling onto Maunakea Street. "Reno, I'm not going." I surprised her and myself with what came out of my mouth.

"How come?" Reno says. "I get everyting—makeup, dresses, ax-cessories. You supposed help me decide how for present your maddah for her final show on dis earth. All her regulars goin' come for pay their respects, so your maddah, she gotta look her best, right?"

"Yeah, I guess," I said. "But—"

Reno held up her hands. "Nevah mind. I so insensative. Painful for see dah dead body, yah? Some people don't even like for touch em, the dearly departed, all cold and ooh-jie kine. I understand. Go." She waved at me, shooing me away. "I do em, dis last ting for my old friend. Don' worry. I can handle."

Reno unfolded herself, pushed her bulk out of the car, and peeled her dresses off the back seat. She held the hangers above her head, fluffing and fluttering her prizes. "Do watchu need for do," she said. "No worry about me; I get my own ride home." She cradled the dresses in both arms and marched into the mortuary, looking like she was bearing the headless corpse of a queen.

•~

I drove without thinking, down Maunakea—Chinatown's street of leis and the homeless—to the harbor, turning Diamond Head, then mauka, away from the sun. As if pulled by the mist and the rain that perpetually crowned the range guarding Manoa Valley, I found myself returning to the home where I once lived and my mother died.

As I pulled into the driveway, I saw that someone had piled some debris in our carport: a litter of papers and a large green-and-brown sack, big as a small man. Only when I parked next to the junk did I realize that the pile covered a man.

At first I assumed it was one of my mother's clients. Reno had told me that not everyone had heard about my mother's death and some seekers still waited outside the house, hoping for a spontaneous reading. She said this reproachfully, since I still could not write my mother's obituary. "Tink of it like you plannin' for one party," Reno told me. "Dah obit is one invitation that needs for go out in time so people get chance for get ready: find dah right dress, put on dah right face, buy one perfect flower arrangement. RSVP, li' dat."

I slammed the car door as I got out. The body didn't move, and when I started to think that I had found another dead person, I heard a mumbling, like someone talking in his sleep. I cleared my throat. The mumbling grew loud enough for me to decipher something like, "Helpings of God, I'll have two scoops."

Inching closer, I planned to wake this person and tell him my mother had died, when—too late, just when I touched what should have been a shoulder—I smelled fermenting mangoes and unwashed feet, the smell of the Manoa Walker.

I'd smelled him before: once, after grocery shopping with my mother at the Safeway in Manoa Market Place, I made the mistake of meeting his eyes. "You!" he had shouted, rushing toward me. "You!" One of his legs seemed shorter than the other, so that when he ran, his arms swinging, his nut-brown hair swarming around his face and shoulders, he looked like an orangutan. "Read and repent! Read and repent!" the monkey man screeched. "God knows, knows all!"

My mother quickly stuffed my untied hair down the back of my shirt, then stepped between me and the Walker. "Go, *Chudang Kaeguri*," she said. "Stink Toad Spirit, go! You cannot claim us. Go!"

The orangutan man reached into his pants and pulled out a handful of brochures. He waved them at my mother's face. "Too late for you, too late, for you have already been claimed," he taunted. "God has claimed you. His flesh is your flesh. Do you forget the promise of his blood? And a promise is a promise is a promise. Ha-ha ha ha-ha!" He shoved a dirty brochure into one of the bags in the cart. "Thief!" he shouted as he scooted away toward KC Drive-In. "Help, someone help! Thief! The devil stole my Bible!"

I felt my face burn as people in front of the stores and in the parking lot turned to look at my mother and me. Eyes unfocused, I rushed the cart to the car. "Beccah-chan," my mother said, tugging me back. "Don't run. Don't let him see fear. Those kind will feed on that opening and come back."

I slowed my pace but pulled my arm away from her. "I'm not afraid. He's just a crazy bum."

"Crazy," my mother said. "But, don't forget, dangerous. Men

who love God like that are angels in disguise. That is a Heavenly Toad in a man suit."

"Humph," I scoffed. "That is a little-kid story." I yanked my hair from my shirt, my fingers combing out the loose strands, which I let fly in the wind.

"Beccah!" my mother yelled as she tried to catch the wisps. "What did I tell you about holding on to what is yours? This is his territory!"

As my mother went on hands and knees on the black asphalt of the parking lot to search for my hairs, I got into the car, where I could hunch over and hide in the back seat.

Later, when I unpacked the groceries, I found the brochure the Manoa Walker had thrown in with the oranges—a tattered advertisement for Instant Checking at Bank of America, with this scrawled on the cover: "A promise is a promise. God is coming for you."

• ~

"Aaagh!" the Manoa Walker yelled when I grabbed onto his leg. Stinking feet wrapped in the remnants of canvas sneakers kicked out from the top of the sleeping bag, like the back legs of a developing tadpole.

I felt a shock charge through my hand and could not loosen my grip. The sleeping bag thumped and banged against me as the Walker cursed and tried to wiggle out backward from his sack, and though I pushed against the struggling man with all my weight, I could not let go. Finally, my palm burning, I fell back, and the Walker emerged, born onto the floor of my mother's carport, bottom first.

He leaped to his feet, then bent over to touch his leg where I had held it. "My leg is burning," he whispered, "and it feels so good." He hopped on one leg and then the other, still gripping the chosen leg, bent double over himself. He stopped, then slowly lifted his head so that our eyes met, and as I stared, his eyes changed from brown to blue. Afterward I told myself that his eyes must have been a hazel that shifted with the light, but the blue I saw was such a vibrant blue, the color found in the ocean of my father's eyes and God's.

When the curtain of blue dropped over his brown eyes, for a moment I thought I saw my father's face shimmering beneath the surface of the Walker's features. "Daddy," I murmured before I could catch myself, before I could quiet the need of the little girl studying the fading image of her father's face.

Then the faces rippled, merged into one, and the Walker straightened, his head pulling taller and taller the body beneath it, until he towered above me as I huddled in the corner of the carport. "You burn with the fires of hell, daughter!" the Manoa Walker growled in a voice as powerful as my father the preacher's must have been. He marched toward me. "Repent before it is too late and join me. Join your mother."

I scooted backward. "My mother is dead," I whispered, a part of me hoping that it was her he was looking for, and that he would leave after he heard the news.

"Jesus was dead!" he yelled. "And he was arisen! So shall your mother and all who have been bathed in the blessed blood of Christ. Whosoever lives and believes will never die, but be Born Again unto the Kingdom of God!"

"No," I said. "My mother was not Christian. She was . . ." I stood slowly, my back to the wall, keeping a wary eye on the Walker, trying to find a word to encompass my mother's beliefs. "She was, uh, Korean," I blurted.

"She is a lamb in God's flock," said the Manoa Walker, "and I've come to collect the one stray. Do not forsake me. Do not deny me." When he took a step closer toward me, I shot my hand out in warning. The palm of my hand, meant to halt just shy of his chest, brushed it so slightly that the flannel of his shirt felt like air on my fingertips. Blue fire crackled between us, and the Walker fell back as if he had been shot. He dropped to the ground, clutching his chest. He curled, forehead to knee, a cooked shrimp shriveling into a C.

And when he stood again, shoulders hunched, with eyes that scuttled in brown and blurry confusion, his head reached only to my shoulder. "Get mac salad wit' the KC special?" he asked, and then he looked at his sleeping bag, at my oil-spotted carport, at me. "Oh no, it happened again, see it happened. Blue light, spaceship, aliens, microprobed." He rambled on, muttering as he scrambled to collect his belongings. "Abductions. *Enquirer* wants to know." He gathered his belongings into his arms and ran down the driveway, scattering several brochures for credit cards and savings accounts along the way.

I sat in the driveway for a while after he left, nursing my hand, which tingled as if I had plunged it into ice water and was just getting the feeling back. My fingers still hummed as I entered the house. I shook my hand, but instead of dissipating, the tingling grew, vibrating through my arms, my shoulders, into my chest.

When the tingling moved into my head, I closed my eyes and almost dropped to the ground. I knelt in the entryway, feeling the floorboards rattling beneath me. Finally the floor settled, and I opened my eyes, to find the colors in my mother's home shimmering, outlining for me what needed to be done. First I fed and watered the spirits, who grew restless in their hunger. I refilled the offering bowls, placing water and some oranges found in the refrigerator on the kitchen windowsill for the Seven Sisters. For Saja, I set out dried cuttlefish—the only meat I could find—on the steps leading away from our house.

I roamed the rooms, as if on a guiderail, checking on each of the talismans my mother had set up, making sure each was secure in its position. Only one, the red-bordered charm my mother glued to the television to counteract negative incoming energy, needed to be restuck. And then the frogs called to me, until—like my mother before me—I moved them from room to room, rotating the ones hiding behind books on shelves, or on the back of the toilet next to the extra rolls of paper, to the bedroom and kitchen so that they got their share of light.

I performed the actions of my mother, caring for the spirits of the house, in order to feel my mother once again. I wanted to be able to feel her next to me, to sense her spirit—for if there really are such things, I knew she would come to me, feeling my need for her, in death as she rarely did in life.

"Mom," I called. "It's me. Beccah." I waited, closing my eyes, stretching my arms wide, waiting for her hug. I would have taken the slightest breeze brushing against my wrist or inner elbow, the slightest rustling of one of the talismans, I would have taken anything, as a sign. I held my arms out until I felt them burn, then dropped them. "Mom," I called out once more. Eyes still closed, I rose and moved through the room. "Are you here?"

After bumping and tripping my way into her bedroom, I gave up and opened my eyes. I walked over to her bureau, where she kept a small altar for the Birth Grandmother, the most intimate of her spirits. The water in one offering dish had evaporated, leaving a faint line at the rim, and the rice in the other dish—as if feeding on its neighbor—had started to dissolve, melting down into a watery gruel. I dipped a finger into the empty water dish, then touched my tongue. I tasted only myself.

Next to the Birth Grandmother's offerings, my mother kept a jewelry box. Made out of rosewood, inlaid with ox horn and mother-of-pearl, guarded by a lock in the shape of a fish, the box held my mother's treasures. I knew what I would find when I opened the box with the key that never left the fish-lock's mouth: frog pins and pendants and earrings given to her by her regular customers, assorted buttons, the gold and jade hoops that she sewed on my clothes for protection, her wedding band, a baby tooth, my umbilical cord, school pictures and report cards, her jade frog.

I rubbed the frog against my cheek and remembered that on the night Reno gave her the necklace, my mother turned toward me just as we were drifting off to sleep. She slipped the chain off her neck and dangled it above my face, so that with each twist of the chain, the little frog kicked the tip of my nose. "Little Frog," my mother said, "I have a story for you.

"Once on a time, there was a little frog who never listened to its mother. If the mother said go north, her child went south. If the mother said go to the river, her child would run away into the mountains." My mother bounced her jade frog up the bridge of my nose and rested it on my forehead, making me giggle.

"Am I the Little Frog, Mommy?" I said, both hopeful and worried that I might be. "That's not me, huh, Mommy, is it?"

My mother hopped the frog over my mouth. "This is how it was between them, from the time the child was born till the time came for the old mother to die. 'My child,' the mother frog said, 'When I die, bury me by the river. Do not, absolutely do not, bury me on the mountain.' Of course, knowing the little frog, the mother frog fully expected to be buried on the mountain."

I opened my mouth, pushed the frog away with my tongue. "What do you want, Mommy? What do you want me to do?" I said. "Ask me and I'll do it. Okay? Just tell me."

The frog caressed my face. "When the mother frog died," my mother continued, "the little frog was so sad it made up its mind that this time it would do as its mother wished. He buried her at the mouth of the river, and each time it rained, he hopped to her grave, croaking and crying to heaven, worried that the river would wash up her corpse and carry it away."

• ✦

That night, and perhaps the night after, I dreamed of frog angels that swooped from the sky like the monkey bats in *The Wizard of Oz*. As my mother and I floated on a river that looked like a purified

Ala Wai, the frog angels plucked my mother from the water and carried her into the sky. I watched my mother—a tiny light against their darkness—beat against the frog angels' sticky-toed talons and flapping wings as they flew higher and higher. I watched and I cried, not knowing how to help, left behind on the banks of the river.

•‿

Now I wonder if I had been remembering the wrong story, if every time my mother said, "Remember the toad," she meant, "Remember the frog." And I wonder if that changes anything. I find myself second-guessing my interpretations of her stories, and wonder, now that she is dead, how I should remember her life.

•‿

I slapped the lock on the box, snapping the hinge, and unearthed something unexpected under the tangle of jewelry: a cassette tape marked "Beccah."

I remember that occasionally one of my mother's clients, new from Korea, would pay her to perform a blessing or an exorcism for the family ghosts left behind. My mother would ask Reno to tape the ceremony, capturing the voices of the spirits as they spoke through her. And when the trance came to an end after two hours or two weeks or however long it took for the unhappy ancestors to relay their grievances, my mother would wrap and pack the cassettes for mailing to their relatives still living in Korea. When I first saw these packages, I remember thinking they were gifts for me and was disappointed when, after my persistent needling, my mother opened one.

"See, Beccah-chan," my mother said after I had ripped the paper off a small package and found a black cassette tape. "This one's not for you."

"Oh," I said, but, unwilling to give up, asked her to play it. "Is it music? I wanna hear, I wanna hear!"

My mother slipped the cassette into our tape recorder. After a prelude of whirs and scratching, my mother's voice—accompanied by a beating drum—wailed out of the recorder.

"Yaaak!" I shoved my hands against my ears. "What are you doing, Mommy?"

My mother slapped down my hands. "You should listen, learn," she said. "This will be you one day."

"Not!" I yelled. "No way. I'm not going to scream like that for nothing."

"Not for nothing," my mother said. "I am crying for the dead. To show proper respect. To show love."

We listened to my mother's cries and moans, to the heartbeat of the drum, until the tape wound down. I knew that as a fortune-teller and spirit medium, she was paid to console or cajole the dead. Sometimes customers, mostly the new immigrants from Korea, paid her to perform ceremonies for lost family members and the dead that had been left behind. They would record my mother's chants to send to relatives and neighbors back home.

There's a possibility I saw this tape, my tape, among the others, or I might have heard her making the actual recording. I would have assumed that this tape was for one of her customers, someone who had failed to pay for or pick up the merchandise. Never would I have thought that my mother performed the ceremony for herself. Never, as a child, did I think about whom my mother had had to leave behind, and whom she cried for.

Instead, when we finished listening to her customer's tape, I told my mother, "I would cry for you, Mommy."

"I know," she answered. "Every year, on my death anniversary, that will be your gift to me."

• ~

I remembered my mother saying this as I fingered the tape she had marked as mine. Under this cassette, bound with a rubber band, was an envelope stuffed with paper and yellowing newspaper articles. I scanned the articles, most of them clipped form the *Korea Times,* reading what I could, and translated something about World War II, the Japanese, and camps. Unable to get far without my Korean-English dictionary, I put the articles aside for later and picked out two official-looking documents. Both, in essence, were missing-persons reports—one from the American Embassy in Seoul, the other from the Red Cross.

"Dear Mrs. Akiko (Kim Soon Hyo) Bradley," they read. *"I am sorry to inform you that we can find no trace of your sisters—Kim Soon Mi, Kim Soon Hi, Kim Soon Ja—presumed dead or residing in North Korea."*

I had to read these opening lines twice more before I understood who was who, that my mother once belonged to a name, to a life, that I had never known about. That the names I had known only in relation to the Seven Stars belonged to women I could have called *imo,* and that my mother, once bound to others besides myself, had severed those ties—my lineage, her family name—with her silence.

I sat, surrounded by the papers, by the secrets she had guarded and cultivated like a garden. I sat and I waited for some way to understand, to know this person called Soon Hyo, thinking that I had always been waiting for my mother, wasting time in the hallway of her life, waiting for an invitation to step over the threshold and into her home.

Mom's REAL name

16

SOON HYO ⟁

My mother died more than once in her life.

Before she died with her head in my hands, leaving me with an emptiness so big I would never fill it until the birth of my own child, she died in March of 1919 on the streets of Seoul.

In the weeks following the signing of the Korean Declaration of Independence, she and her friends from Ewha College joined the throngs of displaced farmers, out-of-work merchants, and idealistic students celebrating in the streets. Day after day, on the corner of her street, she met the boy with whom she hoped to make a yonae, a love match. Holding sometimes a red banner, sometimes a flag, he would wait on the corner with some of their friends, to throw off the gossips. Under cover of their friends and a flying red cloth, they would link arms before becoming part of the river of people meandering through the city.

We were happy, my mother would tell my sisters and me. Not just me, not just my friends, but everybody who marched in the streets. You can't imagine how close we all felt.

Of course, my mother added, either in explanation or in mockery, I was in love.

⟁

The first time my mother was dragged home dead, her own mother had had a premonition. Don't go, she told my mother, I beg you. She wrapped her arms around her daughter, trying to anchor her to the earth of their home, to hold and protect her. But my mother only pushed at the grasping hands, hauling my weeping grandmother across the room and out the door. When my mother finally broke away, my halmoni shouted after her a warning and a curse that sealed my mother's fate: Watch out for him, that no-good, do-nothing-but-yell boy! He'll ruin your chances for a decent match!

• ⁓

My mother—dressed in her pleated white skirt that swung like a bell against her legs, her hair carefully braided and tied with a red bow to catch the eye of her boyfriend—followed where the crowd took her. She dodged the children who sang "San Toki, Toki Ya!" and jumped like mountain jackrabbits, jackrabbits ya! in and out of the parade, and she stole glances at lovers stealing kisses behind their flags. Maybe she thought her own boyfriend would try to kiss her that day.

Several groups of people around her chanted slogans, each trying to outshout the others until their words would be the only ones heard. Her own group of friends were arguing about whether to chant Korean Independence Forever! or Long Live Korea for Ten Thousand Years!—Man Sei, Man Sei!—when my mother became aware of an undercurrent of noise, a strange murmur trickling down from the direction of the Chang Duk Palace grounds, the planned gathering place for the independence celebration.

Listen! one of the louder students said. It's the ghost of the idiot king, farting along the empty halls and wailing about losing his country!

After laughing, perhaps wanting to reassure my mother, my mother's boyfriend explained: Probably just the students from the other side of town.

Their slogans must be louder and better than ours, someone else joked.

Then, over the agreements of Yes, yes, more students, someone and then another someone yelled, Soldiers! but the crowd continued to surge forward.

My mother said that when the people recognized the troops of Japanese soldiers in their Western uniforms, armed and mounted on sleek horses as if ready to charge into battle, a cry went up from the multitude. But instead of sounding angry or fearful, the cry was strangely happy, like one that lovers might utter after a chance meeting in the street.

↑ Japanese kill many students
↓ celebrating Independence

And then it happened.

In unison, as if from some invisible command, the troops, sabers flashing, fell forward, sinking into the crowd. Amidst wordless screams, my mother heard people shouting, Stand! Stand! and for a moment the marchers stood and the soldiers stood, unable to force their way through the compact press of humanity. Then somebody up ahead threw a curse, and somebody else threw a rock or maybe a shoe, and somebody who was close enough cracked a flag stick against a slashing sword.

The soldiers charged for a second time, their weapons hacking a path through the street. In front of her, my mother could see people she knew being sliced and gutted, bleeding and screaming and falling as they tried to turn away. But what was worse, she said, was that behind her, people still did not know what was happening and continued to laugh and shout Korea! Korea! and push forward in their happiness.

One of her friends, maybe her boyfriend, yelled: They're killing us, they're killing us! Break away! And as if releasing a deep breath, the mass of people behind them surged and finally broke, becoming a tidal wave, immense and unstoppable in their efforts to escape.

Caught in the rush, my mother and her boyfriend stumbled

against each other and, their bodies careening out of control, pushed into and over others—I know what it feels like to step on a human body, to feel the rush of blood flood into my shoes, my mother once said—before they finally pitched forward into an alleyway. My mother managed to cover her head and curl her knees into her stomach, waiting to be trampled, when her boyfriend fell on top of her.

When she could breathe again, her breaths sharp with the scent of smoke and blood, she asked the boy to move off her. Only after my mother asked him to move a second and then a third time did she become aware of the comforting feel of his blood blanketing her arms and torso. She said she knew he was dead, but instead of feeling fear or revulsion, instead of pushing away the weight of his body, she wrapped her arms around him, pulling him into her. His stillness and his blood made her feel safe, almost cherished. Nestled beside his cooling body, she slept, until she heard silence and realized her eyes were open. My mother said that from that day on she never closed her eyes, even in sleep.

From underneath the dead boy, from the sides of her eyes, my mother said she saw streets littered with the bright fragments of clothes, hats, shoes, strips of fabric torn from banners and flags, and bodies. And wading through air thick with groans and smoke from burning churches and the fertile smell of blood, the spared and the wounded came to reclaim their dead.

My mother held on to her body and waited.

• ⏑

When my mother's eyes could see again, my grandmother was wailing the death chant and clipping her fingernails to bury next to her.

Never cut your nails at night, my mother would break into this part of the story to warn my sisters and me. Sign of a life cut short.

My mother said she tried to take back her hands and tell my grandmother she was not dead, but according to the story, my grandmother pushed her back down and hissed, "Yes, you are!" Then she wailed loud enough for people on the next street to hear. When she was supposed to catch her breath for the next death cry, my grandmother hissed, "Stupid girl, I'm saving your life."

In order to protect her, my grandmother killed her daughter off. She sent my mother north, to Sulsulham, to marry my father.

•～

It was because she loved me so much, my mother explained. They were burning the homes of suspected revolutionaries and arresting or shooting the people who ran out.

•～

In her special box, in which my mother stored treasures from her past life or for her daughters' future ones, my mother kept two types of clippings. Among the first was a newspaper article from the June 1919 issue of the *Daedong Kongbo* denouncing the official report of the arrest of young hoodlums rioting in the streets and said what my mother said: Most of the city was dead. Churches and homes burned. Forty-six thousand, eight hundred forty-seven Korean nationalists arrested. Fifteen thousand, nine hundred sixty-one wounded. Seven thousand, five hundred and nine—including one boy significant only to one insignificant girl—dead.

The second type of clippings: the burial nails her mother pared from her fingers too soon.

•～

When she arrived in Sulsulham to marry a man she had never seen, someone that had not even been picked out by a matchmaker, who at least would have ensured that their Four Pillars—the year, month, day, and hour of their birth charts—were well aligned, my mother felt her life was over. She was so alone that she knew she could cry forever and never again would there be anyone to comfort her.

My mother did not make her yonae love match, nor did she receive a chungmae, an arranged match, complete with the ceremonial exchange of gifts and celebration. When she arrived in the dust and dead of night, my mother was rushed to her future husband's home. She did not have time to wash or eat or change into her own mother's red-and-blue wedding dress, a dress that should have come as a gift from the groom. She had time only to listen to her future parents' lecture: Marriage is not about love but about duty. About having sons. About keeping the family name. My mother bowed twice to her new in-laws and was married by morning.

My mother never heard her name again.

•⁀

When I was a child, my father would call her anae, wife, and the village ahjimas would mostly call her by my father's name, Kim Uk. Or sometimes ttal omoni, the mother of daughters. Only when the time came to bury her did my sisters and I even wonder what name my mother was born with. In the end, we merely carved Omoni, mother, into the sixth plank of her coffin, the one that faced the sky.

•⁀

My mother died just before winter, during the kimchee-making time. Our family had harvested the cabbage and turnips from our field and were preparing to wash and salt them. My sisters and I had finished our day chores, and our mother had just rolled out the ceramic jars, each as high as her hip, that we would place the salted vegetables in overnight, when she began to complain about how tired she was. Still, she wrung the dripping, salted cabbage until her wrinkled hands stung from the brine. When all the jars were packed tight, my mother rinsed her hands in a bucket of clear river water and went to lie down.

My sisters took that as the sign to prepare the back room for the night and went to spread out our sleeping mats. Instead of joining them, I went to our mother. Mother, would you like some water, some soup, a massage? I asked her, hoping to trade my service for a story. Want me to pull your white hairs?

My mother touched her hands to my lips, then sighed, a long, tired exhalation, as if to shush me, but I knew from the way her eyes closed, lashes sealed against her blue-tinged skin. I put a blanket over her, as if she were only asleep. In Korea, whenever someone died, the oldest son took the dead person's coat up to the roof and invited the spirit to return to the house to feast and prepare for the long journey to heaven. Instead of getting her coat, I, her youngest daughter, went to her special box and pulled out her red-and-blue wedding dress.

I climbed onto the roof, sliding across thatching made slick with ice, and stayed there most of the night, holding her dress open to the wind until my body ached from the weight of the silk and from the cold bite of the stars. I waited on the roof, holding my omoni's dress in the bitter night air, calling for her spirit to come back, calling, Come back, Mother, come back, until finally, after a sudden blast of wind almost knocked me from my perch, I folded the arms of her dress into myself and knew I held nothing.

• ⟿

On the twenty-second anniversary of my mother's death, I try to think of what I will tell my daughter about her grandmother, and I remember the box. In her special box, my mother kept treasures for times other than the present, among them: fingernails and newspaper articles; a red-and-blue wedding dress; gold thread that she was forever saving to sew her first son's, then later her first grandson's, birthday coat; the fine hemp cloth with which she wanted, but would never have the time, to stitch her own shroud.

•～

As I prepare the chesa—laying out the table with my mother's favorite foods, with wine, with a set of chopsticks and spoons for the members of my family, dead and alive, who will never eat from them—my daughter screams her displeasure from the crib she will not sleep in.

My husband has tried to put her in it for the night, but each time she whimpers, I jump to her side. I do not want her to feel the bite of loneliness, to feel she has been abandoned. When I leave her in her basket to take a shower or do the laundry, I hear her frantic screams in the running of the water; yet when I run to check on her, I find her quietly contemplating her hands or toes.

And each night, after my husband has fallen asleep in exasperation, I bring my baby to my bed, where we sleep, cocooned. The milk from my breasts fills her as she sucks from them even in her dreams; and the warmth of her solid body, the gentle waves of her breathing, soothe my own hunger.

Now, as her cries subside into soft hiccuping chirps, I wrap my daughter into a towel, tie her onto my back, and prepare to introduce her to her grandmother. I pour the scorched rice tea and, bowing twice, present it to Induk's spirit in gratitude, to my oldest sister's spirit—wherever she is—in forgiveness, and finally to my mother's spirit in love.

While I sip, I try to think of the words to a prayer I can offer for my mother. I cannot. Instead I will tell my daughter a story about her grandmother. I sift through memory, and this is what I say: She was a princess. She was a student. She was a revolutionary. She was a wife who knew her duty. And a mother who loved her daughters, but not enough to stay or to take them with her.

I will tell my daughter these things, and about the box that kept my mother's past and future, and though she will never know her grandmother's name, she will know who her grandmother is.

Later, perhaps, when she is older, she will sift through her own memories, and through the box that I will leave for her, and come to know her own mother—and then herself as well.

• ~

In the box I hold for my daughter, I keep the treasures of my present life: my daughter's one-hundred-day dress, which we will also use for her first birthday; a lock of her reddish-brown hair; the dried stump of her umbilical cord. And a thin black cassette tape that will, eventually, preserve a few of the pieces, the secrets, of our lives. I start with our names, my true name and hers: Soon Hyo and Bek-hap. I speak for the time when I leave my daughter, so that when I die, she will hear my name and know that when she cries, she will never be alone.

17

BECCAH ·~

According to my mother, the rituals that accompanied the major transitions in a woman's life—birth, puberty, childbirth, and death—involved the flow of blood and the freeing of the spirit. Slipping out of the body along pathways forged by blood, the spirit traveled and roamed free, giving the body permission to transform itself. Necessary but dangerous, these were times when the spirit could spin away forever, lost and aimless, severed from the body.

"This is the blood of a lost spirit," my mother told me when I first noticed the bloodied pad she unfolded from her panties each month. "Every once in a while a woman opens her mouth and a wandering spirit tries to take her body. I'm just spitting it out."

"What? How?" I mumbled, afraid to open my mouth.

"When women are forced to bleed, we have to take care to bind our spirits to us, or they will get confused and wander away. Ejected from our bodies, the spirit flows out on the river of blood, losing its name and its place. Sometimes that *yongson* spirit will try to invade another woman's body—maybe one that reminds them of the body they left behind. Sometimes they will catch a seed in a woman's body and be born again, but most times they will die. See? Like this one." My mother ripped the sticky pad from her panties, rolled it into a wad of toilet paper, and dropped it in the trash.

"Will that ever happen to me?" I asked, unsure if I was referring to losing my spirit or bleeding out a stray.

My mother reached into the box of maxipads and stuck a fresh one on her underpants to catch the blood of more dying spirits. "I will protect you, Beccah," she said, "when the time comes. And I will pray."

•~

But despite my mother's prayers, her charms for my safety, her chants against Saja and Red Disaster, and despite my own efforts to still my body, I eventually bled.

When I felt the knot of pain pulling in my abdomen, pinning me to my seat in Mrs. Abernacke's ninth-grade homeroom, I folded my hands over my belly, picturing a beam of light soaking up the blood. The visualization had worked to suppress menstruation for more than two years, the flash of light cauterizing the wound between my legs, but this time I felt the light merge with my blood, rushing true and deep, thickening as it pounded against my tailbone and *poji* with heavy fists.

While Mrs. Abernacke called attendance, I dropped my head over my desk. I imagined blood, sweet and sticky as syrup, soaking through my jeans and onto the plastic seat. I stayed down, closing my eyes when first bell rang and everyone left for first period. When I opened my eyes again, I saw that the only ones left were me and, toward the back of the room, Fiaso Rialto—whom everyone called Fatso. Fatso, a cushioned cheek piled like dough on the desktop and his large, fat-ringed arms hanging down the sides so that his knuckles grazed the floor by his slippered feet, slept on even as Mrs. Abernacke stalked up behind him. She placed a hand against his neck, a caress really, and when he didn't move, she knocked the back of his head.

"Mr. Rialto!" His head snapped back and he looked around

with red-rimmed eyes. "Naptime ended with kindergarten. Please gather up your belongings and proceed to your next class."

"Huh?" said Fatso.

"Go," said Mrs. Abernacke as she marched over to my desk. I expected a whack on the side of my head.

"Miss Bradley, first bell has sounded. If you don't want detention, please tell me why you are still lounging about in homeroom."

"I, uh, don't know," I stammered.

"Then go on." Mrs. Abernacke folded her hands across her chest, waiting for me to stand.

I slid off the seat, keeping my eyes down, expecting to see a smear of red blood on the chair. Relieved to see nothing but a heart someone had carved, I bent to retrieve my backpack.

"Oh, I see," Mrs. Abernacke said. "You should have just told me. I'm a woman too, you know."

"Huh?" I said.

"It's a natural, though unfortunate, function. Let me write you a pass for the nurse."

"For what?" I asked. I held my backpack between us.

"Please do not play games," she said, looking pointedly at my pants. Then she frowned. "Didn't you watch *The Time of Your Life* in fifth-grade health?"

• ↙

Instead of going to the nurse, I changed into my PE shorts and went home. I tried to sneak my pants into the laundry without my mother seeing, but she found me as I was rubbing Stain Stick against the crotch of my jeans.

"It's time," she cried. "I delayed it for as long as I could, but now it's time." She grabbed the jeans from me, pulled the legs apart and wailed, "Oh, my poor baby! Does it hurt?"

I pushed her away as she tried to hug me. "Quit it," I told her. "It's no big deal, just the facts of life." And then I started to cry.

"*Aigu,*" my mother clucked as she ushered me into her bed-room. "It does hurt. Lie down." She pulled the blankets to the foot of the bed, nestled me into her pillows.

"I swallowed a spirit, Mom," I said, half laughing.

"No," my mother said. "It's your own spirit fighting to get out, wanting to travel. We must make the way safe for it to go and then come back."

"I was only joking," I said. "I'm not a baby anymore that you can fool me with this stuff, you know." And then I groaned as a spirit raked its nails against my womb.

"Shh, shh," she crooned, stroking my hair. When I closed my eyes, I felt my mother move away from me, heard the glass doors open onto the garden.

I slept, sailing in and out of dreams, riding the waves of my first cramping. Through the night, my mother bathed my face and body with water that smelled sharp, like freshly cut grass, like newly unearthed roots. And as she stroked me, I dreamed I was swimming, then drowning, then climbing an embankment that eroded and dis-solved as I scrambled toward the stars. I dragged myself over sand and stone, following the light, until I stepped on a bridge of fire and found a beautiful woman waiting for me.

At first I thought the woman was my mother, then I realized it was myself. "My name is Induk," the woman said through my lips. I looked into the face that was once my own and wondered who she saw, who stood in my place looking at the body that Induk now claimed.

I looked at my new hands, trying to find a clue to my present identity, but as I looked, the hands melted, then dissolved into ash. Quickly I looked at the arms, the feet, the legs, and they, too, disin-tegrated. I knew I was being devoured by flame ravenous as a dragon, fierce as the sun. I waited, a thin column of ash, for the dragon's breath, the wind that would blow my body apart.

"You must come back across running water," Induk said, exhaling, dispersing my ashes like pollen into the night air.

• ✒

When I woke the next morning, my mother said, "You must return across running water." She pulled one of her white ceremonial gowns over my head and yanked my arms. "Come on."

I rubbed my stomach. "I don't feel so good," I whined, hoping she would leave me alone.

"I know," she said. "That's why we have to do this."

"No," I said, scrambling to the other side of the bed. "I have to go to school."

My mother ran to block the door to her room. "I already called, said you were too sick. That we have to go to the doctor."

"Oh," I said, pulling off my mother's gown. "Why didn't you say that's where we're going?"

My mother sighed, then spoke slowly: "Because we're not. I only told them something they could understand."

She lifted the white gown from the bed where I had thrown it, and handed it back to me. I put it on, and when the hem dropped to my ankles, I realized I had grown to my mother's height. "Come on," she said as she walked out the glass doors and into her garden.

I followed her to the back of our lot. When we reached the chicken wire enclosing our property, my mother raised her hands and, like Moses parting the Red Sea, stepped through the fence. I reached the spot where my mother had crossed over, expecting to see some kind of gate worked into the fence, but I couldn't see an opening of any kind. My mother waited. I slipped my fingers through the loops and shook. The fence rattled.

"Here," my mother said. "Look here." She grasped at the barrier between us and gently eased the wire apart. Creaking, the fence split wide enough for me to insert my body, then snapped shut behind me.

I followed where my mother led, watching the muscles of her legs flex as she scrambled over the thirsty tongues of tree roots and loose rocks scattered like broken teeth. I felt my body move like my mother's, bend and dip with hers, as if I lived within her skin. We climbed a skinny path among dank mulch and dying leaves, weaving our bodies through squares of sunlight that wavered and burst like overripe liliko'i as we stepped on them. And each step was accompanied by the music of the river, a white noise I became aware of only when we jumped over a small finger of water.

"She has crossed the dangerous stream in search of the spirit," my mother called out into the moist air.

"Dance," she said to me. "Free your spirit, Beccah-chan, let it loose." She leaped into the air, twirling and pivoting in a space of her own, dancing and singing a song with no words.

"Mom, stop!" I cried, looking about, afraid that—even here in the middle of nowhere, next to a small, unmarked runoff from the Manoa Stream—someone would see my mother as I saw her: flying unanchored to reality, her own dark waters soaking through her tunic until the lines of her used woman's body—the sloping shoulder bones jutting like wings out of her back, the sacs of her breasts swinging from her concave chest, the upturned bowl of her stomach—sharpened under the wet clothes.

"Please not now," I yelled, to both my mother and the spirits she danced with. I vowed that if she went into a trance, I would leave her here in the woods, making my own way back into sanity.

Spinning toward me, she grabbed one of my hands. "Dance with me, Beccah," she said. "Don't you hear the singing?"

She pulled and I jumped, hopping from one foot to the other. "That's it," she told me. "Let the river speak to you. Listen to what it has to say, to what you have to hear."

Her dance slowed. Still holding my hand, she slipped her fingers into the waistband of her tunic pants, pulled out a small pocket knife, and slashed the tip of my middle finger.

I yelled, then popped my finger into my mouth.

"Wait, not yet," my mother said, drawing my finger from my mouth. "Wash it first."

When I dipped my hand into the shallow water of the stream, my mother yelled, "Spirit, fly with the river, then follow it back home." She tapped me on the shoulder. "Okay," she said to me. "Now drink it."

I cupped some of the running water into my hands, brought it to my mouth. I tasted the metal of blood.

"Now you share the river's body," my mother said. "Its blood is your blood, and when you are ready to let your spirit fly, it will always follow the water back to its source."

·~

Like the river in my blood, my mother waited for me to fly to her, waited for me to tell her I was ready to hear what she had to say. I never asked, but maybe she was telling me all the time and I wasn't listening.

Wanting to hear her voice once more, I unpacked the "Beccah" tape—my mother's last message, last gift to me—I had carried back from the Manoa house. But just as when I was a child listening in on my mother's sessions with her clients, just as when I listened to that one tape many years ago, I heard, when I first began playing my mother's tape in the apartment I had chosen for myself, only senseless wails, a high-pitched keening relieved by the occasional gunshot of drums. Still, I listened, but only when I stopped concentrating did I realize my mother was singing words, calling out names, telling a story. I turned the volume knob on the stereo until my mother's voice shivered up the walls, as if the louder the words, the easier I would be able to understand the story.

Kok: I howl into the night air, emptying my grief into the homes of my neighbors, announcing my loss and my love.

As the tape wound on, I rummaged through the kitchen cabinets for paper and pen, wanting to write down my mother's song. I scribbled words I recognized—*kok, han, chesa, chudang, Saja, poji*—words connected to blood and death. After filling several notebook pages with black scrawl, I stopped the recorder. The scraps of paper seemed inadequate, small and disjointed. Needing a bigger canvas, I stripped the sheet from my bed, laid it on the living room floor in front of the speakers, pressed Play on the recorder, and caught my mother's words.

Yom: Preparing your body for its final transition, I lay it down, stretched long against the mat in the main room. I boil ginger root, and with the cooled scented water, I bathe you for a final time. I massage your stiffening limbs, then tuck them close against your body. I wash your intimate places, pull your white hairs, and cut your nails. The loose trimmings I wrap in cloth to bury under you. And through it all I sing.

I sing Hanul, Pada, Ch-onji, sa-nam gwa irum, calling on Heaven, Sea, the four directions of Earth, and I sing your name. I mark the place where you are buried so that you will always find your way.

Abugi. Omoni. Kun Aniya. Mul Ajumoni. I sing the names by which I have known you, all of you, so that you will remember. So that I will remember. So that those who come after me will know. Induk. Miyoko. Kimiko. Hanako. Akiko. Soon Hi. Soon Mi. Soon Ja. Soon Hyo.

So many true names unknown, dead in the heart. So many bodies left unprepared, lost in the river.

Not once did my mother sing my name. And though primarily in English, this tape was not for me, was addressed not to me but to her mother, a final description of her mother's death and feast. Faithful in performing the death anniversary *chesa,* my mother proved to be dutiful and dependable as a daughter in a way she never was as a mother.

When the first side of the tape hissed to a stop, I realized that what I had thought were drums accenting my mother's lament was actually a dismal rapping at my door, incessant but faint. Flipping the tape over, I pressed Play and, with my mother's words wrapped around me, drifted to the door. Through the eye of the peephole, I saw the apartment manager leaning against the door, thumping listlessly with flattened hand, his bowed head a balloon on the string of his body.

"What?" I yelled through the closed door.

Hiram Hirano jumped away from the door, blinking his pink, watery eyes. "Sorry to bother you," he squeaked. "But there've been complaints about your, ah, music."

I watched him fiddle with his balding head, stick a finger into his ear. He snuffled at the door, trying to look into the peephole. "Hallo?" he stammered. "Did you hear me? Hallo? Could you turn it down?"

"My mother is dead," I said.

"Oh," he said, scuttling away from the door as if it were diseased.

Wishing I could turn up the volume even more, I added my own voice, an echo until I stumbled over a term I did not recognize: *Chongshindae.* I fit the words into my mouth, syllable by syllable, and flipped through my Korean-English dictionary, sounding out a rough, possible translation: Battalion slave. ↓ life at camps

Chongshindae: Our brothers and fathers conscripted. The women left to be picked over like fruit to be tasted, consumed, the pits spit out as Chongshindae, where we rotted under the body of orders from the Emperor of Japan. Under the Emperor's orders, we were beaten and starved. Under Emperor's orders, the holes of our bodies were used to bury their excrement. Under Emperor's orders, we were bled again and again until we were thrown into a pit and burned, the ash from our thrashing arms dusting the surface of the river in which we had sometimes been allowed to bathe. Under Emperor's orders, we could not prepare those in the river for the journey out of hell.

The Japanese believe they have destroyed an entire generation of Koreans. That we are all dead and have taken the horrible truth

with us, but I am alive. I feel you, knowing you wait by my side until the time comes for me to join you across the river. I offer you this one small gesture each year, worth more than the guilt money the Japanese now offer to silence me: a bit of rice burned in your memories, and your names called over and over again, a feast of crumbs for the starving.

I rewound the tape where my mother spoke of the *Chongshindae*, listening to her accounts of crimes made against each woman she could remember, so many crimes and so many names that my stomach cramped. Without reference, unable to recognize any of the names, I did not know how to place my mother, who sounded like an avenging angel recounting the crimes of men.

"Mommy—Omoni—is this you?" I cried, but my mother did not pause in her grief, her song for the dead.

I could not view my mother, whom I had always seen as weak and vulnerable, as one of the "comfort women" she described. Even though I heard her call out "Akiko," the name she had answered to all my life, I could not imagine her surviving what she described, for I cannot imagine myself surviving. How could my mother have married, had a child, if she had been forced into the camps? And then, given new context, came the half-forgotten memory of the night my father was taken to the hospital.

From the little consistencies I could gather from her stories, we were living in Florida, in a bungalow adjacent to the chapel on the campus of the Miami Mission House for Boys. What I remember is a small yard in which I played and a small room where I slept by myself. That particular morning, a Saturday that I had been allowed to watch television, I saw *Curse of the Mummy*. Although, remembering its time slot, the movie I saw was more likely to have been *Abbott and Costello Meet the Mummy,* or even *Scooby-Doo and the Haunted House*. But whatever the movie, images of the resurrected dead chased me into the night, into my dreams. I remember the wrapped mummy shuffling toward me—strips of rotting, stinking cloth hanging from outstretched arms—stalking me even as I ran from sleep into the reality of my room. Screaming, feeling the mummy's breath rustle the hair on the back of my head, I jumped from my bed and stormed into my parents' bedroom.

Halfway across their room, I realized it was empty, that there was no one to save me. I waited for the mummy to devour me, but when she reached me, she merely turned my head toward the open window. I opened my eyes and, as if caught in another dream in which I had no control, saw my mother dancing in the alley of our yard and my father on his knees before her, begging her to come inside, come inside before someone saw them.

"Bow down before God, for He alone can heal your wounds," my father told my mother. "Remember the woman of Luke, chapter thirteen. She had been inflicted by evil spirits, suffering for eighteen years, before Jesus put His hands on her, saying 'Woman, you are set free from your infirmity.' Bow down, Akiko, just as that woman did, and you shall be free."

But my mother laughed and spat at my father. "I will never, never again lay down for any man," she said. And she swung around, spinning in circles about him.

My father stood and clasped his hands to his chest. "Forgive her, Father. She knows not what she speaks."

"I know what I speak, for that is my given name. Soon Hyo, the true voice, the pure tongue. I speak of laying down for a hundred men—and each one of them Saja, Death's Demon Soldier—over and over, until I died. I speak of bodies being bought and sold, of bodies—"

" 'Put away perversity from your mouth; keep corrupt talk from your lips, or—,' " my father yelled.

"Of bodies that were burned and cut and thrown like garbage to wild dogs by the river—"

" 'Or ye shall be struck down!' " My father grabbed my mother's shoulders and shook her.

"I'm the one! I'm the one to strike you down, and God down too!" my mother screamed, charging my father, scratching at his face.

But my father was the one to strike *her* down, pushing her into the damp ground in an attempt to cover her mouth. "Quiet! What if someone hears you speaking like this? The boys, the brothers? What if Beccah hears you? Think of how she would feel, knowing her mother was a prostitute."

My father held my mother in his arms, cradling her as she moaned and pounded against him. "Shush," he murmured. "It is not for me to judge. But know that 'The sins of the parent shall fall upon their children and their grandchildren.' I ask you to protect our daughter, with your silence, from that shame."

I fell asleep in my parents' bed that night, listening to the sound of my mother crying, and when I woke, I was in the hospital. I spent most of the next few weeks in the hospital, roaming its corridors, dreaming in front of the candy machines, sliding on the slick white floors, waiting for my mother to emerge from my father's room. When I asked to see him, my mother said, "Wait, wait until he is better," but I never saw him again. On our final visit to the hospital, I remember hearing the words "heart failure," "complications," "pneumonia," "I'm sorry." And as the doctor bent toward my mother and me, offering his condolences, I asked not about my daddy, but about the candy in the vending machine.

•~

I clawed through memory and story, denying what I heard and thought I remembered, and tried to pinpoint my mother's birth date, her age during World War II. Flooding my mind with dates and numbers, I wanted to drown my mother's voice, wanted to reassure myself that these atrocities could not have been inflicted on her, that she was just a child when she claimed to be a comfort woman. I began to scratch dates on the bedsheet—*1995, 1965, 1945, 1931-2-3—*

when the manager came back. I recognized his feeble knocking, but the voice that called my name from outside the door was Sanford's, whom I had listed on the rental agreement as the person to contact in case of emergency.

I did not need to get off the floor in front of the speakers to know what was happening behind the door. Hiram, bug-eyed and sweating, would be backing away after having performed his obligatory knocking. Sanford would be waving the timid manager down the hallway while fretting with his hair and expression, concerned with looking supportive yet boyishly handsome.

I didn't rush to open the door upon hearing his voice, and I knew Sanford's mask must have slipped. "Beccah!" he roared, pounding the door. "It's me."

I turned the knob of the volume down. "Who?" I said, then twisted the knob back toward high.

Sanford stopped pounding for a moment, then yelled out his name as if it were a question.

About to take pity on him and open the door, I heard my mother call me, weaving my name into her chants, her prayers for justice.

Beccah-chan, lead the parade of the dead. Lead the Ch'ulssang with the rope of your light. Clear the air with the ringing of your bell, bathe us with your song. When I can no longer perform the chesa for the spirits, we will look to you to feed us. I have tried to release you, but in the end I cannot do it and tie you to me, so that we will carry each other always. Your blood in mine.

I remembered watching my mother lay out the offerings for the dead before she would feed me, remembered her dancing over me with strips of cloth torn from the sheets of my bed. And while I had felt invisible, unimportant, while my mother consorted with her spirits, I now understood that she knew I watched her. That in her way, she had always carried me with her.

Feeling my mother's arms around my waist, I walked to

the door. "I'm speaking to my mother," I told Sanford through the cracks.

"Your mother is dead," Sanford said, speaking to me as I had spoken to my mother, as if she were unstable. Dangerous.

I looked at Sanford, made small through the tunnel of the peephole. When I was in high school, the art teacher taught us to look through a square made by our fingers, in order to focus on what we wanted to paint. I often looked at my mother through the finger frame, trying to put her in perspective. I liked the way my fingers captured her, making her manageable. Squinting my eye through my lens, I could make her any size I wanted. I could make her shrink, smaller and smaller, until she disappeared with a blink.

I looked at Sanford as I had looked at my mother, fitting him in the space between my fingers, and slowly, slowly, with infinite gentleness, brought my fingers together until he shrank smaller than the lines in a standard obituary, smaller than newsprint.

"I have to leave you, Sanford," I called out, while he slammed his weight against the door. I watched him rub his shoulder, then dropped my hand and closed my eyes. With my mother's voice filling the apartment, her words swirling around my shoulders, I thought how easy—in a pinch, with a blink—it was to make someone disappear. "Goodbye," I told him. "My mother is calling me."

18

BECCAH ᴗ

Reno and I fought over my mother's body.

"What's this? And this? And this?" I pointed into the rented casket, at the black eyeliner circling my mother's eyes, the blush slashing across her cheeks toward her temples, the bright-orange lipstick, the feathered headpiece perched on her piled hairdo.

"What?" Auntie Reno placed her hands on her hips. "Whatchu trying for say?"

I glared at her pursed lips, done up in the identical shade of tangerine as my mother's, and snorted.

"Whass your problem? If you no like Koral Kiss, then I change em; I know not everybody can wear em like me."

"Yeah, Reno. It's the lipstick. And the purple eye shadow— looks like somebody beat her to death. And the clothes and the hootchy-kootchy feather thing—straight from the strip show in Vegas or what?" I leaned over the coffin. "This isn't my mother," I told her. "This is you. Just like it's always been you."

Reno slammed her hands down on the edge of the casket so hard the feathers on my mother's headpiece quivered. "Goffunnit, girlie. You wait. You da one leave dis in my hands. You da one say, 'Auntie Reno, I no can dress my maddah. Auntie Reno, I no can fix her face. I no can touch one dead body. I no can even write one suckin' obituary.' "

She marched around my mother, toward my side of the coffin. "So what den? If her own daughtah not goin' take care her, den who? Me. Auntie Reno. Thass who. And dis dah tanks I get."

Instead of backing up when she stomped toward me in her tottering heels, I stepped forward. "Oh, Auntie, thank you thank you thank you," I sneered. "Always, all my life, I've been thanking you. And for what?"

"What!" Auntie Reno screeched, bringing the mortician running into the room. "For what—for what?"

The mortician smoothed the front of his coat and cleared his throat, oiling his voice. "Ladies, may I assist you in some way?"

Reno turned toward him, bringing her hand to her forehead. She wobbled, the bulk of her body threatening to drop onto the young man. "I sorry, sir," she breathed. "For one moment, I was overcome wit grief."

The mortician touched her on the shoulder, a practiced move: sympathetic yet unintrusive. "I understand. This is a difficult time for the ones left behind." He glanced at my mother. "She was a beautiful woman," he said, then, looking back at Auntie Reno, added, "Your sister?"

I snorted, and Reno fluttered her eyes. "Jus' like. I dah one help her when she first move to Hawaii. I dah one gamble on her, give her her first job." She raised her voice and, turning her face from the mortician to give me stink-eye, said, "I dah one manage her business, take care her daughtah when she was, ah, feeling indispose."

I forced a laugh. "Thank God for Auntie Reno," I crooned into Reno's scowl. "What would we have ever done without her?"

"You bettah believe it, sistah," Reno spat.

The mortician lifted his hand in my direction, placing it tentatively between Reno and me. "Uh, you must be Ms. Bradley, daughter of the deceased."

I ignored him. "Oh, I believe it, Reno. And what would you have done without my mother? Without all the money she made for you? How could you have made all those gambling trips? How could you have sent all your own kids to Punahou—at least until they got kicked out?"

Reno slapped the mortician's arm down and narrowed her eyes. "What exactly you tryin' for say?"

The man inched toward the door. "Eh, Frank! Frank," he called toward the front room.

I glared at him. "Do you mind? We're trying to have a private conversation."

Reno pushed at my shoulder. "Eh, no take it out on him, he's jus' doing his job." She narrowed her eyes at me. "Unlike *some* people, leaving dah dirty work for others."

The mortician backed against the door. "Frank, I said, try come," he shouted, his job English fraying under stress. "Please! Dis only my first week, and look, get one 911 in here!"

Reno bustled over to the man. "Hush you, boy," she clucked, patting his hands. "No worry 'bout us. We jus' havin' one difference of opinion." She smiled. "You was saying?"

The man rubbed his hands across the thighs of his pants. "No, really," he said, pasting a smile across his face. "I nevah said—I wasn't saying anything. In fact, uh, if you'd please excuse me, ladies, I, uh, should check on the arrangements for the next group."

When Reno moved toward him, saying, "No need go; we finished here," I grabbed at her arm. The man escaped.

"Reno," I said. "We are not finished."

"Den what?" Reno yelled. "I wen ask you before: Whass your friggin' problem?"

"And I told you, Auntie Reno. It's you," I said. "You my

friggin' problem." I stretched toward my mother's head, snapped the feather off the hat, and waved it in front of Reno's face, where it dangled at an angle like a furry finger. "Ever since I met you, you used us. Used my mother, treated her just like a puppet on your string. I watched you over the years, saw how you got when she went into her trance—like every minute was gonna make you richer and richer. And it did, didn't it? Never mind that she might not have come back to us each time. You never cared about her. Or me, either. Just about what was in it for you!"

Reno reached for the feather, but I jerked it from her hands before she could touch it. "Thass not true," she protested. "Outta the goodness of my heart, I—"

A laugh, hot and harsh, melted my throat. "Cut the crap, Reno. It's me you're talkin' to. Not my mother. I know you made a ton of money off us."

"Now listen, honey—"

"Don't call me that!" I shouted. "How dare you call me that, like we're so close, when you never invited me even once into your home!" I threw the feather at her. It fluttered, then drifted into the coffin between us.

Reno dropped her chin. "I sorry," she whispered, her lids flickering as her eyes tracked the feather. "I nevah even tink. I jus' figgah I always see you at your maddah's. But you know, you nevah wen ask, either. . . ."

I shrugged. "Whatevahs." I felt drained suddenly, numb. I sank into a folding chair set up next to my mother's coffin and leaned my forehead against the black lacquered wood. "Whatevahs, Reno. I'm tired. I don't care anymore. Keep everything," I whispered. "The money doesn't matter to me. You're the only person I got left, and I can't even trust you."

"Beccah," Reno said, settling her body onto the seat next to mine. "If your maddah wasn't laying dead in front of us right now,

so help me God, I slap your head jus' for tinking what you tinking."
She raised her arm, as if to put it around my shoulders, hesitated,
then let it drop back to her side. "You was her daughter, dah one
come from her own body. But you nevah know shit about her,
did you?"

Reno grabbed my shoulder. I tried to shrug her away, but she
pushed down, tightening her grip. "Get up," she said, using me to
lever herself up. Then she pulled at me until I stood. "And look. Try
really look at your maddah."

I looked into the coffin once again, surprised when a tear fell
from my face onto my mother's, splattering against a Maybelline-
bronzed cheekbone.

"Dis what I see," Reno said. "One tough woman. You tink she
so out of it all the time, Beccah? Dat she so lolo I can jus' steal her
money—not dat I would, mine you—an' she not goin' know it?"

I wiped the back of my hand across my eyes.

"If you tink dat, den you dah one dat's lolo." Reno leaned over
and placed a palm against my mother's cheek, moved her thumb to
blot a smudge of lipstick. "I tell you, your maddah knew me like no
one else. Dat was her gift. She would look into a person's heart and
know em—their heartache, their weakness, whatevah. Because she
knew suffahrin' like I no can even imagine."

"Reno," I asked, interrupting, "what did you know about—"

Reno threw her hands into the air. "Eh, no ack up wit me
again, girlie," she said, misunderstanding my question. "I telling
you I know what I know. Your maddah was one survivah. Das how
come she can read other people. Das how come she can see their
wishes and their fears. Das how come she can travel out of dis world
into hell, cause she already been there and back and know the way.

"An' I tell you someting else," Reno said, prodding me in the
chest bone with her pointing finger, "before you disrespect me or
your maddah again. She knew what it was like for be one orphan,

having to beg for everyting, every scrap of food or whatevah. She no want you to know dat feelin', like you all alone, no one to turn to. She love you more dan anyting in dis world. So she take care you."

Reno grabbed my hand, and when I didn't pull away, she stroked it, rubbing my fingers between her own.

"I don' know if you know dis," Reno said, "but dat Manoa house yours, free and clear."

I twisted my neck to look at her, searching her face.

"Yeah, for real." Reno smiled. "Your maddah smart enough for buy em outright, jus' before dat big Japanee real estate boom. I tell you, she made one killin' on dat house."

I jerked my hand from hers. "I'm sure that made you happy. You must've made a nice commission."

Reno clicked her tongue against her teeth. "Stupid, why you no lissen? I tol' you dat was before the market wen skyrocket; dah commission was manini."

"I bet. Compared to what you were used to making off her trances," I sneered, unwilling to give in and forgive.

Reno ignored me. "I'm telling you, your maddah was so sharp. You know she save all her money for you? She knew exactly what she made, down to dah last cent in dah Wishing Bowl. She even know wen you wen sneak money for school lunch, field trip, stuff li' dat."

My mouth must have dropped open, because Reno laughed. "You nevah know, eh?" she said. "I tell you, my Vegas and Nevada was dah same way. You kids always tinkin' you can fool wit your maddahs." She shook her head, her smile slipping. "No one could fool your maddah. She told me for set up one special account in your name. Check me every week too, cause dat's how good she know me. My strengt' and my weakness too."

Reno waddled over to the makeup bag she had propped against the table supporting my mother's coffin and pulled out a square of linen. She rolled one end into a sharp point, then dabbed it into the corners of her eyes. She blew her nose, then sniffed. When she turned toward me again, her nose was red, the foundation rubbed away from the tip.

"Who you see?" Reno asked, gesturing toward my mother.

"My mom," I said, without looking, without thinking. Then: "I don't know."

Reno shook her head. "You better tink long and hard, Beccah. Den you better look again."

Laid out in death, my mother looked shriveled, barely big enough to fill the coffin. I don't remember her looking so old; she was fixed in my mind's eye as a middle-aged woman. I must have stopped seeing my mother when I reached intermediate school. In Reno's flashy clothes and dramatic makeup, my mother looked like an old lady pretending at youth.

"Reno, I don't mean to reject what you've done," I ventured. "But this isn't right. This isn't how I knew her or want to remember her. Not with the makeup and the fancy gown. Not with all the people paying money to see some kind of final performance, to gawk at her one last time." I traced a finger over the crow's-feet beside my mother's lavender-dusted eyes, surprised at how smooth she felt, how soft.

"I think we should cremate her," I said, unable to look up and face Reno's anger or disappointment. "Then I want to do something private, for just her and me, maybe, if you don't mind."

I waited, my head bowed, fingers gripping the edge of the coffin, for Reno's screams of outrage, her accusations of ingratitude. I waited, my neck growing stiff, my fingers tight and cramped, until Reno cupped my chin, lifting my face. She smoothed my bangs, tucking them behind my ears in the way my mother had done when I was a child. "Do whatchu gotta do," she said. "She your maddah."

I closed my eyes, leaning into the fingers that felt like my mother's. "What about the big ceremony you've been planning?" I whispered. "What about all the gifts and money? You don't mind canceling?"

Reno combed my hair with her fingers, tickled my ears with her nails. Then, taking a deep breath, she said, "I ain't canceling. *I* goin' do what I gotta do, too. I still her friend and business managah."

I jumped away from her, opened my mouth to yell, when she held up her hands. "Try wait, try wait," she said. "Lissen: your maddah no need even be here. I jus' goin' hold one closed-casket ceremony. No one goin' know 'cept me an' you an' her."

"Oh my God," I said. "That's too much even for you. You can't."

"I got to," Reno said. "Dis for her other self, dah one she showed to people. You know, Beccah, she was one business woman too. One performah." She shrugged. "An' I already wen complete the obit, so no worry. Dah undahtakah sent em to dah papahs, goin' come out today."

She wiggled her eyebrows. "By the way, whatchu tink of dah guy? Kinda cute, eh? Dat ehu hair, hapa-lookin' face, mmm-hmm." Reno smacked her lips. "Not like one undahtakah at all. More like one shoe salesman at Liberty House, one upscale one. I already wen ask, too. He available."

"Don't change the subject," I groaned. "Besides, what did I tell you about matchmaking?"

"Yeah, yeah, I know," Reno said. "You not interested." She sighed. "Too bad you one mahu."

"I'm not!" I laughed, feeling boxed into a corner. "I like men, okay!" I choked, shocking myself by saying that in front of my mother, even though she was dead.

Reno patted my head. "Yeah, yeah, if you say so. Sex is fun no mattah how you slice em. But I got for tell you, it also means you gotta care, take some responsibility for dah other guy and for yourself too." She held up her hand. "I know, I know how you young folks are—Vegas talk like you too. No like strings attached—shit, whass dat? No strings? Dah world no work dat way, girl. Dis world ain't nothin' but strings.

"Besides," she added, bending over the coffin, "I was talkin' for myself. Whatchu tink—me an' dah mortuary man?" She plucked the feather from my mother's chest, then waved it at me, flirting.

I smiled though my throat burned. "Go for it, Auntie," I croaked.

Reno handed me the purple plume, then unraveled her hand-kerchief. "Now you talkin'," she said. She dabbed at the makeup under her eyes, wiping away the smeared mascara. Then, wrapping a clean part of the cloth around her fingers, she licked it. And without looking up at me, she bent over the coffin to rub the makeup off my mother. Lick by lick, gentle and diligent as a mother cat, Auntie Reno cleaned my mother's face.

• ➤

When I returned to prepare my mother's body, the mortician led me into a room resembling a kitchenette. She had been taken out of the display casket and repositioned on what looked like a tall metal picnic table. Her dress had slipped off one shoulder and hung down her arm; I could see where bits of the masking tape Reno had used to tighten and secure it in the back had loosened and let go.

"If you need help with anything," the mortician said, "like turning her, or anything, just let me know. They can be pretty heavy. Dead weight, yeah."

I chuckled. "You must get a lot of jokes like that."

"Huh?" he said, frowning.

I cleared my throat and bit my tongue. Afraid I would laugh if I looked into his puzzled face, I pawed through my satchel. I unpacked my mother's ceramic offering bowls, strips of linen cut from the bedsheet I had written on when I listened to her tapes, and flowers from the garden —ginger, ʻuki ʻuki, hibiscus, honeysuckle— and when I looked up, the mortician was gone.

I filled the bowls with water, placing them on the long table next to my mother. "Hi, Mommy," I said, my voice cracking. "I don't know if I'm doing this right, but . . ."

I unpinned the hat, the feathered lavender stem protruding like a broken bone, and uncoiled her hair so that it hung over the top of the table. Brushing until the ends of her hair whipped around my arm like a living thing, I began to sing.

"I remember," I sang without knowing the words. "Omoni, I remember the care. Of the living and the dead." I gathered the strands pulled free from her scalp, then packed them into a small drawstring pouch once used to hold jewelry. "I will care for your body as your spirit crosses the river. I will stand guard. I will send you on your way."

Untangling vines of honeysuckle from the bouquets of ginger and ʻuki ʻuki flowers, I curled them whole into the water bowl. "A rope of scent, Omoni, purity and light. Hold tight and I will guide you past Saja in Kasi Mun," I sang out. "And if you fall, if he lures you into hell, wrap the vines around you, and I will be your Princess Pari, pulling you through. *Pururun mul, Kang-muldo mot midu-riroda . . . Moot saram-ui seulpumdo hulro hulro sa ganora.*"

I floated whole hibiscus into the bowl and tore the delicate flesh of the white ginger and ʻuki ʻuki, sprinkling them into the water as well. "Mugunghwa for courage and independence, Omoni. And for Korea. I remember. I remember. Ginger and lily for purity and rebirth. I know."

When the blossoms, saturated, sank to the bottom of the bowl, I dipped a strip of linen into the water. Ink-black spider legs, fragile and minute as cracks in glazed porcelain, wiggled out from the words I had scribbled on the material. I touched the ink, and when my finger came away clean, I touched my mother's eyelids and her cheeks, dipping her in blessed water. I rinsed the strip in the bowl of water, wrung it dry, and blotted her lips. "This is for your name, Omoni, so you can speak it true: Soon Hyo. Soon Hyo. Soon Hyo."

I unbuttoned and untaped the gown and tried to wrestle her arms out of it. When I started to sweat, I cut it off her, letting it hang in tatters along her sides. My mother lay naked under her dress, in the body that had always embarrassed me both in its foreignness and in its similarity to mine. I looked now, fighting my shame, taking her body piece by piece—her face, her arms, her legs, working in a spiral toward the center—until I could see her in her entirety, without guilt or judgment.

I fit one of my hands against my mother's, palm to palm, fingertip to fingertip, mirror images. I remembered as a child I coveted my mother's jewelry, especially her rings, and wished my fingers would grow so that I could wear them. I'd pull on them, exercise them with finger flexes, measure them. And somehow, without my marking the exact day, without my even noticing until now, my hand had become my mother's.

"I will massage your arms with perfumed water blessed by the running river. I will massage your legs until they are strong enough to swim you to heaven." I cleaned and cut her nails and placed the cuttings in the drawstring bag. I pushed the bag under her, let her weight settle over my hand before I eased away. "See?" I said. "Your spirit can travel without worrying about what is left behind."

After I washed her, I shook out the damp strips of cloth and, one by one, draped them over the length of her body, wrapped her arms and legs. Her words, coiled tightly in my script, tied her spirit to her body and bound her to this life. When they burned, they would travel with her across the waters, free.

I heard that the ceremony Reno held for my mother in the mortuary chapel was standing room only. The Borthwick chaplain and the Buddhist priest delayed their joint service, helping to place extra folding chairs in the aisles and in the entryway, and still people crammed shoulder-to-shoulder in the doorways.

"So touching," Reno said, dabbing her folded handkerchief against her eyes. "Lot of people wanted to pay their respects to your maddah. Even Mrs. Pyle—you know dah one you used to call Ol' Lady Pilau cause her stink halitosis?—said a few words, though she was all habut at your maddah cause your ma wen tell her her stink-breat' no go away until she stop talkin' stink about everybody else. And still she no learn," Reno said, waving a hand in front of her nose. "Could smell that woman from outside dah door. Hooey!

"An' of course, everybody in dah business was there: Mr. Lee from the Good Fortune and Prosperity store, Reverend Hwang from dah Palolo temple, even dat oddah fortune-teller, dah Laotian one in Kaimuki, she came. Was one good turnout." Reno sighed and patted her belly, as if she had just feasted on a good meal.

"So, Reno," I asked, "nobody knew? Nobody asked to see her one last time?"

Reno scowled. "Whatchu tinking? Dis one funeral. People get mannahs, you know. Most dey did was kiss the coffin lid, bow coupla times in front dah picture I put on top. Get one, though, wen trow herself on top the coffin, crying louder dan one cat. Geez, I no even know who she was, too."

And on their way out of the chapel, all of the mourners showed how much they loved my mother and the daughter most didn't even remember she had. In her memory, they dropped envelopes stuffed with money and miniature frogs into the Wishing Bowl for the family she left behind, for a final blessing.

•～

I had picked up my mother's ashes the morning of Reno's ceremony. After flipping through an album filled with pictures of urns
offered by Borthwick—from the elite faux-marble canister to the
Borthwick basic, which sold for seventy-five dollars and looked like
a plastic candy jar with a screw-top lid—I decided I would bring
my own container. I emptied out one of the drawers in her jewelry
box, scattering ropes of necklaces, fistfuls of gold and jade charms,
rings. I sifted through the rings until I found one that I had especially pined for as a girl—a braided gold band studded with pearls
that my mother called "ocean tears"—and slipped it onto my wedding finger.

•～

When I presented the drawer from the jewelry box, expecting the
mortician to fill it with my mother's ashes, his mouth dropped
open. "Ah, ahh, umm," he stammered.

"I know this is unusual and it doesn't have a lid, but look,"
I said, waving a box of Saran Wrap at him. "Just cover the top
with this."

"No, well, you see," the mortician said. He took the Saran
Wrap I thrust into his belly and stared at it, then at me. He hadn't
gelled his hair back, as he had the last time I saw him, and the sun-
bleached tips dipped into his eyes. He shook his head. "You don't
understand."

"It's just temporary," I snapped, thinking he wanted to try to
sell me one of his urns. "I plan to scatter the ashes."

"It's not that," he said. "It's, well, it's too small to hold everything. Try wait. I'll get her; you'll see what I mean." The mortician
walked to a display cabinet and selected a squat black vase.

I swallowed and shoved the drawer and the plastic wrap into
my bag before he returned. The mortician slid the vase onto the

counter between us, and when he lifted the lid, I could see that the urn was filled with ashes. More ashes than I thought there would be. Gray soot flecked with bone and silver.

"Fillings," the mortician said, almost apologetically, when he noticed me staring at the bright specks.

I started to cry, thinking there was more to a body than there should be, and less.

"Don't worry, no worry," he said, sounding worried himself. "I take care you. Wait, wait, okay? You can have one, watchucall, complimentary urn." He bent down to open one of the counter's drawers and stood up, popping open a fold-out gift box like the ones on sale at Longs or Payless for a dollar fifty.

•➤

About to sprinkle my mother's ashes in the garden behind our house, I heard the song of the river. The music had always seemed faint to me, but now it drummed in my ears. I carried my mother through the break in the fence and traveled the path we took the year she blessed my wandering spirit.

I stepped into the stream, letting the water bite through my shoes, the cuffs of my jeans, with its cold teeth. Bending down, I cupped a handful of my mother's river and held it over her box of ashes. "Mommy," I said as the water dribbled through my fingers. "Omoni, please drink. Share this meal with me, a sip to know how much I love you."

I opened my mother's box, sprinkling her ashes over the water. I held my fingers under the slow fall of ash, sifting, letting it coat my hand. I touched my fingers to my lips. "Your body in mine," I told my mother, "so you will always be with me, even when your spirit finds its way home. To Korea. To Sulsulham. And across the river of heaven to the Seven Sisters."

•➤

Later that night, I stepped into water again. In my dreams, I swam a deep river, trying to reach the far shore, where my mother danced around a ribbon of red. I swam for hours, for weeks, for years, and when I became too tired to swim any longer, I felt the pull on my legs. I struggled, flailing weak kicks, but when I turned and saw that it was my mother hanging on to me, I yielded. I opened my mouth to drown, expecting to suck in heavy water, but instead I breathed in air, clear and blue. Instead of ocean, I swam through sky, higher and higher, until, dizzy with the freedom of light and air, I looked down to see a thin blue river of light spiraling down to earth, where I lay sleeping in bed, coiled tight around a small seed planted by my mother, waiting to be born.

ACKNOWLEDGMENTS

My love and thanks to the following people who helped make this book a reality:

My mother, Tae Im Beane, for her stories, true or not.

My sister, Dawn Myung Ja Chamness, and her friends who had a good time correcting my Korean.

The Bamboo Ridge Study Group, for helping me see the novel in a short story.

Cohorts Cathy Song, Juliet S. Kono, and especially Lois Ann Yamanaka for advice and inspiration on matters both professional and personal.

Leslie Bow, Elena Tajima Creef, and Laura Hyun Yi Kang for their sharp, savvy, and fast responses that helped pull everything together.

Alice Chai and Elaine Kim for their scholarship and activism in Korean and Korean American communities.

Keum Ja Hwang for speaking out.

Youngsook Kim Harvey for her research on Korean shamans, including her book *Six Korean Women*.

Susan Bergholz for keeping an eye on the small details and the big picture.

Kathryn Court and Beena Kamlani for their intensive readings and necessary tweaks.

My husband Jim, for his steadfast support and determined love, through the highs and the lows and always.

A PENGUIN READERS GUIDE TO

COMFORT
WOMAN

Nora Okja Keller

INTRODUCTION

Comfort Woman

In *Comfort Woman*, Nora Okja Keller tells the devastating story of Akiko, a young Korean woman who was sold into prostitution in the Japanese "recreation camps" of World War II, and Beccah, her daughter by an American missionary. Throughout the novel, Keller explores the legacy of Akiko's pain, the manner in which she represses the wounds of her past, and its splintering effect on her relationship with Beccah.

Desperate to escape the scene of her torture, Akiko marries someone she does not love—an American missionary who takes her away from Japan, but mistakes her silence for devotion, and neither understands nor properly cares for her. Soon, she gives birth to Beccah, the child that she loves passionately, but to whom she will never reveal her traumatic past. As the novel unfolds, the two women are living in Honolulu, where Beccah must fend for herself when her "crazy" mother slips into trances, communicating with spirits of the dead. Akiko and Beccah are mother and daughter, but they have traded the roles of nurturer and nurtured. They speak the same two languages yet rarely communicate their true feelings. Akiko buries her pain, a choice that keeps her from enjoying a fully loving relationship with Beccah. In turn, Beccah resents her mother and isolates herself—so much so that while she spends her days writing the obituaries of strangers, she feels little when the time comes to measure the value of her own mother's life.

What are the consequences of a life filled with secrets and repression? The spirit world becomes Akiko's sanctuary, her ticket to survival. She escapes pain through her trances and, ultimately, through her death. As a result, Beccah must create her own rules for living and for loving, recognizing and translating the other gifts that her mother has left behind. By deciphering the foreign words uttered in the tape recordings that hold the key to her heritage, by preparing her mother's dead body for a new life in the spirit world, and by learning the truth of her mother's past, Beccah can move toward the future.

AUTHOR QUESTIONS

Fortunately for us, there has been a surge of Asian-American writing in this country, especially by women authors. Why do you think this is? How does your heritage as a Korean-American set you apart from writers of Japanese, Chinese, Filipino, or Vietnamese descent?

Whenever I get a question that asks me to speak outside of myself, to speak authoritatively on historical and sociological issues, my first response is "How should I know?"

I don't have the proper perspective to say, definitively, this is how being a Korean-American woman is different from being Vietnamese or Filipino or Polish or French or whatever. I can only speak from this one body, this one mind, this one life's experiences.

But I do recognize that I am writing in a time that is more receptive to various voices than ever before. In the seventies, the big name in Asian-American literature was Maxine Hong Kingston. (What a gift *The Woman Warrior*, the first book I had ever read by an Asian-American writer, was to me; I began to realize I didn't have to hide my ethnicity in order to become a writer.)

And the eighties were dominated by Amy Tan. The nice thing, the important thing, about the nineties is that there is no one writer that has become the tokenized "It" for Asian-American literature. Kingston and Tan helped push the door open for a new generation of Asian-American writers, both male and female.

Also, there are more Asian-American writers writing now because, generationally speaking, it is a matter of time. The majority of Asian-Americans currently writing are second- and third-generation. Writing is a luxury that is not often an option for the first-generation immigrants. It's something that comes after food is put on the table; it comes after there is a home in which to put the table. My mother, who came to America in the sixties and raised five children here alone, never wished for me to become an artist. Like many immigrant parents, she was worried about her children's security in this new country. She wanted me to be an X-ray technician or a dental hygienist ("They make steady money—Americans are always breaking bones and cleaning their teeth") so I'd always be able to eat.

Growing up in Hawaii you must have been exposed to a wide variety of races and racial blends. How do you think your life in Hawaii shaped your experiences as an Asian-American and as a writer?

I used to think that I could live anywhere, that place didn't matter because I could adapt, find a niche in any community. But I think that type of arrogance was born from the fact that I grew up secure and accepted in Hawai'i. There are not many other places in the United States where a child who was half Korean and half German could have blended in. Being *hapa,* the Hawaiian term for mixed-race, was not just considered normal, but was celebrated. I had single-race friends say that when they grew up, one of their goals was to have *hapa* children. The funny thing is, I never considered that a strange thing for them to say.

It also wasn't strange to see people of different races loving each other and hating each other, even in the same family. That's just the way it is in Hawai'i. It's a small place where the differences between people have a tendency to seem petty and small next to the overwhelming richness of the land, which has its own stories and personalities and life.

And as a writer, I've been nurtured by the people from Bamboo Ridge, a press that for twenty years has been dedicated to publishing writers from Hawai'i. I love these guys and the time we spend together. Every month we meet to discuss writing, books, and I have learned not just about things like narrative structure and plot, but about life and generosity of spirit.

Your novel is based on historical fact, and on a chapter in history that few people seem to be aware of. Obviously you felt some responsibility to get the facts out about what happened to these Korean women during the Second World War. Did this responsibility ever feel like a burden? Did the facts ever get in the way of the fiction you wanted to write?

I first heard about "comfort women" in 1993. Keum Ju Hwang, a woman who survived the comfort camps of World War II, was speaking at several American universities in order to "bear witness," to bring to light this chapter in history.

At that time, there was very little information about comfort women available in English. I contacted one of the professors who helped bring Hwang to the University of Hawai'i—Alica Chai—and she was able to provide me with some documents and essays that she had translated from Korean.

With these documents, I had facts—proof that the camps existed, that hundreds of thousands of women were forced into prostitution there—but I had very little detail, very little personal testimony, about what it was actually like for the women in these camps. I had to imagine their daily lives, their physical and emotional anguish, the aftermath. Taking that leap was scary, and quite often I tried to resist it by postponing writing certain sections for weeks.

Spirits play an important role in your novel—but they're not commonly a part of American cultural life. Can you tell us a little about the role spirits play in everyday Korean life? Would it be unusual for a young girl to find her mother setting out offerings for various spirits in order to ensure her well-being?

Again, I'm not an expert, an authority on daily Korean life. I don't know about the "typical" Korean household, but mine was infested with ghosts. To name a few: There was my aunt who died in toddlerhood and somehow we children took to leaving offerings of candy for her spirit. Another ghost followed my sister home from school one day—it must have been a disruptive student in life; we'd sometimes hear that one running up and down the stairs in the middle of the night. And there was my mother's ex-husband, who was killed by a drunk taxi driver in Pusan, and also my grandparents, for whose thirsty spirits my mother set out bowls of water. Those were the ghosts particular to my family, but there were also larger spirits, such as the Birth Grandmother, prominent in Korea's shamanic tradition. From what I understand, shamanism is still very much alive and relevant in Korea, so much so that there is a waiting list of a year and a half to consult the best shamans.

Dreams figure prominently in the lives of your characters. Did they play a role in the writing of this book?

Yes. I often tell people that my dreams were haunted after I attended the lecture given by Hwang. Throughout the writing of this book, my dreams were filled with images of war and women, of blood and birth. And the only way I could exorcise these images was through writing.

You have said that when you were younger you felt "embarrassed and alienated" from things that were Korean. How have your own experiences affected the ways you will teach your daughter about her ethnic heritage?

I didn't want to be Korean when I was a teenager. Koreans were my uncle and mother, fresh off the boat, smelling like garlic, talking with tongues thick with accent or in a gutturally fast, spit-flying *foreign* language. I wanted to be American.

So I pretended I couldn't understand what they said. I ignored them, and also part of who I was. I know I hurt my mother. I knew it then and I know it more so now, when I am a mother myself.

My writing, through which I both explore and reclaim my ethnic heritage, is also an apology to my mother and family for my adolescent shame; it is easier to write "I'm sorry" than to say it.

There is a certain rightness, a joy and a satisfaction, when I hear my older daughter define herself as Korean, when she begs my mother to speak to her in Korean, the language of her grandmother's stories.

A few years ago, thinking about some of these same issues, I wrote an essay called "My Mother's Food." What follows is an excerpt.

A Bite of Kimchee

I became shamed by kimchee, by the shocking red-stained leaves that peeked out from between the loaf of white bread and carton of milk, by the stunning odor that, as I grew to realize, permeated the entire house despite strategically placed cartons of baking soda. When friends I invited to my home pointed at the kimchee jars lined up on the refrigerator shelves, squealing, "Gross! What's that?" I'd mumble, "I don't know, something my mom eats."

Along with kimchee, I stopped eating the only three dishes my mother could cook: kalbi ribs, bi bim kooksoo, and Spam fried with eggs. (The first "American" food my mother ever ate was a Spam-and-egg sandwich; even now, she considers it one of her favorite foods and never gets tired of eating it. At one time in our lives, Spam was a staple. We ate it every day.)

I told my mother I was a vegetarian.

One of my sisters ate only McDonald's Happy Meal cheeseburgers (no pickle), and the other survived for two years on a diet of processed-cheese sandwiches on white bread, Hostess Ding

Dongs, and rice dunked in ketchup.

"How can you do this to me?" my mother wailed at her American-born children. "You are wasting away! Eat, eat!" My mother plopped helpings of kimchee and kalbi onto mounds of steaming rice. My sisters and I would grimace, poke at the food and announce: "Too fattening."

When we were small, my mother encouraged us to behave like proper Korean girls: quiet, respectful, hardworking. She said we gave her "heartaches" the way we fought and wrestled as children. "Worse than boys," she used to say. "Why do you want to do things like soccer, scuba, swimming? How about piano?"

But worse than our tomboy activities were our various adolescent diets. My mother grieved at the food we rejected. "I don't understand you girls," she'd say. "When I was growing up, my family was so poor we could only dream of eating this kind of food. Now I can give my children meat every night and you don't want it."

"Yeah, yeah, yeah," we'd say as we pushed away the kimchee, pushed away the Korean-ness.

We pushed my mother, too, so much so she ended up leaving Hawai'i. After she moved away, wanting to travel and explore the America she had once—as a new bride barraged with foreign language, customs, foods—been intimidated by, I ate kimchee only sporadically. I could go for months without a taste, then suddenly be hit with a craving so strong I ran to Sack-n-Save for a generic, watery brand that only hinted at the taste of home. Kimchee, I realized, was my comfort food.

When I became pregnant, the craving for my own mother accentuated my craving for kimchee. During the nights of my final trimester, my body foreign and heavy, restless with longing, I hungered for the food I myself had eaten in the womb, my first mother-memory.

The baby I carried in my body, in turn, does not look like me. Except for the slight tilt of her eyes, she does not look Korean.

As a mother totally in love with her daughter, I do not care what she looks like; she is perfect as herself. Yet, as a mother totally in love with her daughter, I worry that—partially because of what she looks like—she will not be able to identify with the Korean in me, and in herself. I recognize that identifying herself as Korean, even in part, will be a choice for her—in a way it wasn't for someone like me, someone recognizably Asian. It hit me then, what my own mother must have felt looking at each of her own mixed-race daughters: how strongly I do identify as a Korean-American woman, how strongly I want my child to identify with me.

Kimchee is an easily consumable representation of culture, digested and integrated by the body and hopefully—if we are to believe the lesson "You are what you eat" that episodes of "Mulligan Stew" taught us in elementary school—by the soul as well.

When my daughter was fifteen months old, she took her first bite of kimchee. I had taken a small bite in my own mouth, sucking the hot juice from its leaves, giving it "mother-taste" as my own mother had done for me. Still, my daughter's eyes watered. "Hot, hot," she said to her grandmother and me. But the taste must have been in some way familiar; instead of spitting up and crying for water, she pushed my hand to the open jar for another bite.

"She likes it," my mother said proudly. "She is Korean!"

When she told me this, I realized that for my mother, too, the food we ate growing up had always been an indication of how Korean her "mixed-blood" children were—or weren't—at any given time. I remember hew intently she watched us eat, as if to catch a glimpse of herself as we chewed. "Eat, eat. Have some more," she'd say, urging us to take another serving of kimchee, kalbi, seaweed soup, the food that was linked to Korea and to herself.

Now my mother watches the next generation. When she visits, my daughter cleaves to her, follows her from room to room. Grandmother and granddaughter run off together to play the games that only they know how to play. I can hear them in my daughter's room, chattering and laughing. Sneaking to the doorway, I see them "cooking" plastic food in the Playskool kitchen.

"Look," my mother says, offering her grandchild a plate of plastic spaghetti, "noodles is kooksoo." She picks up steak. "This kalbi." My mother is teaching her Korean, presenting words my daughter knows the taste of.

My girl joins the game, picking up a soft head of cabbage. "Let's make kimchee, *Halmoni*," she says, using the Korean word for "grandmother" like a name.

"Okay," my mother answers. "First salt."

My daughter shakes invisible salt over the cabbage.

"Then garlic and red pepper sauce." My mother stirs a pot over the stove and passes the mixture to my daughter, who pours it on the cabbage.

My daughter brings her fingers to her mouth. "Hot!" she says. Then she grabs the green plastic in her fist, holds the cabbage to my mother's lips, and gives her *halmoni* a taste.

"Mmmmm!" My mother grins as she chews the air. "Delicious! This is the best kimchee I ever ate." My mother sees me peeking around the door.

"Come join us," she calls out to me, and tells my daughter, who really is gnawing at the fake food, "Let your mommy have a bite."

QUESTIONS FOR DISCUSSION

1. Do you think that Akiko is "crazy"? Did she possess special powers? When Reno says, "Das how come she can read other people. Das how come she can see their wishes and their fears. Das how come she can travel out of dis world into hell, cause she already been there and back and know the way," is she making a connection between the psychological trauma Akiko suffered as a result of her experiences as a comfort woman and her ability to communicate with spirits?

2. Both Akiko and Beccah seem to lead double lives. Akiko is torn between the spirit world and the world she occupies as a working single mother and Beccah between her life as an American teenager and as a person of Korean descent. How else is the theme of identity woven throughout the novel? Does either woman ever discover who she really is?

3. Why do you think Akiko keeps the truth about her past a secret from Beccah? How did this secret affect their relationship? How might it have changed their relationship had Akiko revealed the secret while she was alive?

4. There is so much tension between Akiko and Beccah, it's hard to detect the love that they share. How is theirs a typical mother daughter relationship? How are the normal conflicts that flare up between mothers and their—especially adolescent—daughters made more complicated in Akiko and Beccah's relationship?

5. Why do you think Akiko clings to her Japanese name—assigned to her in the army camp—instead of reclaiming her Korean name, Soon Hyo? What is significant about the fact that we don't learn of this Korean name until near the novel's ending?

6. Keller has set her novel in Hawaii, a place that is foreign to many Americans who associate it with images of pristine beaches and tropical delights. How is Keller's Hawaii different from these clichéd images? What did you learn from her portrayal of this state that has its own dialect and richly varied culture?

7. Discuss the character of Auntie Reno. Is she a real friend to Akiko and Beccah? Does she take advantage of Akiko's vulnerability? What does she teach Beccah about her mother? How does she represent the clashing of cultures that is so prevalent in Hawaii?

8. Water, especially water that flows in rivers, is a recurring motif in the novel. What does it represent in Beccah's memories, and in her passage from youth to adulthood? What role does water play in Akiko's memories? Why do you think Beccah chooses to scatter her mother's ashes in the river behind their home?

9. What do you think of the novel's alternating narrative voices? Why do you think Keller chose to structure her novel this way? What are the advantages of knowing Akiko's story before Beccah learns it? Whom do you think we get to know better: Beccah or Akiko?

10. The term "comfort woman" is painfully ironic given the agonies endured by Akiko and the other women forced into prostitution by Japanese soldiers. How does Keller extend the irony of this term throughout the novel? To what extent are Beccah and Akiko uncomfortable? How are their lives devoid of comfort? And how does each learn, ultimately, to be a comfort to—and derive comfort from—the other?

NORA OKJA KELLER was born in Seoul, Korea, and now lives in Hawaii with her husband and two daughters. In 1995 she received the Pushcart Prize for "Mother Tongue," a short story that is a part of *Comfort Woman.* In 1998 she received the American Book Award, and in 1999 the Elliot Cades Award for Literature. She is currently working on her second novel.

For more information about other Penguin Readers Guides, please call the Penguin Marketing Department at (800) 778-6425, E-mail at reading@penguinputnam.com, or write to us at:
Penguin Books Marketing Department CC
Readers Guides
375 Hudson Street
New York, NY 10014-3657

Please allow 4–6 weeks for delivery.
For a complete list of Penguin Readers Guides that are available on-line, visit Club PPI on our Web site at:
http://www.penguinputnam.com

Also from Nora Okja Keller

Fox Girl

Set in the aftermath of the Korean War, *Fox Girl* gives a powerful voice to the abandoned children of American GIs. Hyung Jin, "fox girl," is disowned by her parents, but finds kinship in her fellow outcasts Sookie, a teenage prostitute kept by an American soldier, and Lobetto, who makes his living off the streets by pimping and running errands. Shunned by society, they dream of an American ideal that they will do anything to attain. *Fox Girl* is at once a rare portrait of the long-term consequences of a neglected aspect of war and a moving story of the fierce love between a mother and her daughter that will ultimately redeem Hyung Jin's life in America.

ISBN 0-14-200196-1

FOR THE BEST IN PAPERBACKS, LOOK FOR THE

In every corner of the world, on every subject under the sun, Penguin represents quality and variety—the very best in publishing today.

For complete information about books available from Penguin—including Penguin Classics, Penguin Compass, and Puffins—and how to order them, write to us at the appropriate address below. Please note that for copyright reasons the selection of books varies from country to country.

In the United States: Please write to *Penguin Group (USA), P.O. Box 12289 Dept. B, Newark, New Jersey 07101-5289* or call 1-800-788-6262.

In the United Kingdom: Please write to *Dept. EP, Penguin Books Ltd, Bath Road, Harmondsworth, West Drayton, Middlesex UB7 0DA.*

In Canada: Please write to *Penguin Books Canada Ltd, 10 Alcorn Avenue, Suite 300, Toronto, Ontario M4V 3B2.*

In Australia: Please write to *Penguin Books Australia Ltd, P.O. Box 257, Ringwood, Victoria 3134.*

In New Zealand: Please write to *Penguin Books (NZ) Ltd, Private Bag 102902, North Shore Mail Centre, Auckland 10.*

In India: Please write to *Penguin Books India Pvt Ltd, 11 Panchsheel Shopping Centre, Panchsheel Park, New Delhi 110 017.*

In the Netherlands: Please write to *Penguin Books Netherlands bv, Postbus 3507, NL-1001 AH Amsterdam.*

In Germany: Please write to *Penguin Books Deutschland GmbH, Metzlerstrasse 26, 60594 Frankfurt am Main.*

In Spain: Please write to *Penguin Books S. A., Bravo Murillo 19, 1° B, 28015 Madrid.*

In Italy: Please write to *Penguin Italia s.r.l., Via Benedetto Croce 2, 20094 Corsico, Milano.*

In France: Please write to *Penguin France, Le Carré Wilson, 62 rue Benjamin Baillaud, 31500 Toulouse.*

In Japan: Please write to *Penguin Books Japan Ltd, Kaneko Building, 2-3-25 Koraku, Bunkyo-Ku, Tokyo 112.*

In South Africa: Please write to *Penguin Books South Africa (Pty) Ltd, Private Bag X14, Parkview, 2122 Johannesburg.*